# Summer
# at
# Croftwood
# Cinema

Victoria Walker

For James
I'm going anyway
x

# 1

Patsy Clements was just about ready to throttle Oliver. He'd said he would be an hour and that was over two hours ago. Admittedly, Oliver's, the coffee house which Oliver owned and Patsy worked in, had been busier than usual for a Thursday lunchtime and neither of them would have expected that in the middle of March but still, she couldn't help being annoyed with him.

'I'm so sorry Pats,' he said, flustered as he came through the door, immediately swapping his coat for one of their distinctive canvas aprons which had 'Oliver's' emblazoned across the front.

'That's two ninety-five, please,' she said to her customer before turning to Oliver and brushing some dust off the sleeve of his trademark floral shirt. 'It's fine, don't worry.' Because annoyed as she was, he was her best friend and would do anything for her, so she pushed her irritation aside and carried on serving.

They worked through the rest of the lunch queue together before a lull gave them a chance to talk properly.

'That was busy for a Thursday,' Oliver said, beginning to

tidy away some of the mess that had built up behind the counter. 'I'm sorry, I would have been back sooner except...'

'What?'

He had a mischievous look on his face which told Patsy that he'd been up to something. Almost straight away she got caught up in his excitement, and was keen to hear whatever it was.

'I bought the cinema!'

'What, you mean you've hired out a whole cinema?' She had no idea why he would do that. It must have cost a fortune.

'No, not hired it out, I've actually bought the cinema here, in Croftwood!'

'What? Who buys a cinema?'

Oliver took her hands in his, his eyes bright. 'Me, Pats. I do.'

'You mean the one in the park? Hasn't it been closed for years?'

'Yes, it's been closed since 1997. And... it's mine!' He crouched down slightly as if he was about to grab her and swing her around or something equally exuberant.

'You've bought the cinema in the park? Are you bonkers? It's derelict. What are you going to do with it?' As she said the words, Oliver let her hands fall, along with his face. The tiny pang of guilt that she felt for bursting his bubble was quickly overtaken by common sense, because she knew she was right. It was an old 1920s building on the edge of the park and had been neglected for years, long before its doors had closed.

'Come on Pats, it's not derelict. It's completely intact apart from the window. Once the foliage is cleared, it'll be fine.'

'So you're going to open it as a cinema?'

'Yes, but more than that.' His eyes were shining again and Patsy knew that whatever she thought, he was behind this idea and nothing was going to stop him. 'Even when we run it as a cinema, we'll offer food, have a proper bar, really nice seats, you know, make it into a real destination. And it'll be flexible so we can use it for functions and events.'

'Well, that does sound cool. So you and Amy are doing it together?'

He shrugged, looking a little sheepish. 'She knew I was planning to go to the auction but I didn't let on how interested I was in the cinema. The thing is, after we went in on this place together, she lost interest… I want this to be mine. And actually, Pats, I was hoping you'd agree to help me get it up and running.'

Riding on a surge of infectious enthusiasm from him, her first instinct was to accept, especially now she'd heard his vision for the place but it was immediately replaced by a reality check.. 'I'd love to say yes, Ollie but you know things are a bit tight.'

'It's not about the money. I haven't got time to be across all of it myself. I need help and it needs to be someone I know I can get along with and someone who won't take any messing around from me or anyone else.'

She smiled, loving how Oliver turned her no nonsense frankness into a positive trait. Something that she knew he found mildly infuriating, he also realised might be useful.

But however brilliant it sounded, Patsy wasn't sure she could accept. For the past three years since she'd returned to Croftwood and started working for Oliver, she'd been careful to keep her life simple. She didn't earn a fortune working at the coffee house but it was enough to cover the rent and bills on her tiny flat and to keep her in knitting wool. Having got herself into a position where she was self-sufficient and felt safe, she wasn't sure she was brave enough to push herself out of that comfort zone, however tempting.

'I don't know anything about renovating derelict

buildings, or about running a cinema. How much use can I be?'

'To be honest, it's pushing my budget to get someone professional in to help but if you're willing to mix it up with working here, I can manage to pay you barista wages for the extra hours and I'd make it right for you financially once it's up and running. A stranger isn't going to do that for me on a promise.'

That sounded more feasible. 'Let me think about it,' she said, pulling him into a hug. 'Congratulations, it's really exciting even if it sounds like I'll be left in the lurch with this place even more often.'

Oliver grinned. 'It'll be fine. I'm going to turn the flat into a project office so I'll be around all the time.'

'You're giving up your bachelor pad?'

Oliver lived upstairs in a very masculinely-decorated flat, heavy on tweed and leather. He shrugged. 'I'm at Amy's most of the time anyway and lots of my stuff is there already. It'll force me to finish the job.'

Oliver disappeared upstairs and one of their newest regulars came up to the counter for a refill.

'Same again?' Patsy asked.

'Yes, please.' Toby had spent almost every day over the past two weeks in the coffee house, sitting at his laptop with a fresh coffee every hour or so and a sandwich for lunch. He treated it like an office, although Patsy hadn't managed to find out yet what he actually did. One of the perks of the job were the little insights you got into the lives of the regular customers and Toby had established himself as one of those relatively quickly. He always looked as if he was at work, wearing a shirt and smart dark jeans with brown leather boots, and he wouldn't be the only customer who used the coffee house as an office. It was so cool, with its plank-top tables and trailing greenery that even a local designer held all

4

of his client meetings over coffee and there was a woman who wrote rhymes for greetings cards, spending most of the day gazing out of the window with a pencil in her mouth. Perhaps the signs that were dotted around the place served as inspiration, Patsy's favourite being, 'May your coffee be strong and your Monday be short.'

'Having a good day?' she asked.

'Not bad thanks. You look as if you are?'

Until he'd mentioned it, Patsy hadn't realised that she had a big grin on her face. She was pretty excited about Oliver's new project.

'Oliver's bought the cinema, the one in the park.'

'Wow, that's quite something. I can imagine whatever he does with it will be a real boost for the town.'

Patsy handed over his coffee. 'For sure. It'll be nice not to have to trek to Worcester to see a film at least.'

Toby laughed. 'It's only six miles, but it's easy to forget how close it is when there's no need to leave Croftwood most of the time.'

Although the town of Croftwood was small and centred around the high street, with the library at one end and the Post Office at the other, it had everything most people needed. You couldn't go clubbing or eat at a different restaurant every night of the week but if you were happy with a Chinese takeaway, a couple of pubs and excellent coffee, it was perfect.

Patsy watched Toby return to his table, the laughter gone from his face almost immediately as he went back to whatever he was doing on his laptop.

She smiled. If Oliver's vision for the cinema could match up to what he'd done with the coffee house, Toby was right, it would be brilliant for the town. And it'd be nice to have a new challenge in her own life, after three years of making coffee and keeping herself to herself, it might be just what she needed.


Once they'd closed up for the night, Patsy waved to Oliver as he drove off in his Mini to Amy's house in Worcester, before she headed through the churchyard towards the old part of the town where she lived. The streets were tree-lined avenues and most of the houses were Victorian. Patsy lived on the third-floor of a Victorian villa conversion. The tiny dimensions of her attic flat along with the killer stairs were made up for by the flat roof she could climb out onto through her bedroom window. In the summer, the leaves of the enormous oak tree which rose higher than the house, grazed the edge of the roof and provided privacy from the overlooking windows of the neighbouring house. But despite the day having been bright and sunny, now that the sun had dipped beneath the horizon, the March evening was too chilly for her to consider climbing out there tonight.

She unlocked the door to her flat, closed it behind her and then made sure to flick the latch to deadlock it and put the chain across for good measure. Catching her reflection in the mirror, she rolled her eyes. Her thick chestnut hair was half in and half out of the bun she'd piled it into that morning and the cheap mascara she'd bought in a moment of thriftiness had migrated to her under-eye area over the course of the day. She sighed as she pulled the pins out of her hair and rubbed her fingers under her eyes. Not that anyone was going to see her, but she had principles.

Once she'd made a quick dinner of pasta and arrabbiata sauce, her absolute favourite, she put the TV on and settled in front of the latest Scandinavian boxset she was bingeing through on Netflix. She liked to have something on while she knitted, and the socks that she had on her needles were plain enough that she could knit and still read the subtitles.

Her mind was still on the conversation she'd had with Oliver. The offer he'd made her was tempting but now that she had a chance to think seriously about his proposal, the idea of getting involved in anything long-term, however exciting it might sound, frightened her. She'd known Oliver for years, since she'd lived in Croftwood as a teenager and when she appeared again three years ago, he'd given her the job at the coffee house when she'd really needed it, without asking any questions. Of course, back then he was in the first throes of his relationship with Amy and he needed someone to hold the fort for him while he attended to her demands. Patsy had never quite taken to Amy, finding her high-maintenance and an odd choice for Oliver, but they had been together for all of that time and it was hypocritical of her to think she knew any better given her own relationship history. Anyway, the job at the coffee house had been the perfect solution for both of them and Patsy would be forever grateful.

Something like this which would move her out of the comfort zone she'd built for herself was a big step. When she was at the coffee house, she was her old self; confident, feisty, Oliver called her, but it was easy with him. They were best friends and could be completely honest with each other. It crossed her mind that Amy might not like her being so involved with the project, especially when she was effectively being cut out of the deal. It would be interesting to see if that ended up being the case and a tiny part of her hoped maybe some sparks would fly. She loved a bit of harmless drama occasionally. But whatever she might think, she was happy to accept that he was happily settled with Amy and she wanted to support him in this next phase of his life.

Maybe she should speak to him, tell him why she was worried but that would mean telling him everything and no-one knew everything. Most of the time she didn't even think about it because she'd managed to get to a place in her life where she'd started to leave it behind and if she did say yes to Oliver, it felt like she'd be cracking open the door of her fortress. Opening it even a tiny bit felt dangerous because who knew where that might lead. Even feisty-Patsy might not cope in the face of that.

# 2

Overnight, Patsy had gone back and forth, thinking over Oliver's proposal and had eventually resolved to put aside her fears.

'Okay, I'm in,' she said the following morning when she arrived at the coffee house to find him arranging the pastries in their baskets ready for the early crowd.

He dropped his tongs onto the counter and hugged her. 'That's excellent, thanks Pats. That's one less thing for me to worry about. I thought you'd be on board but because I hadn't asked you before the auction and you didn't seem that keen yesterday, I was a bit worried. I'm not sure I can do this without you.'

'Of course you can, it'll be much better if I'm involved though. God knows the mess you'd make of it on your own.'

He grinned and she knew it was going to be okay. He was so easy-going and had no expectations of her. She completely understood where he was coming from with the vision he had for the coffee house and she could already imagine the kind of plans he had for the cinema.

'The first thing we need to do is find someone who can

take on some of your hours here. Don't worry,' he reassured her. 'I meant what I said yesterday. I'll pay you the same as I would normally, just that some of your hours will be working on the cinema project now instead.'

'No problem. Have you got anyone in mind or do we need to put a notice in the window or something?'

'Rosemary mentioned that Linda's nephew Jack is looking for some hours. He's in sixth form so can be pretty flexible. I'll see if we can get him in to meet us.' Rosemary and Linda worked together at Croftwood Library and were regulars at the coffee house. 'The other thing we need to do is go and have a proper look at the place. I'm meeting the architect there tomorrow morning. I wonder if we could get someone to cover the coffee house so you can come with me? I'd love you to be in on all the discussions right from the start.'

'We could ask Beth. She's back from university for reading week, I'm sure she'd fill in.' Beth was their old Saturday girl and had left the previous summer to go to university in Sheffield. 'I'll text her.'

'Morning, guys.' Jess was the owner of the fabric and yarn shop a little further down the high street, The Croftwood Haberdashery. It was one of the more modern fabric shops which was busily inspiring a new generation of seamstresses to make clothes that people actually wanted to wear, and where there were sewers, there tended to be knitters so Jess stocked a range of yarn too.

'Morning Jess, what can I get you?' Patsy asked.

'A latte, please, and a pain au chocolat as I'm by myself this morning.' Jess was wearing the kind of dress Patsy always wished she'd be lucky enough to find in a charity shop. It was dark grey with huge dusky pink blooms over it and the style was pure 1950s with a skirt that probably had a stiff net petticoat underneath.

'No workshops today?'

'No, but that reminds me. We've got six in tomorrow. Can I order coffee and pastries?'

'Yes, sure.' Whenever the shop was running a class, they placed their order and Patsy or Oliver would drop it to them. It was a bit of a pain having to make sure that two of them were in on those mornings and although it didn't seem worth it for six coffees and pastries, it always resulted in the participants coming into them for lunch. 'Tenish like usual?'

'That'd be perfect, thanks. I love your cardigan by the way.'

'Thanks, I only finished it last week. Just in time for the last of the cold weather hopefully.'

Jess hosted the fortnightly Knit and Natter club at the shop, so she'd seen the cardigan throughout its progress.

'Can you wear it to Knit and Natter on Wednesday so I can take a photo of you in front of the wool wall?'

'Um, okay,' Patsy said hesitantly, knowing that the picture would be headed for Instagram.

'I can chop your head off if you want?' Jess was used to camera shy customers and was willing to compromise for content.

'You're on. See you Wednesday. Or tomorrow if I do the delivery.'

'Thanks!' Jess turned to leave, her skirt twirling spectacularly around her, making Patsy resolve, as she did almost every time she saw Jess, to learn how to sew as soon as possible.

The following morning, Patsy headed straight to the park to meet Oliver. There was a wide path that ran through the park and the cinema was just to the right of the park entrance, at the end of a narrower path. The side of the building closest to the park boundary was gradually being devoured by rhododendrons, although Patsy could imagine that it would be a beautiful riot of colour in the summer. As it was, there were already carpets of crocuses celebrating the arrival of spring and the trees were beginning to come into bud.

The old cinema was a fairly nondescript brick building with heavy wooden double doors which had been painted red once upon a time. There was a circular window above the door, in the gable of the roof which unfortunately, despite being at least ten metres off the ground, had been the target of some stone-throwing and was smashed. Being the only window that she could see at least meant that hopefully, as the doors were intact and sturdy, the building was as good as impenetrable and wouldn't have been vandalised inside.

'Morning Pats,' Oliver said as he pulled a bunch of keys out of his pocket. 'Might as well get inside while we wait for Matt. I can't wait to see it.'

'Haven't you been inside before?' Patsy asked, not that keen to be the first to enter an abandoned building after so many years.

'No, I saw photos of the inside in the agent's details,' said Oliver, seeming unconcerned about flouting the golden rule of Homes Under The Hammer.

'Hold your horses!' Someone bellowed from across the park. It was a blonde-haired man in jeans and a sports jacket, carrying an armful of hardhats and a portfolio case. 'Christ, Oliver, don't go in there without one of these.'

'Alright mate, thanks.' Oliver took a hard hat and handed it to Patsy. 'This is Matthew Garvey, our architect. Matt, this is Patsy Clements, my business partner.'

'Nice to meet you.' He handed Oliver a hard hat and took one for himself which had MATT written across the front.

'In case we forget your name,' said Patsy, pointing at it.

'What? Oh right,' he said dismissively, without even pretending to think it was funny.

Patsy waited until Matt's back was turned and rolled her eyes at Oliver as they giggled and then followed Matt into the building.

There were a couple of high-beam torches inside the door which Matt and Oliver took charge of. The building smelt old and musty and dust motes danced around in the beams of torchlight but already, Patsy could see the charm of the place. In the foyer was a small ticket kiosk decorated with intricate wood mouldings and next to it a counter with a few empty jars on shelves behind it, presumably where drinks and snacks had been sold and a flight of stairs were opposite that. It was spacious, taking up the whole width of the building with doors at either side which led into the main part of the building.

'Watch your step,' Matt warned as he pulled the doors closed behind them, losing the daylight.

Oliver headed straight through the door to the left, into the cinema. Patsy went in between him and Matt, benefiting from the light that each of their torches provided. Once they were through the door, Oliver shone his torch to the far wall. Even in the dim light, it was clear that the place was completely untouched.

They walked down to the front, the floor gently sloping away from them towards the screen, passing the rows of burgundy velvet seats. Oliver turned around and shone the torch up to the ceiling, illuminating the whole space.

'Wow, it's bigger than I thought it would be,' he said.

The ceiling was decorated with plaster mouldings but everything had been painted dark red at some point, erasing the beauty of the place but thankfully not the possibility of bringing it back to life.

'I don't remember the balcony,' said Patsy, as Oliver shone his torch across the upstairs which spanned halfway over the ground floor. 'Although the last time I came here was to see 'Santa Claus, The Movie', so perhaps I've just forgotten.'

'Or you weren't posh enough to sit upstairs. It was more

expensive.'

Patsy gave Oliver an indignant shove.

'You can see the projection room,' said Patsy, pointing to the small square window high in the back wall. 'Is all the equipment still in there?'

'It looked like it on the photos,' said Oliver, 'and there was a list of fixtures and fittings, but it doesn't mean anything to me.'

'We'll need to check the integrity of the balcony structure,' said Matt, who was wandering up and down underneath shining his torch in a way that made him look like he knew what he was doing, which he probably did.

The cinema screen was torn on the top left corner, exposing the metal frame but revealing a large space behind which they went to explore through a door at the one side.

'Blimey, there's quite a lot of space behind here,' said Oliver. 'What's that?' He was pointing at a large wooden panel on the back wall which looked like a huge barn door.

'Ah,' said Matt, knowingly, and irritatingly, thought Patsy as they waited for him to expand. 'I'd heard that this once used to be a small theatre. This is the original scene dock door.'

Patsy and Oliver looked blankly at him so he sighed and then expanded.

'They needed a huge door to get scenery in and out. That's why it's almost the height of the back wall. The opening's been bricked up from the outside but I expect it was too much trouble to get this down, it's so huge that they left it. Amazing. Look, it's on huge runners. It'll need a lot of work to get them working again, but what a bit of luck.'

The space was full of old chairs and other junk. 'If we cleared this, the door would open straight into the park and we could use it as a function room,' Oliver said.

'That would be amazing,' said Patsy. 'You could string

lights in the trees behind, it would be gorgeous.'

'We could have a small bar over on that wall to save people walking through the auditorium to get a drink. Yes, this could be brilliant,' said Oliver.

Patsy was starting to worry about the enormity of the task ahead and she wasn't sure exactly what part Oliver expected her to play. Still, at least now she'd seen it they could sit down and make a proper plan.

They headed upstairs although Matt wouldn't let them go onto the balcony until he'd had it structurally assessed, so the only place left to explore was the projection room. The stairs that led up to it were narrow and there was a door at the top which was locked. Oliver handed the torch to Patsy while he went through the keys to find the right one.

'I bet it's that one, the little one with the chunky top.'

Oliver tried the suggested key and after a bit of jiggling, the lock turned.

'Christ!' Oliver leapt backwards as soon as he went in, after a startled pigeon flew towards him on its escape out of the broken round window. 'And you can stop laughing,' he said to Patsy who had backed out of the door and was staying well clear. 'I'd like to see you stay calm in the face of an attacking pigeon,' he said, so indignantly that it only made her laugh even harder.

The room was dominated by a huge projector which had two massive reels on a large metal frame behind it. They were at least a metre in diameter, one above the other. There was a panel full of switches on the wall next to the tiny window that looked out over the auditorium. It looked a bit home-made to Patsy, not that she knew anything about that sort of thing, but because of the pigeon problem, the whole room was fairly unsavoury and Matt gave it no more than a cursory look before they all headed downstairs again, being sure to close the door and lock it to stop any pigeons infiltrating the rest of the building.

'So, what do you think?' Oliver asked Patsy once they were back outside.

'I think it could be amazing. It's a bit daunting though, there does seem like an awful lot to do.'

'It's structurally better than I would have expected, subject to a survey of course,' said Matt.

'Of course.' Patsy couldn't hide her sarcasm but did at least manage not to roll her eyes, since he was looking right at her.

'Thanks for coming along, Matt. Let me know what the next steps are.'

Matt and Oliver shook hands while Patsy stood there knowing she wasn't going to be offered a handshake.

Matt turned towards her and held his hand out. Patsy began to smile in disbelief — maybe she'd got him wrong. Then he said, 'Hardhat,' and she was glad she hadn't already stuck her hand out. Dick.

Once Matt had gone and Oliver had locked up, they began strolling back to the coffee house.

'I'm totally up for it,' he said. 'Now the coffee house is established it's the perfect new challenge.'

'Well, aside from the pigeon, it's won me over,' said Patsy. 'I forgot to ask earlier, what did Amy say?'

Oliver looked at her and bit his bottom lip.

'You haven't told her?'

'I will. I just…'

'You're scared?' She gave him a gentle shove and smiled at him to let him know she was teasing, even though she didn't think she was far from the truth.

'I just need to find the right time. You know what it's like.' For a moment, he looked lost in thought but then the brightness was back. 'I'm so excited, I can't wait to see how it all comes together.'

Patsy was feeling the same way. Seeing the building had

started her thinking about what they might offer by way of food and drinks. She could envisage a drinks bar in the foyer next to the ticket booth, which she hoped would stay because she loved the nostalgia of it.

Patsy's phone buzzed with a text from Beth to say that The Croftwood Haberdashery's order was ready to be delivered.

'Come on, Ollie. We've got to get back to the coffee house to sort the delivery for Jess.'

She linked her arm through his as they speeded up their stroll, thinking that very soon there might not be enough hours in the day for either of them. They really needed to get Jack or someone else on board as their third barista as soon as they could if they were going to have the time to devote to the cinema, because it was going to take a lot of it.

# 3

Oliver had invited Patsy round to Amy's for dinner so that they could make a start on a proper plan for the cinema. He'd offered her their spare room for the night so that she didn't have to take the last bus home from Worcester which was at the ridiculously early time of 10.30 pm, so she'd packed an overnight bag and a bottle of wine and was looking forward to eating something she hadn't cooked herself for once.

Since they'd looked around the cinema, she'd had lots of ideas that she wanted to share with Oliver but they never had a chance to talk when they were at work. Their shifts did overlap but that was because the two of them both worked lunchtimes, the busiest part of the day. Today, Patsy had stayed all day so that Oliver could go to the wholesalers and she could get a lift to Worcester with him once they'd closed.

'Have you talked to Amy yet?' she asked, as they both climbed into his Mini and she chucked her bag over onto the back seat.

He looked at her and she knew the answer before he could say anything.

'Oliver! We can hardly have a planning meeting at Amy's

house if she doesn't know anything about it. She'll go mad. 'I'll tell her as soon as we get there. It'll be fine.'Oliver! It will not be fine. She'll think we're in it together and we didn't tell her.'

'I'm… okay. I don't think she'll be happy about it but it's business. My business.' He paused and glanced at her. 'And she can't go off on one if you're there.'

'You chicken. Why does she think you've invited me?'

Another sheepish look from Oliver told her everything

'Oh for chrissakes Ollie, grow a pair. She's your girlfriend. If you can't talk to her, what are you even doing?'

'I know, I know,' he said, shaking his head. 'Look, just come back with me, I'll say your heating's broken down and you need to stay. And then I can tell her while you're there and you can pretend I'm telling you for the first time too. Please.'

He attempted to look forlorn but she frowned at him, making sure he knew it was a lot to ask but he grinned, knowing equally well that she would do it for him.

'I can put on my best acting skills for the night, I suppose but it feels a bit weird staying the night without being invited.'

'It's fine,' he said, glancing over at her. 'I'm inviting you. You're my best mate, Pats. It's not that weird to invite a friend over. If it makes you feel better, pretend that it's my house.'

'I hope it's nicer than that. I think Amy's taste probably runs to a higher standard than your man cave.'

'There you go, back into your stride now.' He grinned as he looked in his rear-view mirror.

That was the best thing about working with Oliver: the banter. They could be completely honest with each other. Well, day-to-day stuff that didn't matter, at least on her part. Her personal life was non-existent and that was part of the reason she could be so open about everything else because there was nothing to hide. If he wondered why she never pursued relationships or showed any interest in men, he never said. He never pried, never asked anything about her, and she appreciated that massively. The fact that his life played out mostly right in front of her, in the coffee house, was part of the reason why she had so much to say and he took it in the spirit it was intended.

'So what did you think of the cinema?' she asked him. 'Was it what you'd expected?'

'Yes, I think it was. It was a bloody relief that there were no nasty surprises. I know after the roasting I got from Matt about how naive I'd been to go in head first without checking it out thoroughly that I was really lucky, but I had a good feeling, you know?'

'Mmm, I know what you mean. As soon as we walked in, I could totally imagine how it could look. Maybe a bar next to the ticket booth. We will keep that, won't we?'

'Oh, for sure. I think we need to keep anything that gives us that nostalgic vibe, unless it's something naff from the eighties.' He turned off into a side street and pulled up outside a Victorian semi. 'Here we are.'

Patsy grabbed her bag and followed Oliver up the path. He let himself in.

'Ooh, you've already got your own key. Nice.'

Oliver rolled his eyes but he looked pleased. 'Well, it made sense.'

'Hey Amy!' he called out.

Amy came into the hall. 'Oh Patsy, were we expecting you?' she asked, pointedly looking at Oliver and making Patsy cringe for him.

'My heating's broken down and Ollie kindly offered me a bed for the night.' Anything she could do to help Oliver out in the face of this uptight excuse for a loving girlfriend. He threw her a look of gratitude.

'Hope that's okay Ames,' he said, attempting to placate her with a kiss and receiving a reluctantly offered cheek. 'The spare room's opposite the top of the stairs if you want to take your bag up, Pats. Make yourself at home.'

'Thanks.' She headed upstairs, hearing Oliver and Amy move into the kitchen with the beginning of a conversation about however was Amy going to stretch a two-portion risotto three ways, with Oliver patiently suggesting garlic bread from the freezer before the door closed behind them.

The spare room was pretty sparse, a double bed upon which Patsy dumped her bag before taking her coat off, a chest of drawers and a bedside table. Patsy opened a drawer. It felt nosey but it wasn't as if it was Amy's bedroom, that would be a step too far. It was full of neatly folded clothes which wasn't that surprising since Amy never seemed to wear the same thing twice. Although to be fair to her, she would have had to make room for Oliver's clothes in her wardrobe so perhaps she had been kind by moving some of her things out.

She looked in the other drawers to find them all filled with more clothes, a couple of drawers of bikinis and other summer holiday paraphernalia. She was killing time, conscious that she ought to give them a few more minutes alone before she ventured back downstairs.

'Glass of red?' asked Oliver, beginning to pour before she'd had chance to even utter the words, 'yes, please.'

'Thanks for inviting me to stay, Amy. Your house is lovely.'

'You're welcome,' she said, as she busied herself with chopping a lettuce. 'It's no fun having no heating, even in March.'

After a delicious dinner of butternut squash risotto with a colourful side salad and garlic bread, they headed into the lounge with their glasses of wine and the rest of the bottle. Amy crouched down by the fireplace and began to light the fire. Patsy mouthed, 'Tell her!' to Oliver, who was sat opposite her on the other sofa. He nodded vigorously, looking very sincere, yet said nothing.

'What was that auction like that you went to the other day?' Patsy asked, giving Oliver a determined look while he responded by shaking his head and waving an arm until Amy turned around.

'Um, yes, it was interesting.'

'Did they sell the old cinema in the end?' Amy asked, sitting on the sofa next to him and laying her hand on his thigh, making Patsy want to childishly mime sticking her fingers down her throat, but she resisted.

'Well, actually,' Oliver began with a laugh that was far too jovial, 'I ended up bidding for it.'

'Good one,' said Amy with a giggle, obviously thinking he was joking.

Patsy was starting to enjoy herself. She shouldn't be pleased seeing her friend squirming like this as he attempted to confess that he'd made a fairly big decision without even mentioning it to his girlfriend of three years, but she was and it was his own fault he was in this situation.

'No, really Ames.' He gulped the last of his wine down and refilled his glass without offering either of them any.

'But we're business partners, Oliver.' Amy's tone was as pinched as her face.

'In the coffee house, yes but you don't want anything to do with running it any more so I didn't think you'd be interested.'

'You could have asked me.'

Now, she sounded hurt and Patsy couldn't help but sympathise with her. Oliver should have spoken to her about it, even if it was to explain that he wanted to go it alone.

'I'm sorry. It was a spur of the moment thing. If you want to come in with me on it, you're more than welcome.'

There was silence. Patsy wondered whether it would be strategically best to say goodnight and head upstairs but she felt that Oliver probably still needed whatever moral support he could get to dig himself out of this hole.

'Blimey, Ollie, that's crazy!' she said, trying to convey that the news was a surprise and that she thought it was a bit bonkers, to make it a more realistic reaction. As soon as it came out of her mouth she realised it sounded like she was on Amy's side.

'My thoughts exactly, Patsy,' Amy said, confirming her suspicions. 'Buying somewhere like that on a whim…what were you thinking? We don't have the money and you don't know anything about refurbishing something that size. It's one thing tarting up a high street unit to be a coffee shop,' Patsy willed Oliver not to correct her and say it was a coffee house. 'And quite another taking on an entire building which has lain derelict for years and years.'

Oliver seemed to grow in stature throughout her little speech. Whether it was the slur on his business by referring to it as a coffee shop or whether it was the insinuation that what he'd achieved with Oliver's had just been tarting up what was already there, which was definitely not the case, Patsy could see that Oliver was suddenly thinking clearly. No longer scared of Amy, he was going to explain himself, as he should have done all along.

'This project means a lot to me. I'm part of Croftwood now, and seeing an opportunity that could give something amazing to the town, I was always going to take it. I know I should have told you my plans but I was going to do it with or without you and to be honest, I knew you'd think it was mad and I didn't want you to burst my bubble. It was the thrill of my life when I won that auction, I've never had a feeling like it. Yes, it's a lot to take on but I know I can do it. I'm not saying it's not scary, because it is. But it means everything to me.'

Patsy looked on with pride that her friend was finally standing up for himself and explaining so eloquently what he wanted. How could Amy not be won over by that?

'Fine, if it means that much to you, do it. But I'm having nothing to do with it.' She stood up and flounced out of the room.

Patsy and Oliver sat in stunned silence, staring at each other until Patsy found the whole thing simply so hilarious that she burst out laughing, grabbing a cushion to stifle the sound. Oliver began shushing her but soon was also laughing into a cushion.

'That went well,' he said, once they'd recovered. 'Shame you're in the spare room because I think that's my bed tonight.'

'Want to top and tail?'

'I'll take the sofa. I think sharing a bed with you, however innocently, might send her over the top.'

'I'm sure it'll be okay in the morning,' she said, reaching over and squeezing his hand. 'She needs time to think it over. And if she wants to do the project with you, please don't worry about what we'd decided because I'm more than happy to carry on being a barista.

'Thanks, Pats. But whatever happens, we're in this together. I might keep it on the down low for now though,' he smiled.

But how were they going to get from here to the point where Amy would be fine with it all, and fine with Patsy being involved? It seemed impossible.

# 4

Oliver was very quiet the next morning on the drive in. They had left before Amy was up; Oliver looked like he'd had no sleep at all having slept on the sofa which was only a two-seater. Patsy kept glancing at him but he kept his eyes on the road, focused. She knew his mind wasn't on the drive, he was worrying about what had happened the night before. And she was worried about him. It was quite a situation he seemed to have engineered himself into and despite her delight at the drama that had unfolded before her, she didn't want Oliver to be in the place he was now.

They worked in almost total silence, getting the coffee house ready to open for the day, only interrupted when the pastry delivery arrived and Oliver briefly turned on his usual chatty charm and exchanged a few words with Jake. He ran an artisan bakery from a barn conversion on the outskirts of town and his vanilla custard cruffins were to die for.

Patsy decided enough was enough. 'Let's stop for coffee before we open. We hardly ever do this end of the day together, let's have a treat.'

Oliver shrugged but scooped up two fresh cruffins and

made his way over to their favourite table, tucked in the corner and screened from the big windows that looked out onto the high street by shelves of trailing foliage, while Patsy made a couple of lattes.

'You need to get it off your chest before we open, otherwise we're not going to have any customers. I know you can't be fake-cheerful all day.'

He sighed and pulled a chunk off his cruffin. 'I should have told her, right at the start. I still could have bought the place even if she'd thought it was a bad idea.'

'So why didn't you?'

'Because… I didn't want her to suggest going in on it with me. That's awful isn't it?'

Patsy rolled her eyes. 'Do you think I didn't know that? You said the other day that you were annoyed that you started this place together and now she's washed her hands of it, it's no wonder you don't want the same thing to happen again.'

'She has no enthusiasm for stuff like this. You were really excited when I told you.'

'Once I got past thinking you were mad, yes. And I do get why you wanted to go it alone but I can't spend the day with you if you're in this mood. Seriously.'

There was a knock at the door.

'I'll let you get that so you can practice your cheerfulness,' said Patsy.

It was Rosemary, the librarian. She always insisted on being let inside before they were actually open. Their breakfast chat was over, so Patsy gathered up their cups and plates and headed back over to the counter where Oliver was already making Rosemary's regular cappuccino.

'Morning Rosemary.'

'Good morning, Patsy. Have you telephoned Jack about the job you're offering?'

Rosemary was always straight to the point, everyone was used to it but it made Patsy smile because of Rosemary's assumption that the job was Jack's purely by virtue of her recommendation.

'It's on my to-do-list today. Do you think he's going to fit in here?'

'He's Linda's nephew,' Rosemary said, as if that was the only trait needed to be a successful barista. It wasn't worth an argument. She'd give him a couple of trial shifts on the off-chance Rosemary's instincts were right.

'Sure, thanks for the tip-off. I'll bring your coffee over if you want to take a seat.'

Rosemary tipped her nose in the air and headed over to where she always sat, at a table for two, facing the window so that she could people watch.

'Putting all this stuff with Amy aside,' Oliver began, once Patsy had delivered Rosemary's drink, 'I want to start planning.'

'Me too. Let's not lose the wave of enthusiasm.'

Oliver gave her a pointed look. 'I am still enthusiastic. It's just a little glitch.'

'Okay. Let's plan then.'

'So the way I see it working is that I'll oversee all the refurbishment, any building work and decoration. If you could take on responsibility for the bar area and kitchen that would be great. Then we can work together once we get nearer to the end on all the fun stuff like marketing and branding. What do you think?'

'That sounds good to me. So, organising suppliers, designing menus, that kind of thing?'

'Exactly. Because that stuff takes a lot of time and if it's down to me, I won't have time to start on it until it's too late and it's too important to rush.'

'It sounds to me like you're planning on opening a

restaurant. What are you going to do about getting the actual cinema up and running again?' Rosemary called over to them.

Oliver looked at Patsy with wide eyes. 'We hadn't even mentioned the cinema. How does she know?' he whispered.

'She knows everything,' Patsy murmured, sliding her gaze across to Rosemary who was waiting, with eyebrows raised, to hear their plan.

'You are planning to present films?' Rosemary said.

'Well, obviously,' replied Oliver, before whispering to Patsy, 'God, I hadn't even thought about that. I don't think either of us know anything about it do we?' Oliver said.

Patsy shook her head. 'That projection room… well, I wouldn't know where to start.' Oliver took a large gulp of coffee. 'Who knows if that stuff is even going to work, let alone whether you can still use it. Maybe it's something like a glorified DVD player these days.'

'Worcester University has got a Film Society,' said Rosemary. 'I understand it's very popular. When I worked at the university library a student asked me if we had any books on projecting, because he was learning how to do it. You ought to get in touch with the university, they might be able to offer some advice.'

Oliver swept his arm across to Rosemary as if he was introducing her. 'Thank you Rosemary.'

'I don't mind following up on that,' Patsy offered. 'It could be quite good fun to find out a bit more about it.'

'Okay. God, that could be a money pit that I've not even considered. I was so worried about the structure after Matt going on about all these hidden things there could be, even though it looks fine on the outside, I never even thought about that.'

'Let's not worry until we know what the situation is. It might be fine,' said Patsy, as she reached over and rubbed his hand reassuringly.

'Yeah, I guess so.'

'Come on, it probably only needs a good clean and it'll be as good as new.'

Oliver grinned. 'Thank goodness for you and your relentless optimism.'

'Someone needs to be the positive one around here.'

Oliver raised an eyebrow and shot her a resigned smile. At least he looked happier than he'd been this morning.

'And thank you Rosemary. We'd be on the back foot if you hadn't mentioned that. Can I offer you a pastry on the house?'

'Perhaps tomorrow, thank you Oliver. I must be off.'

'Good lord,' Oliver said when she'd gone. 'That could have been a disaster. I'm such an idiot. No wonder Amy thinks it's a bad idea.'

'It is not a bad idea, but we do need to sit down and make a proper plan. Now, finish your cruffin before the morning rush starts.'

That evening, Patsy went to Knit and Natter at Jess's shop. The shop was long and narrow, the front filled with bolts and rolls of fabric from floor to the very high ceilings, then further on, past the cutting table and the till was the yarn. Patsy's favourite part of the shop. It was packed from the floor to the rafters with yarn of all colours and thicknesses, all of it beautiful and arranged pleasingly by colour. Although Jess wasn't a big knitter, she knew every ball of yarn she stocked and what you needed for anything you wanted to knit. Then through the yarn room was the workshop room where a large wooden table lent itself to sewing, knitting or tea and a chat.

'I heard a rumour that Oliver has bought the old cinema in the park. Is that true?' Jess asked as soon as Patsy walked in, after checking that no-one was within earshot.

'Yes. He's got some good ideas for it. We're going to run it as an events space as well, something more flexible than just a cinema.'

'Wow, that sounds exciting. It looks like a wreck from the outside, is there a lot to do?'

'The inside is pretty untouched but it's a bit of a mess. The architect, Matt, is getting some surveys done but he thinks it's structurally sound.'

'Is it common knowledge yet? I thought I'd better check because I heard from Rosemary,' she said, giving Patsy a knowing look.

'I have no idea how Rosemary found out but I think it's okay if people know. Although if you see Amy, it might be better not to mention it. It's a bit of a sore point.'

'Ah, right.' Jess opened her mouth, presumably to ask what that was all about but they were interrupted by Mary and Penny, a couple of the regulars. 'Help yourselves to tea and coffee, ladies, you know where everything is.'

Patsy loved the Knit and Natter evenings. She always took very simple knitting because anything that required counting or any concentration on the pattern inevitably ended up being pulled out afterwards because it was full of mistakes. A sock was perfect for covering the knitting aspect so that she could pay full attention to the nattering.

'Have you seen that the cinema was sold at auction last week?' said Carol to the group.

There followed a lot of reminiscing about the last time everyone had been to the cinema, who they'd been with, how much it had cost and all sorts of other things that brought the old place back to life for Patsy. It made her realise how important it was going to be to refurbish the cinema in a way that would keep alive all of these memories and feelings people had for the place. It might not look the same in the end — hopefully it wouldn't — but that didn't mean that they couldn't try and keep the spirit of the place intact while they brought it back to life. It hadn't occurred to Patsy that all of these people were bound to be invested in its future, given that they all held a piece of its past within them.

'I hope whoever's bought it gets rid of the seats. They were so uncomfortable, my bottom was always asleep by the end of the film,' Sue said, with a nostalgic smile.

'I wonder if they'll keep the balcony? It was always a treat to sit up there when we were kids.'

'Oh, they're sure to. It's the charm of the place.'

'If it's structurally sound,' Patsy found herself saying.

'You know something,' said Penny, looking at her with a raised eyebrow. 'Since when do you ever say things like that?'

There was no point hiding it. 'Okay, you've got me. Oliver's bought it.'

'Has he really? Well that's something to natter about!'

The rest of the evening was taken up with Patsy being interrogated about what it was like inside and what they were planning to do and everyone was very excited by the end. She also had plenty of offers of help for everything from upholstery and cleaning, to Mary whose daughter was a graphic designer. In the end she was glad she'd told them. It was better than them hearing it from Rosemary and knowing she'd known and not told them. And anyway, it just showed that in general, everyone thought it was great that the cinema would be up and running again. And all she needed to do was find out exactly what was what with the technical side of things.

# 5

After a combination of googling and Facebook stalking, Patsy managed to contact someone at the Worcester University Film Society and had arranged to meet a guy called Ed on the university campus to see if she could get a bit more information about the technical side of running a cinema.

She was waiting in the Costa coffee shop, expecting to be meeting a young man between 18 and 21 years old when a man in his thirties came up to her.

'Patsy?'

'Ed? Oh, hi, thanks for meeting me.'

'No worries, I'll just grab a coffee.'

Despite his age, he was dressed very much like a typical student, in jeans, Converse trainers and a hoodie. He was tall and slim with dark brown hair which was grown out of what had probably been a decent haircut and now was marginally on the cool side of unkempt. He was wearing glasses with heavy black frames which Patsy found particularly attractive, to her surprise.

'So, you want to find out about being a projectionist?' he asked when he sat down opposite her with his coffee and a few sachets of sugar.

'Sort of. My friend has bought the old cinema in Croftwood and neither of us know anything about the technical side of running a cinema. We need to find out if the equipment that's there is going to work, that's the main thing.'

'That's an exciting project,' Ed said, as he emptied three sachets of sugar into his coffee and started drinking it without bothering to stir.

'Yes, there's quite a lot to do and to be honest, we hadn't thought about this side of it at all.'

Ed frowned. 'But it's a cinema, isn't that the only side?'

'We're opening it as a sort of boutique cinema with a bar and a food offer and we're hoping the space will be flexible enough to be a venue we can hire out for functions.'

'That sounds cool.' He nodded thoughtfully. 'But you're not going to get very far with being a cinema if you haven't sorted out your projection box.'

Patsy was momentarily stunned that he was being so frank and her first reaction was to be offended. Clearly he thought they were idiots for not having considered the practicalities. But he was right and Patsy recognised her own brand of telling it like it is in Ed.

'That's absolutely true and that's where you come in.'

'I'd love to have a look at it, if that's okay. How long's it been closed? I wonder what kind of kit you've got?' His face lit up as he spoke. He was obviously passionate about this and Patsy felt like she'd struck gold on her first attempt at finding someone who might help.

'It's been closed for over twenty years. I wouldn't even be able to start to describe what's there, apart from a couple of huge spools sitting behind the projector.'

'Oh, it's a tower system, awesome. We use a platter system here but I know how to deal with a tower. It's a lot simpler.'

'That's a good start then,' said Patsy, with a sigh of relief that she wasn't going to lose her prized advisor before they'd even left the coffee shop. 'I'll get the keys off Oliver and maybe we can meet there in a couple of days? Can I have your number and I'll text you.'

'I'll put it in your phone,' said Ed, holding out his hand.

Patsy unlocked her phone and handed it over, taking the opportunity to look at him more carefully while he wasn't watching her. He was actually wearing quite expensive clothes that at first glance, maybe because she had been thinking 'student', had appeared scruffy.

'There you go. So I'll wait to hear from you?'

'Great. I've got Thursday off, so maybe sometime then?'

'Works for me, I haven't got any lectures on Thursday.'

'Well, thanks for your time, Ed,' said Patsy, standing up. She felt a bit awkward, should she shake his hand or something?

'No problem, thanks for getting in touch. It's great to be able to help with something like this.' He held out his hand to her. He had a strong grip and when he looked at her and smiled, she could have got lost in his gorgeous brown eyes. And not only his eyes were gorgeous; Patsy felt a surge of attraction that she hadn't experienced for years.

'See you Thursday then,' she said, hurriedly pulling her hand from his grip and leaving before she blushed right to the roots of her hair and he saw exactly what she'd been thinking written all over her face.

On the bus journey back to Croftwood, Patsy couldn't stop thinking about Ed. It was so long since she'd even thought about a man in that way, the attraction she'd felt towards him had come over her in a wave from nowhere and left her feeling a little bit stunned. Since she'd left Dan and moved back to Croftwood, the last thing on her mind had been starting a new relationship. Things had been so bad with him that she found it hard to imagine what it would be like to have a relationship that you could classify as normal. But today, Ed had made her feel differently, and although it was quite scary, another part of her was excited to know that at least she wasn't dead inside. She had been attracted to Ed and it had ignited a little spark that she would be very careful with until she knew whether he felt the same.

Of course, he could have a girlfriend, a wife even. It wasn't unheard of for students, especially mature ones, to be married. It would be odd if he wasn't in some sort of relationship, Patsy thought as self-preservation kicked in and she sabotaged the thoughts she'd briefly entertained that he could be the man to lead her out of her lonely existence. And did she really want to go out with a student? They might be similar in age but they were at completely different places in their lives. It would never work.

But he seemed lovely. Patsy looked in her contacts and found his number. He'd put himself in as Ed followed by the nerd face emoji which made Patsy smile and remind herself that she'd met him for ten minutes and maybe that wasn't enough to go on either way. She would see how things went when they met on Thursday and not over-think it in the meantime.

Back at the coffee house, Oliver was sitting at the table nearest to the counter with his laptop open. He looked up when she came in and then seeing it was her, relaxed back again, smiling.

'Good meeting?'

'Really good. He's massively enthusiastic about coming to see what we've got, so that's a good start.'

Toby was the only other person in the coffee house which wasn't that unusual for the time of day and he made a move to come to the counter.

'Another coffee, Toby? I can bring it over,' she called as she swapped her coat for an apron.

'Thank you, much appreciated. I'll pay for two next time I come up,' he said and went back to his laptop.

'What do you think he does?' Patsy whispered to Oliver on her way back from taking Toby's coffee over to him.

Oliver shrugged. 'He hasn't been coming in long enough to have found out yet. I did see him heading in the direction of Portland Avenue the other day so maybe that's where he lives.'

Patsy's eyes widened. Portland Avenue was one of the nicest roads in Croftwood. If Toby lived there he had a detached Victorian house on a wide, quiet road lined with mature lime trees. Every time one of those houses came up for sale, she and Oliver had a good look at them on Rightmove to see how the other half lived.

'If he lives there he must be making some serious money doing whatever that is.' She waved her hand discreetly in his direction.

'Quite. We'll find out,' said Oliver easily. 'We always do. So what's the next step with the cinema guy?'

'Oh, we're going to arrange to meet up on Thursday so I can show him the projection box. Is that okay with you?'

'Course it is. I can hold the fort here. Which reminds me, I need to ask Linda if Jack's still interested in a few hours here.'

'Sorry, Ollie, I meant to ring him the other day. Let me get his number off Linda and give him a call.'

'Would you? That would be great, thanks. I've got the accounts to do and I'm seeing Matt later about submitting the plans. Do you want to sit in on that?'

Patsy scrunched her nose. She was keen to see the plans but her first impression of Matt was that he was a bit condescending towards her. Because they were inevitably going to work together, perhaps she should suck it up and go to the meeting to get things off on the right foot. Maybe her first impressions were wrong. It had been known. Since they were meeting upstairs in Oliver's flat, she decided to go but regretted her decision almost before they'd started.

'Are you a qualified architect?'

'Well, no, obviously not.' Even Oliver seemed taken aback at Matt's response to Patsy's suggestion that they put a dividing wall in the foyer to make a corridor between the foyer and the entrance to the stalls.

'You can't 'just' put walls in wherever you want to. You have to consider the flow of the building. And there are all sorts of other considerations like fire escapes...all sorts of things.'

Matt seemed exasperated and was running his hands through his hair.

'Is everything alright, mate?' Oliver asked him.

'Sorry. It's been one of those days. Apologies, Patsy, I didn't mean to snap at you.'

'No problem.' It had confirmed her suspicions about him but she appreciated the apology, nevertheless.

'The most important thing for you guys is to get the necessary planning permission in place as soon as possible and the quickest way for that to happen is to make the fewest changes possible.'

His tone told Patsy that he was struggling to keep calm in the face of two people who didn't know what they were talking about and she wondered what had happened to him to put him in such a mood.

'We need planning permission to open up the brickwork at the back so that the old scene dock door can work and we need permission to fit the extraction system into the side of the building where the new kitchen is going to be.'

'Those are the most important things to get us up and running,' Oliver said, looking at Patsy for her consensus.

'Yes, but we haven't talked about exactly what we're going

to do to the inside. What if there are other things we ought to be putting on the planning permission that we haven't thought of yet?'

Matt exhaled impatiently but to his credit, took a breath and said, 'We can always put in amendments at a later date. It's not now or never, we're just ticking off the big things first.'

'Okay, that's fine then,' Patsy said.

'I'm sorry, Oliver. If we're agreed on that, I'll submit for you tomorrow but I could do with calling it a night. It's been a long day.'

Patsy briefly felt sorry for him. He did look tired.

'That's fine, mate. I appreciate you doing this with us tonight.'

They shook hands and Matt gave Patsy a weary smile. All of a sudden, tired, cross Matt was somehow more endearing than condescending Matt had been.

'I'll be in touch,' he said, and headed downstairs to the coffee house to be let out by Oliver.

'Want me to walk you home?' Oliver asked Patsy when he came back upstairs.

'No, of course not. But thanks for the chivalrous offer. So what's with Matt? Is it a bad work day or something else?'

Oliver shrugged and Patsy knew she was an idiot to think that a man and his friend would discuss anything personal.

'I don't know. He's recently been through a divorce, maybe it's something to do with that?'

'Mmm, maybe.'

Patsy walked home wondering how it could be that she could go three years without entertaining the idea of having a man in her life to now, in the same week, two men had... what was it even? Had an effect on her? Made her notice that she was a woman capable of being attracted to men? Whatever it was, it was disconcerting. Especially because somehow, Matt was in the mix even though she had an inkling he had misogynistic-arse tendencies. But her heart had ached for him when he'd said goodbye and she'd seen that look in his eyes. What was going on?

# 6

Patsy had texted Ed and arranged to meet him at the entrance to the park at eleven o'clock on Thursday morning. She had the keys from Oliver and was going to go back to the coffee house afterwards to let him know what Ed thought of their projection set-up.

'Hey, Patsy,' said Ed, arriving at the park entrance wearing an outfit almost identical to what he'd been wearing the day she'd met him but with a smart black wool peacoat, the collar turned up against the chill of the bright spring day. In contrast, Patsy was wearing a navy blue teddy fur coat which had seen better days. Feeling decidedly down at heel compared to Ed, she decided right then that this was going to be its last winter.

'Hi, Ed. Thanks for coming. Shall we go straight in?'

'Lead the way,' he said, gesturing with a sweep of his hand.

She followed the path towards the door with Ed behind her, which made her extremely self-conscious. She could feel his gaze on her back and wondered what he was thinking. As well as the slightly scruffy coat, she'd chosen to wear some old-favourite purple flared corduroy jeans and she suddenly worried what he would think. They weren't especially fashionable but she loved the way they looked with her Red or Dead T-bar shoes. Now though, as she walked along, imagining him critiquing everything he could see, she was convinced that he'd think she was dressed like a five-year-old from the 1970s.

Luckily, Matt had left the hard hats inside the doorway and Oliver had reminded her to make sure they used them. He'd also made her get some masks, given that there was at least one pigeon that had taken up residence in the projection box and apparently Matt had gone on to Oliver quite a lot about the health hazards related to pigeon poo.

'Are the hats and masks an indication that it's a right state inside?' asked Ed.

'It's not, although there was a pigeon in the projection box because the window's smashed. Look.' She pointed to the round window above them, where helpfully, a pigeon flew through as they stood there.

'Yes, I see. So that probably needs boarding up before the equipment gets ruined by pigeon shit.'

'It might be too late for that.'

Grabbing a torch each, they went into the auditorium first where Ed marvelled about how it was a time warp and Patsy explained their plans, such as they were.

'Shame the screen's ripped,' he said, shining his torch on it. 'They cost serious money to replace. Although if we can repair the tear we might be able to shift the projector to the right slightly and then we'd miss the worst of it.'

It boosted Patsy's confidence in the whole project for him to be referring to doing things as 'we'. He was obviously pretty keen to be involved and thank goodness because the comments he'd made, even in their first meeting, had made her realise how much she and Oliver didn't know about running a cinema. It had started to feel worse than Oliver not looking around the building before he bought it.

They made their way up to the projection box and Patsy made as much noise as she could when they opened the door to frighten the pigeons out.

'You go first,' she said to Ed, just in case there were any birds planning to jump out at her.

He headed straight for the projector which seemed to have escaped the worst of the pigeon detritus.

'Oh, yes. This is similar to the model we have at uni. Not exactly the same but I know where I am with it. And the tower, apart from being a bird perch at the moment looks to be in good nick. All of it will need dismantling and cleaning but I think it'll work.'

'What's all that other stuff?' Patsy asked, pointing to the unit which had all the switches.

Ed grinned. 'This stuff is the sound. That's not so much my area of expertise, you'd need to get an engineer to check it out. I mean, we'll be able to tell if it works but if it doesn't that's where my knowledge ends.'

He walked further into the room, past the projector.

'Ah, nice little making-up table in here.' He turned round and surveyed the room, nodding his head, which Patsy took to be a good sign, even if she couldn't see his expression because of the mask. 'Top priority, get the window boarded.'

'Okay. I'll tell the boss. Look, do you want to come for a coffee? My friend Oliver runs a coffee house in town and he's the one who bought this place, he'd love to meet you and hear what you think.'

'Yes, sure, that'd be good.'

They made their way back outside and took big lungfuls of fresh air as soon as their masks were off. They looked at each other and laughed.

'Great minds,' Ed said, taking Patsy's hardhat from her

and dropping it inside the doorway with the others before Patsy locked the door, asking Ed to double-check that it was secure before they strolled through the park together towards Oliver's.

'Do you live in Croftwood?' Ed asked.

'Yes, I've got a flat the other side of the park.'

'And what do you do?'

'I work at Oliver's, that's my friend's coffee house. Named it after himself but it kind of works.'

Ed nodded thoughtfully. 'So he's a bit of an entrepreneur?'

'I suppose he is. I've never really thought about it, but buying the cinema makes him one for sure. He's a good friend, massively helped me out when I moved back to Croftwood.'

'Where did you move from?'

'I grew up here but moved to Birmingham and came back a couple of years ago.'

'Wow, it's quite different to Birmingham, a bit on the quiet side, in comparison.'

Patsy shrugged. 'It was great living in the city for a while but you know, it's not as if every night is a night out or every day is a day out.'

Ed frowned, a confused look on his face.

'I suppose what I mean is that it's cool to live somewhere like that for the nightlife or the culture or whatever but actually, you don't take advantage of those things every day if you live there. And on a daily basis, Croftwood is a much friendlier place to live.'

'Working at a coffee shop must be good for that, meeting people, I mean. Same with my job, really.'

'What, being a student?' Patsy laughed at his description of it being a job.

'I'm not a student,' he said, as if it should be obvious. 'I'm a lecturer.'

It made a lot more sense, although Patsy was surprised a lecturer could get away with dressing so casually.

'Well, in my defence, you look like a student.'

'Helps to get them on side,' he said, grinning.

'What do you teach?'

'Computer Science.'

That threw Patsy. Her own background was in that field, although it felt like a lifetime ago. It was a coincidence that she would put to the back of her mind. That wasn't who she was anymore. But now she knew what he did, Ed began to make sense to her. He was a cool nerd. They arrived at the coffee house and as Oliver was busy serving a customer, Patsy went behind the counter to help.

'Take a seat, Ed. What can I get you?'

'Cappuccino, please.' He headed over to a table in the window.

'So that's the film bloke?' asked Oliver, as he steamed the milk for Ed and Patsy's coffees while Patsy dealt with the rest.

'Yes, Ed.'

'You're blushing, Pats. Got a soft spot for him already?'

'Shut up, he's nice. Be nice.'

'I'm always nice. Does he know his stuff?'

'Definitely. And he seemed to think there's nothing a good clean wouldn't solve for the projector and the spinny wheel bit.'

'Did he teach you that technical term? It's impressive…'

Patsy whipped him on the leg with a tea towel.

'Ouch! Come on Pats, I'm only joking. Sorry,' he added when he saw the fierce expression on her face.

'Just bring the coffee over okay? And come and sit down with us for a minute while you haven't got any customers.'

Patsy went to join Ed, and Oliver followed her with a coffee for each of them.

'Hi Ed, nice to meet you, I'm Oliver Jones.'

Ed stood up and shook Oliver's hand.

'So Patsy tells me you think we might be okay with the projection stuff?' Oliver said. 'I must admit, I was worried I'd bitten off more than I can chew. I was so focused on the hospitality side of things, I didn't even think about the bloody cinema.

Ed smiled. 'The projector and the tower need a good clean. Like I said to Patsy, the sound equipment isn't my area, you might have to get a specialist in to take a look but once the window's boarded up and you've evicted the pigeons, we can have a proper look.'

'That sounds great. Thanks for coming over, I really appreciate it. Sorry, looks like I've got another customer.' Oliver took his coffee and left Ed and Patsy to it.

'Do you think I'm in there then?' Ed asked after Oliver had left. 'I'd love to have a go at restoring that projector.'

'In the absence of anyone else, no offence, I think you can assume the job's yours if you want it. I don't think we can pay you much though.'

Ed shrugged. 'It's not about the money. I'll enjoy it and I might recruit a couple of students from the Film Society to give me a hand. They'd be more than willing to give their time for free in exchange for beer.'

'That sounds more than fair.'

'Well, great, I look forward to getting started. Look, thanks for letting me get involved in this, Patsy.' He looked at very earnestly and her stomach flipped a little bit as she looked into his eyes.

'It's no problem, I mean, you're really the one doing us a favour. There'll be plenty of beer for you as well, or whatever your drink of preference is.' She tried to keep herself sounding breezy as her imagination ran away with her, producing images of them sipping wine together at the bar in the foyer of the cinema.

He looked at his phone. 'Sorry, I'd better be off. I've got a lecture at one.' He stood up, looked awkwardly at her for a split second, then said. 'Right, see you then.'

Patsy said goodbye and watched him walk up the high street, his hands in his coat pockets and she felt oddly bereft. She didn't know when she'd see him again, and suddenly that seemed like a problem. She wondered whether he felt like there was something between them in the same way that she was starting to. The fact that he'd agreed to help them out, well maybe that said something. Or maybe she was reading too much into it and he genuinely loved faffing around with projectors.

She snapped out of her daze and noticed Toby smiling at her from his desk of choice for the day, a couple of tables away.

She smiled back. 'Having a good day?'

'Not too bad, thanks. Nothing meaty as yet. I'm a lawyer. Give advice online,' he said.

'What do you call meaty?'

'I love a dispute. Anything apart from contract queries which are dull or family issues, they're always sad.'

'It must be quite interesting not knowing what you're going to get asked.'

'Yes, it is generally. More varied than anything I've done before. Less pressured too.'

Patsy decided that she'd learned quite a lot about Toby for one day so decided not to ask what he'd done before. That could wait until another day.

'Can I get you a refill?'

'That'd be great, thanks.'

She joined Oliver behind the counter where he was busy making a hot chocolate for someone and turned to serve the next customer.

'An espresso please,' the woman requested. Her eyes were red-rimmed, she'd obviously been crying.

'That's one-fifty please. Take a seat and I'll bring it over,' she said, gently.'

The woman nodded and rummaged in her bag. 'Oh god, I've forgotten my purse!'

Fresh tears rolled silently down her cheeks and she turned to leave.

'It's okay, it's —' on the house, she was about to say but Toby beat her to it.

'It's on me.' His tone said that there was no question that he was paying.

'Thank you, that's so kind of you,' said the woman and headed over to the table in the furthest corner from them.

'That was really nice of you,' Patsy said to him as he tapped his card, paying for his own coffee as well.

He shrugged and gave her a resigned smile. 'Forgetting her purse on top of whatever else is going on…it was the least I could do.'

He took his coffee and headed back to his laptop while Patsy made the espresso. Such a small but hugely compassionate gesture for a complete stranger to make. Anyone could have done the same but Patsy could count on both thumbs how many people had ever done that during one of her shifts at the coffee house, aside from Oliver who regularly gave away the odd cup to someone who might be having a bad day. Toby was one of the good ones and knowing now what he did for a living, well that was something to remember for another time.

# 7

Work finally started on the cinema a couple of weeks later, when spring was in full swing. Matt the architect had wanted far too many meetings for Patsy's liking and she had quickly lost the will to live. Oliver agreed that as the project manager, he would deal with the strategic decisions. The guilt she'd had at feeling like she was picking and choosing only the interesting bits was quashed as soon as she realised Oliver seemed to have no limit to how many meetings he was prepared to have. She would much rather cover his hours at the coffee house while he did that than have to be involved in endless discussions about health and safety issues any more than she had to be. But with every meeting they had with Matt, the clearer it was to her that she had got him wrong. Not to say that his constant haughty reminders about wearing hard hats didn't get on every single one of her nerves sometimes, but she didn't dislike him quite as much as she had in the beginning.

Scaffolding had been erected around the building and some of the greenery surrounding it had been cut back to accommodate that. The first part of the plan was to make good the outside by replacing the guttering and any broken tiles on the roof. The bargeboard and soffits were all being painted and the window had been repaired.

Inside the auditorium, in the stalls, they'd peeled back a corner of the carpet to find a beautiful wooden floor which amazingly seemed sound.

'The floor is beautiful,' said Patsy when she and Oliver were waiting for Matt.

'I know. Matt's asked me what we want to do. I don't think we've got much choice other than to carpet it again. I mean, you don't want people clomping around on noisy floorboards in a cinema.'

'Sorry I'm late,' said Matt, rushing in looking flustered and with two small children in tow.

'No problem at all, mate,' said Oliver. 'Are you sure you don't want to do this another time?'

'There's never a good time at the moment. They won't be any trouble.'

He herded his children, a boy and girl who were no older than about five, into the back row of the stalls and spoke to them in hushed tones which Patsy could tell was a major warning to them to behave themselves.

'So, the floor,' he began. 'What do you think?' He turned around, distracted by the children who were already out of their seats and running across the back row. 'Flo! Sammy! What did I say?'

The children stopped in their tracks, briefly but then carried on as soon as his back was turned. Patsy could tell he was going to lose it.

'Do you mind if I give them a job to do?' she asked.

He raised his eyebrows and grinned. 'If you can do anything that means they'll behave themselves for five minutes, be my guest.' His tone told her he had serious doubts that she'd be able to do anything.

'Got some Post-It notes?' She knew he did because his files were covered in them. He handed her a stack which she split in half. She called the children over to her, knelt down and chatted to them for a minute, handing them each some Post-Its.

'The floor. I think it's gorgeous but too noisy to have in a cinema,' Patsy said, while Matt was still looking at his children who were now quietly sitting in each chair in turn, having a quiet word with each other and then putting a Post-It note on the chair, or not, before moving onto the next one.

'What are they doing?'

'They're marking which chairs are uncomfortable or broken.'

'You're a genius,' he said, exhaling and turning his full attention onto the meeting now that the children were occupied. 'Okay, you're right about the floor. I think we need to look at a floor covering that's as practical as this wooden flooring would be because when it's being an events space, it's the perfect solution, easier to keep clean than carpet. But you need soft surfaces to help the acoustics overall, not only to keep the noise of footsteps down.'

'Have you come across anything that you think could work?' Oliver asked.

'I'll bring some samples to the next meeting. We're ruling out carpet then?'

'I think so, but let's look at the costs as well before we finalise,' said Oliver.

They walked down the stalls to the area behind the screen so that Matt could explain what was going to happen next with the scene dock doors, passing the children who were solemnly discussing one of the chairs. Matt caught Patsy's eye and gave her a grateful smile.

'Thanks. They can be a handful.'

'They're not angels like this all the time?'

'You wouldn't believe what five-year-old twins can get up to when they put their heads together.'

Once they'd said goodbye to Matt and the twins, who'd made him promise that they could come back to help with the chairs another day, Oliver and Patsy headed up the stairs to inspect the projection box which had been cleaned. The room didn't look that different because although it smelt better and, thank goodness, the floor wasn't covered in poo, it was still so dark in there. The light from the window was sucked up by the black walls as soon as it passed through the glass.

'There's not much to see, is there?' Patsy said as she wandered in, further than she'd been before now that no birds were going to frighten her to death.

Oliver was examining the projector and peering through the small window in the wall which looked out into the auditorium. 'I don't know, I think it's quite exciting. I can understand how your man, Ed, finds all this interesting. I might hang out with him and find out a bit about it, if that's not going to cramp your style.'

'You're such an idiot, Ollie. He's not my man, anyway.'

'Not yet.'

'Oh, for god's sake.'

'I saw the way he looked at you when you were making coffee. He was watching your every move. He likes you.'

'He was probably just desperate for a coffee. And he hasn't been in touch or anything so he's obviously not interested.'

'Give him a chance Pats, he's probably trying to play it cool. Or he has no idea what he's doing, which wouldn't be that surprising for one of those nerdy types.'

'I'm not sure either of those excuses make him ideal boyfriend material. And even if I did like him, he's the first man I've even thought I might be interested in for years. I don't think I'd be lucky enough for him to feel the same way.'

'Well, we'll see, won't we?' Oliver said. 'You need to let yourself go, have a bit of fun with him if that's what you want.'

'I might not have had much luck with men in the past but I think I can set my sights higher than having a bit of fun.'

'Definitely, Pats. I was only suggesting not to take it too seriously when, like you said, maybe he's not going to be the love of your life.'

But what Patsy was wondering again, was how it was possible that in the same week she had met Ed and felt that spark of attraction, she'd also noticed Matt. She couldn't say that she fancied him in the same way that she felt something for Ed, it wasn't an instant attraction, obviously, but there was definitely something about him that intrigued her and she was beginning to enjoy their sometimes barbed exchanges over the plans for the cinema, maybe even looked forward to them. Perhaps Ed had somehow awoken something in her that had been dormant since Dan and now her attraction beacon was working again. It sounded ridiculous but that was how it felt. Maybe Oliver was right and she shouldn't think too hard about it all, just see what happened and do whatever made her happy. It made a nice change, anyway.

It had been a couple of weeks since Ed had been to Croftwood and Patsy hadn't heard from him since. Having tentatively arranged that she would let him know when things were underway, now that the projection box had been cleaned felt like the ideal time to get in touch.

**It's done and all the pigeon poo is gone so we're ready when you are! X**

She immediately regretted the kiss. It felt too much. She was used to almost exclusively texting Oliver, so it had been automatic.

**Great, can't wait to get started!**

He hadn't reciprocated the kiss. That meant he had actively decided not to and her heart sank a little bit. He probably wasn't interested.

**I've got the day off on Sunday. Cinema at 11am? I'll bring the coffee! X**

It was important to sound breezy. And not to look as if she'd rethought the kiss.

**Works for me. See you then.**

Hopefully he'd assume the kiss business was something that she did all the time. Feeling that she had nothing to lose after all, she texted a reply.

**Looking forward to it :-) X**

# 8

On Sunday morning, Patsy called in at Oliver's to collect coffees for her and Ed on her way to the cinema. It was her day off and the place was quiet now that the Sunday morning brunch crowd had thinned out. It had been drizzling on and off which was probably persuading people to stay indoors and embrace a lazy start.

'Two lattes, please,' said Patsy, as she helped herself to two pain au chocolats and a handful of sugar sachets.

'Help yourself to the pastries, Pats,' said Oliver, rolling his eyes and smiling at her as he started steaming the milk. 'What are you up to this morning?'

'I'm meeting Ed at the cinema. Now that it's clean and pigeon free, he's keen to get started. Is it okay to give him a spare key?'

'Sure. Maybe ask him to let you know when he's planning to be there so someone knows if he's there by himself. Health and safety, you know.'

'Okey dokey. It's quite exciting isn't it?'

'Mmm hmm,' said Oliver. 'The project or seeing Ed?'

Patsy took a moment to consider her answer. 'Okay, if I'm

being honest, both. I did get a little flutter when he texted me so I think that's a sign.'

'He texted you? So he must be keen too.'

'Well, I started the texting,' Patsy admitted. 'He might be keener on the cinema project than he is on me.'

'He's probably using that as an excuse. Maybe he's a bit shy. I mean, he teaches computers so maybe he doesn't have that much experience with women?'

'Not everyone who's into computers is a social outcast. But maybe you're right. We'll see how it goes.' She tucked the pastries inside her bag and picked up the coffees. 'See you in the morning.'

'Have a good time, Pats. See you tomorrow.'

Patsy walked through the churchyard towards the park, enjoying the signs of spring that were still emerging. Even though the patches of crocuses that had been sprinkled across the grass were almost gone, there were still plenty of daffodils, the trees were blossoming and there was a hint of the scent in the air.

Ed was waiting outside the cinema with a big holdall at his feet.

'Morning,' he said.

'Morning.' Patsy passed him one of the coffees. 'Shall we have coffee before we go in? Seems a shame to be inside since it's stopped raining.'

'Okay,' he agreed and they headed for a nearby park bench. 'You're right, it's a glorious day now but still a bit cloudy if you look over there.'

While he laid his waterproof coat along the bench for them to sit on, Patsy pulled the pastries out of her bag. 'I got these too. And some sugar for you.'

'Thanks.' He took three packets of sugar and emptied them into his coffee then took a pastry. 'You remembered about the sugar.'

'No-one takes three sugars these days, it's pretty memorable.' She looked at him and smiled. It felt a bit awkward between them, she didn't know why. Perhaps once they got started it would be okay.

'I'd like to say it's my only vice but that's probably not true.'

'If you count that as a vice, I think you're probably doing okay.'

He smiled. 'Looks like things are really starting to happen,' he said, gesturing to the cinema with his cup.

'Yes, they've finished the roof so I think taking out the back wall is the next thing to do before the scaffolding comes down.'

'That sounds like a big job. What kind of timescale are you on?'

'We're hoping to finish by the end of July and then we'll have the grand opening in August so that we can still make the most of the park before the end of the summer.'

'Well, that's plenty of time for sorting out the projection box.'

'Cool. It does seem that we keep forgetting about that side of things even though that's our main attraction.'

'Shall we make a start? I mean, you don't have to stay, you can just let me in if you've got things to do.'

Patsy tried hard to gauge whether Ed wanted to be by himself or whether he was being polite.

'I'll hang around for a bit, if you don't mind. It's quite interesting and I think out of me and Oliver, at least one of us needs to have some clue about the projection side of things.'

Ed grinned and when Patsy smiled back at him, she found herself caught in his gaze for what seemed like minutes until he bent down to pick up the holdall and lifted his coat off the bench.

Patsy fumbled in her bag for the keys. 'Right, let's go in

then.'

Since her last visit to the projection box, some working lights had been installed. The main electrics in the building still needed replacing but in the areas that needed it there were temporary lights.

'Blimey, it's quite a transformation,' said Ed as they walked into the projection box. He opened the holdall and pulled out a roll of lining paper. 'Okay, we're going to dismantle the front of the projector. It's the only way we can clean it thoroughly,' he added when he saw Patsy's look of alarm. 'Don't worry, I'm going to meticulously catalogue the parts so there'll be no problem putting it back together.' His confident tone did nothing to reassure Patsy. It seemed so drastic but she had no choice but to put her faith in him.

'So where do we start?'

'We'll lay out this paper over there on the floor.' He pulled a black marker pen out of the bag. 'I'm going to work top-down through the projector, removing all the parts. I'll pass each part to you, you put it on the paper, draw a rough outline around it and number it sequentially. Okay?'

It sounded simple enough. 'Okay.' Patsy took her coat off and hung it behind the door on one of a set of coat hooks which she'd never noticed before. Ed did the same.

Also in the holdall were a set of tools which he laid on the floor next to the projector.

'Right, ready?' He handed the pen to Patsy. It seemed like a whole new level of responsibility of the sort she hadn't had in a long time.

'Ready.'

'Okay, I'm on the top sprocket.'

Patsy wasn't sure if she needed to know that but repeated, 'Top sprocket, top sprocket,' to herself while she waited, in case the term went clean out of her head while she waited. After a couple of minutes he handed her a metal tube with spikes going around either end of it. It was pretty dirty, she could only tell it was metal because of the weight of it.

'Okay, top sprocket.' She placed it on the paper that they'd laid out and drew around it, writing 1. Top Sprocket next to it. One down, quite a few to go.

Ed continued to hand her pieces, many of them sprockets and all of them filthy. They worked in companionable silence, only speaking to reference the parts as they concentrated on the job in hand.

'Okay, that's the first lot out,' said Ed. 'It's in good nick if you ignore the dirt.' He took a packet of wipes out of the holdall, pulled out a couple and handed them to Patsy before taking some more for himself.

'God, that's disgusting,' Patsy said, looking at the dirt that had come off her hands.

'Yep, and there's more where that came from.'

'So what's next?'

Ed looked at his watch. 'That's a good place to stop. Best to tackle it in chunks, I think.'

Patsy pulled out her phone and was shocked to find it was three o'clock. 'Wow, time flies when you're having fun.'

'I appreciate the help, Patsy. You did a great job,' he said gesturing to the floor where around forty pieces of projector were carefully laid out.

'I've really enjoyed it. I'm happy to help anytime if I'm free, just let me know. Oh, I have these for you.' She pulled the spare keys out of her pocket and handed them to him. 'So you can come and go as you please, but you need to text me if you're coming so we know who's in the building.'

'Thanks, that's great. I'll probably come over on the odd evening. Is it okay to leave this stuff here?'

'Yes, of course. Mi casa es su casa, or whatever the phrase is.' She could feel herself blushing.

'Have you got any plans for the rest of the day?' Ed asked

as he pulled his coat on.

'Not really. I'll probably go home, sit on the terrace if the sun's out.'

They walked down the stairs together. Was he going to ask her out for a drink? Or dinner? She locked the door and they stood looking at each other briefly, Patsy's expectation that he might suggest going on somewhere together building by the second.

'Well, thanks. I'll let you know when I'm over here again.'

'Right.' He turned to walk away and Patsy watched him. Then he turned around and her heart lifted. He was going to ask her.

But he smiled, awkwardly, and then carried on walking.

Patsy began walking in the opposite direction, towards home. Her heart was sunk into her boots. Was it her? She felt she was reading the situation completely wrongly. Maybe she was out of practice, it had been so long since she'd had any interest in the opposite sex. Was it as Oliver had said and he was shy? He was a grown man, for goodness sake and it was hardly as if she was some flippy-haired sure-of-herself intimidating woman. She felt she had given him every opportunity to say something, if he wanted to. So either she'd got it wrong and he didn't want anything more than friendship, or else, maybe she was going to have to make the first move. That was a particularly frightening thought. She wasn't sure she'd ever made the first move before, definitely not with Dan. He'd very much been the pursuer. And before Dan, it had just been the odd snog in a nightclub and who ever remembered how those things started?

At home, Patsy made herself a gin and tonic, dug her sunglasses out of a drawer and took a blanket off the arm of the sofa before climbing out of the window onto her little terrace to enjoy the sun now that the rainclouds had disappeared. Once she was settled in her chair with the blanket across her, she could well believe it was summer. The sunshine always made her feel better.

After a few sips of her drink, she decided that she'd give Ed one more chance to make his move and then, if there was another opportunity like there had been today, when she thought he was going to ask her out, if that happened and he passed it up again, maybe she'd put on her brave pants and ask him herself. What did she have to lose? Getting turned down by a computer science lecturer wasn't the worst thing that had ever happened to her. It was a long time since she'd taken any kind of risk in her personal life, a long time since anything had happened in her personal life at all, and the very fact that she was considering asking someone out told Patsy everything she needed to know about how perhaps finally it was time to move on.

# 9

Every Friday and Saturday night, the Worcester University Film Society put on a film for its members. It was as much about the running of the whole thing, from selling tickets and refreshments to the projecting of the film and Ed was one of the members of staff who could be called on by the students for help with the technical side of things. This Friday, he was filling in at the last minute for a student who was ill although he suspected that it was more likely because of a party that they didn't want to miss. At the start of term when everyone committed to the rota, there were huge amounts of enthusiasm but when it came to it, the idea of missing a night out to soberly project a film by yourself, wasn't that appealing. Ed could understand that and he didn't mind doing the odd shift to keep his hand in anyway. What else would he be doing on a Friday night?

He left the house and walked along the alley which skirted the edge of the racecourse, crossed the river at the Sabrina bridge and took the path on the opposite bank of the river towards the campus. He had a bottle of wine stashed in his bag; once the film was on, the hard work was over and it was fine to relax and watch from the back corner seat which was always reserved for the projectionist. It was quite usual for the students to bring their own drinks with them, so no-one would bat an eyelid.

As he walked, it occurred to him that he could have invited Patsy along to see him run the film. He wasn't sure how interested she was but it was a genuine reason to have contacted her and if it hadn't been such a last minute commitment he might have thought of asking her. Although, there was still over an hour before the film actually started. He needed to get there early to open up but maybe it wasn't too late?

He paused to pull his phone out and typed a quick message.

**It's short notice, but if you're not busy I'm running the film tonight if you want to see how it's meant to work :-)**

He carried on walking but was almost holding his breath in anticipation of Patsy's reply. It was the best opportunity he'd had so far to ask her out without having to be too obvious about it. Now that he had his own key to the Croftwood cinema there was no need for her to be there with him anymore and he'd been wondering when he would see her again.

**Sounds great! When and where?! X**

With a huge grin on his face, Ed texted her directions and then carried on his way with a spring in his step.


Patsy hugged her phone to her chest. Ed had asked her out. Kind of. She knew she shouldn't read too much into it because it was almost a work thing. A demonstration of how an actual film gets projected was almost like a training session and although, to her surprise, she had become quite interested in the technical side of the cinema, she hoped it was more to do with Ed wanting to see her than him being desperate to impart his projectionist knowledge.

She had ten minutes to get ready and still be able to make the next bus to Worcester. She was changed into her leggings and a sweatshirt for a night in front of the television so she ran into the bedroom and picked up the dress she'd worn that day. It was navy-blue with a bright floral print, had a round neck, long sleeves and a tie-belt but Patsy's favourite thing about it was the skirt which was long and gathered in three tiers. She pulled on some bright pink tights and her battered black biker boots and she was good to go. Luckily all she needed was a refresh of mascara and some lipgloss and she was happy with herself. She grabbed a bar of her favourite sea salt dark chocolate from the cupboard — the only sweet treat she kept in the flat — and skipped out of the door.

Ed's directions were pretty thorough and when Patsy arrived, the lecture theatre which doubled as the cinema, was a hive of activity. She queued with the students and paid three pounds for a visitor ticket, realising that she had no idea what film they were showing.

'Hi, I'm looking for Ed?' she asked the girl who was manning the door into the auditorium.

'The projection box is round the corner.' She pointed Patsy in the right direction.

The door was closed, so Patsy knocked and then opened it and tentatively peeked inside.

'Patsy! You made it, come in.' Ed looked so pleased to see her, it gave her hope that maybe there was more to it than a training session.

The projection box was small, only around five metres by three and was dominated in one corner by something that looked like a giant tiered cake stand, with three stainless steel discs, maybe over a metre each in diameter. In the opposite corner to that was the projector which stood taller than Patsy and was a good deal smarter than the one at Croftwood.

'Wow, this is amazing. Quite a bit fancier than our set-up.'

'It's a bit more modern,' admitted Ed, 'but it does the same job. I haven't started yet, I wanted to show you right from the beginning.'

Patsy looked out at the auditorium through the window next to the projector. 'It looks like it's getting full already. Have you got time to show me?'

'It only takes a couple of minutes and we've got a bit longer than that.'

He went over to the big contraption in the corner where Patsy could see that a huge reel of film was lying on the top disc. Ed picked up the end of the film from the middle of the reel, looped it around a plastic roller and then pulled it over his head and across the room to the projector.

'Oh my god, it's going to be like that the whole time? Stretched across the room?'

'Yes,' Ed grinned. He was clearly in his element and Patsy wasn't sure it was about her after all. This was something he was passionate about and he was enjoying sharing it with her. 'Yours won't be like that because you've got the tower which is instead of this kind of platter system. Your film will be behind the projector. Come round here.'

Patsy squeezed into the space between the side of the projector and the wall and watched Ed weave the film through the projector, from the top to the bottom, around all the sprockets. They were exactly like the ones she'd carefully laid out on the floor in the cinema only these were bright and shiny and she couldn't imagine that theirs would ever clean up to that kind of standard.

'Come here and look through the gate.' He pointed to where he meant. It was almost the only place inside the projector where the film was flat; everywhere else it was in loops around the sprockets. 'This is where the light is going to shine through when we switch it on. You have to make sure that a whole frame of film is in here when you lace up, otherwise when you start the film, the picture will be split.'

There was a lot to take in and Patsy was a little overwhelmed by all the technical information but she leaned in to see what he was talking about. In the close quarters of the projection box, it was the closest she'd ever been to Ed and she could smell him. It felt so intimate and made her catch her breath. Examining the film gave her a few seconds to compose herself. 'No pressure then,' she said, aware that she sounded breathy. 'Has that ever happened?'

'No, it's the first thing you learn and, touch wood, no-one forgets it. There are other things that are more likely to go wrong.'

Once she'd moved out of the way, he went back and checked the projector while Patsy stared at his side profile, feeling like she'd discovered a secret. She knew what he smelt like and it wasn't aftershave wafting all around the room, it was him and it gave her butterflies.

He laid the end of the film on the floor then briefly switched the projector on. Patsy was surprised at how quickly the film ran through, making a loopy pile on the floor. Once there was enough film to reach back to the platter, he switched it off and picked up the end he'd laid on the floor ready for the next step.

'See, once it starts running, it'll wind back onto the platter with the start of the film in the middle ready for next time,' he said as he wound the end of the film around the centre circle. 'Saves rewinding it. That's one of the main disadvantages of a tower, the rewinding.'

He switched something on and the film tensioned between the projector and the platter.

'Now we need to put the lamp on and we're good to go.'

He pressed a button on the projector and a loud buzz signalled that the lamp was lit, as well as light escaping from a tiny window in the back of the projector. Ed turned the lights off in the room.

'Is it time?'

'Just waiting for the go ahead from front of house. But we're ready.'

They stood together in the small space next to the projector. The sense of anticipation was palpable. Patsy could feel the adrenaline radiating from Ed and she understood why he liked it so much. Everyone in that auditorium was relying on what was going on in this box. It had to be perfectly executed and the pressure involved in pulling it off seamlessly was clear. There were so many things to know and remember and Patsy imagined that it would be easy to make a mistake.

'Okay, we've got the thumbs up,' Ed said as he looked out of the window. 'Everything will happen at once so stay there and don't move for a sec.'

'Okay.'

Ed flicked the projector on and it whirred into life. He turned some buttons, flicked something on the projector and did another dozen things all at the same time. Then he looked through to the screen and at the same time was adjusting something on the projector with his left hand.

'There, all done.' He turned and grinned at her. His eyes were bright and Patsy thought he'd never looked more confident. Maybe that would translate into him finally telling her if he liked her.

Ed pulled a bottle of wine out of his rucksack. That was a good sign.

Patsy took out her chocolate.

'We've got the refreshments covered between us,' said Ed. 'Shall we?' He gestured to the door.

'Is it okay to leave it?' With the film travelling back and

forth across the room, Patsy felt like it would all go wrong unless Ed stood next to the projector for the duration of the film.

'Yeah, it'll be fine and we'll be watching it so we'll know if anything goes wrong. We'll get booed, which will give us a clue if we don't notice.'

'Don't even joke about it. I had no idea all of this was going on every time I go to the cinema.'

'Well, it doesn't go on in many places anymore, all the big cinema chains have gone digital.'

Patsy led the way out of the projection box, realising that she still didn't know what the film was going to be.

Ed closed the door, laughing at Patsy's worried expression. 'Honestly, it'll be fine.' He picked up two plastic cups from the refreshment stall and quietly opened the door at the back of the auditorium. He let Patsy into the back row first and then sat down next to her. His eyes were on the film straight away, as if he was checking it, then he gave Patsy a thumbs up and poured the wine for each of them. He handed her a cup and they silently chinked them together before settling down to watch the film.

It was Jaws of all things. Patsy didn't think she'd ever seen it all the way through and even though everyone laughed when they saw the shark which did look like a big plastic prop compared to the CGI wonders they could produce now, there were still plenty of jumps and screams. Each time, she and Ed looked at each other and laughed and near the end, the part when they were on the boat, the calm before the storm, she felt his hand slip into hers and she knew she'd been right to give him the chance to tell her before she jumped in ahead of him. Tonight was on his terms. It was his place, his passion and he'd needed that to give him the confidence to take the leap.

Patsy's heart swelled in the darkness as she squeezed his

hand and felt a squeeze in return. This was the start of something. The first time in a long time that she'd felt special to someone and the first time in a long time that things had felt so right. The only person she'd been close to in the past three years was Oliver and their friendship meant everything to her. But this, with Ed, was something else entirely and right in that moment when the lights were still down, before they could spoil anything by having to talk about what had happened between them, she was so happy she thought she might burst.

# 10

On Monday morning, Patsy was still on a high after Friday night when Ed taking her hand had told her everything she wanted to know. They'd both been on cloud nine after the film and had said very little to each other while Ed switched everything off and locked up. He'd walked her into town to get the last bus back to Croftwood, holding hands the entire time and they'd had the briefest of kisses before she got on the bus and went home, feeling as if she was the luckiest girl in the world.

She'd been holding the fort at Oliver's during the morning rush while Oliver went to the weekly site meeting at the cinema.

'Oh my god, Pats, you've got some weird dreamy look on your face,' he said, taking his coat off and hanging it behind the door to the flat. 'Did he finally sweep you off your feet?'

Patsy could feel herself blush. Was it that obvious? 'What are you talking about?' she said defensively, knowing that resistance was futile because Oliver could read her like a book.

'He did. Well, good for Ed. It was about time. Spill the

beans then, how does a nerd proposition the woman of his dreams?'

'He's not a nerd.'

'Ah, so he did proposition you! I knew it!'

As irritating as it was that Oliver was absolutely right, Patsy couldn't help but grin and tell him everything. Not that there was much to tell but it felt like her world had shifted and she knew Oliver would understand that.

'At least he didn't push it on the first date,' Oliver said, with a protective tone to his voice.

'It wasn't meant to be a date, he was showing me how to run a film. It's just a coincidence.'

'It isn't. No-one, not even a nerd, asks a woman to something like that without an ulterior motive.'

'His motives were very pure.'

'I know, and that's good. He's a good bloke. And I'm really pleased for you. Only joking about the nerd stuff.'

He pulled her into a quick hug.

'No you're not, but it's okay because the nerd stuff is fine by me.' She made an espresso for Oliver while he was putting his apron on. 'How was the meeting?'

'Yeah, great. They're going to start taking down the brickwork on the back wall today to open up the door and it sounds like we're on schedule at the moment which is good.'

'That is good. I can't wait to see what the place looks like when the back door's open. I hope it's how I'm imagining it.'

'They've started taking the old chairs out. I thought we ought to try selling them. I mean some of them are a bit of a mess but if we can make a bit of money on them, that would help. Would you have time to look into it?'

The first thing that crossed her mind was how disappointed Matt's children would be that their chairs had gone. She'd have to come up with something else for them to do if they came with him again.

'Yes, definitely. It's a great idea. I wonder if it's worth getting the Gazette involved? See if they'll do an article about the project and then we can say where we're selling the chairs. I bet there are local people who would love to own a bit of Croftwood Cinema nostalgia.'

'That's a great idea. I'll leave that with you then?' He was looking at Patsy as if she might turn him down.

'Oliver, don't sound like you're scared to ask me. I want to help, I told you that.'

'I only worry because I'm not paying you properly.' He sighed. 'I feel like I'm taking advantage of your good nature.'

'Shut up. I'm happy to do it for barista wages. We made a deal, right? I'm happy to do whatever needs doing. Okay?'

'Okay. Thanks. And you have got a boyfriend because of me, so I suppose that's something.' He was grinning, knowing he'd get a rise out of her.

'As if that was anything to do with you. Now bugger off and clear those tables.' She flicked him with a tea towel for good measure.

She grinned as she watched Oliver clearing the tables. It felt great to have found Ed. It was a long time since she'd been in the first flush of a relationship and it made her feel like a teenager again. She hoped he'd text her to say he was coming over to work in the cinema so that she could meet him there. He'd warned her that he was busy with marking assignments so maybe he wouldn't have time this week but the anticipation of the next time she'd see him was keeping her going.


That evening, Patsy pulled out the old laptop that had come with her to Croftwood but never been touched. Unsurprisingly, the battery was dead so she had to wait for it to charge up before she could power it up and start looking for an outlet for selling their chairs. It had felt like a necessary break from her old life, when she'd worked on computers all the time, to not do that in her new life. That wasn't her job anymore and she hadn't missed it. Until now. It was odd having a keyboard at her fingertips again. Feeling the programming power she used to crave back in her hands. But she was going to continue, as she had for the past three years, to resist the urge to do anything other than browse the internet. Tonight, she wanted to make sure that there was somewhere they could sell the chairs before she got the local paper involved, so they were ready to catch the momentum if there was any.

Eventually she settled on eBay because although it wasn't the cheapest option, it was the best way to sell to non-locals and easy to sell multiples if people wanted more than one chair. She was shocked to find that even the ropiest of similar looking seats sold for over a hundred pounds. And to think they'd almost gone into a skip. How many chairs did they have? They could be sitting on a nice boost to their funds.

Glancing out of the window to see how close to dark it was, Patsy decided to nip over to the cinema and count the chairs and maybe take a few photos so she could get started on the listing. Going while it was still daylight felt okay but she really didn't want to be in there alone in the dark, it was too creepy.

It was less than a five-minute walk to the park. Patsy unlocked the door of the cinema, grabbed a hardhat and turned on the working lights in the auditorium. Most of the seats were still in their rows but some were laid flat having been unbolted from the floor. Patsy counted the seats in one row and then began to count the rows when she heard a noise coming from inside the foyer. She froze for a second, then backed herself towards the wall into the shadows. She could hear someone coming. Why hadn't she locked the door behind her? Someone could have followed her in.

She heard the auditorium door open but not close, as if the person was stood in the doorway. From the position she was in she couldn't see who it was without revealing herself.

'Hello?' they called.

'Ed,' she called back with relief, emerging from her hiding place. 'What are you doing here?'

'Christ, Patsy! You scared me to death.'

'You're supposed to tell me when you're coming,' she said, making her way over to him.

'Sorry, I forgot about texting to let you know.' He put his hands into his pockets as she reached him. 'I had an inkling that if I texted you, you'd probably come as well and I wouldn't get anything done,' he said with a smile.

'That's true, I would have come straight over and helped you with your sprockets,' she said with a lighthearted tone so as not to let on that she was upset. It was hard not to be offended that he seemed to have been avoiding her on purpose.

'Haha, see? I'm not going to be able to look at a sprocket in the same way again.' He grinned and Patsy softened a little.

'So how have you got on?'

'Do you want to see?'

She nodded and he led the way up the stairs to the projection box. 'Anyway, what were you doing here, loitering in the dark?'

'Counting chairs. We're going to sell them and it turns out they go for a fair bit more than we realised. I was greedily working out how much we might get.'

'Right. So you texted Oliver to say you're be here alone, did you?'

'Well, no. But it's different.'

'No it isn't. What if it wasn't me lurking around? It's so quiet in the park no-one would have heard you scream.'

'Alright, Ed! That's basically all you need to say to make sure I never come here by myself ever again. You make it sound like I'm one step away from being in a horror movie.'

'Sorry,' he said. 'Let's take your mind off things with some good old-fashioned manual labour.' He handed her a cloth. 'If you could start with cleaning these,' he said, pointing to some of the parts she'd carefully laid out the last time she was there, 'that would be great. Really shine them up, get into all the tiny gaps. They need to look like the ones in the projector at Uni.'

'These will never be as shiny as those,' said Patsy, choosing one that didn't look too bad to begin with.

'They will. Challenge extended.' He looked at her with a quizzical raised eyebrow and a lop-sided grin that made Patsy's insides quiver.

'Challenge accepted.'

She made herself comfortable on the floor so that she could watch Ed work as she cleaned. He was cleaning the projector itself, now that it was empty of all the moving parts. He had a bottle of water that he poured into a dish and dipped a toothbrush in before gently using it to brush the dirt off. He'd laid a sheet on the floor which was gradually being covered with debris as he cleaned.

He was lost in his task and Patsy was lost watching him. He was quite sexy and she never thought she'd think that of a man who only wore an unending supply of hoodies and jeans. She'd thought her type was a less cultivated version of Oliver. Someone a bit more comfortable-looking but with his sense of style and attention to grooming. But she'd been wrong. Ed was a contender. There was something about him, maybe a culmination of lots of tiny things that added up to make him attractive to her. On Friday, she'd been sure that they were on the same page. Tonight, she wasn't so sure. Or rather, he didn't seem so sure. He was a man of relatively few words, she had come to realise over the past couple of weeks, and a man who was tentative and unsure about sharing his feelings. But on Friday, he'd shown that given a bit of time he could make the moves she was hoping for.

They had started something that she'd thought they both wanted to continue and as she watched him examining the inside of the projector as if there was nothing more important in the world, she smiled and hoped that at some point that gaze would fall on her again. And she could wait if that's what she had to do.

The next day, Patsy mentioned the enormity of the chair selling task to Jess when she called in for a well-earned coffee once the Haberdashery had closed for the evening.

'There are more than four hundred chairs. I mean, when we decided to sell them, I thought there would be a couple of hundred but it's deceiving when you see them set out in rows like that, you'd never think it was as many.'

Jess nodded sympathetically. 'It is quite overwhelming, but four hundred chairs, that could make such a lot of money, I bet they'll go like hot cakes.'

'Hopefully. I'm going to try and get the Gazette interested, that might help shift them. We're going to need to get them out before the builders start on the inside.'

'And how's it going with you and that projectionist guy? Oliver said you had a date on Friday.' Jess looked eagerly at Patsy as she took a sip of coffee.

'He did not tell you that,' said Patsy, mortified to hear that Oliver had actually said it was a date, when it hadn't started out that way at all. 'It wasn't really a date, he asked me if I wanted to watch him project the film, for research purposes.'

'It sounds like a date in disguise,' said Jess perceptively.

'Well, I do like him but I think I've come to realise that he's a slow worker when it comes to relationships. Honestly, I thought there was something between us and then on Friday, he made his move but then last night when we ran into each other at the cinema it was as if that had never happened.'

'Hmm. Maybe he's not very practiced at that kind of thing?'

'So Oliver's told you his theory that he's a nerd who doesn't know what he's doing when it comes to women?'

Jess giggled. 'Not exactly in those words. Look, as long as you're happy, nothing else matters, does it? Just make sure he doesn't mess you around.'

'Thanks. To be honest, Ed is the first guy I've been interested in for such a long time that I'm quite rusty on the protocols myself. But at the risk of sounding like a fourteen-year-old, I did think we were probably going out with each other after Friday night.'

'In that case, maybe you should tell him that,' said Jess gently.

Perhaps she should, but pointing out to Ed that she'd thought they'd embarked on a relationship implied that he hadn't noticed, which wasn't a conversation she wanted to have at all.

# 11

On Monday morning, Oliver had arranged for Beth, who was back for the Easter holidays, to hold the fort at the coffee house for half an hour while he had his weekly site meeting with Matt and the builders and Patsy met the chap from the Croftwood Gazette. Beth was about to leave again to go back to university so it was just as well that Patsy had finally organised for Linda's nephew Jack to come in for a trial.

Although the cinema was closer to her flat than the coffee house was, Patsy went into town to meet Oliver so that they could walk there together. It was nice to have chance to catch up without being interrupted by customers.

'Good job on getting the paper involved, Pats.'

'Rosemary had a contact from something they'd helped her out with for the library.'

'It'll be brilliant publicity for us and hopefully they might want to follow the project until we open.'

'Hey, one thing at a time, it's all about the chairs today.'

When they arrived at the cinema, Matt was waiting outside with a fistful of hardhats from which Oliver and Patsy diligently took one each and placed on their heads. Patsy wished she had remembered about the hats because she would have done her hair differently. The hat squashed the nicely backcombed bouffant she'd created that morning to inject some glamour into her half ponytail.

As they were about to go inside, Patsy noticed a portly middle-aged man walking towards them next to a younger chap with a massive bag slung across his shoulder.

'Do you think that's them?' she asked Oliver.

'Looks like it. Are you happy to sort them out by yourself while I meet with Matt?'

'Yes, of course. Go on, we'll catch up later.'

For some reason, Patsy felt nervous being left as spokesman for the cinema but at the end of the day, it was about the chairs. It wasn't going to be difficult.

'Morning, Patsy is it?'

'Hi, yes.' She took the hand he was holding out to her.

'I'm Gareth and this is Pete our photographer.'

'Great, come on in. Oh, can you put one of these on, please? Health and safety,' she said apologetically gesturing to the pile of hard hats by the door.

She led the way into the stalls where most of the chairs were lying on their backs, having been unbolted from the floor. While Gareth chatted to her about what the plans were, Pete wandered around, periodically crouching and peering at the chairs from different angles. It was distracting and oddly fascinating.

'Don't mind him,' said Gareth. 'He's sussing out the best shots.'

'Oh, no, that's fine.' Patsy drew her attention back to Gareth and realised she'd missed the last thing he'd asked her which was presumably why he'd explained about the photographer. 'Sorry, what did you ask me?'

'Are you only selling them online or can people pop in and have a look?'

'Oh. I hadn't thought of that. I suppose not, because it's a bit of a building site but it's a good idea. Maybe say that they can do that by prior arrangement. I've got our email address I can give you.'

'Okay, well I think I've got plenty to go on. We'll focus on the regeneration angle, folks love that. Saving an old building, that kind of thing. And we'll push the nostalgic angle with the chairs. Hopefully you'll get rid of some of them. Got quite a few to flog, haven't you?'

'Yes, over four hundred.' Patsy's stomach lurched slightly at the enormity of the task ahead which was literally laid out in front of her.

'Okay, let's get Pete in to take some shots. Where do you want her, mate?'

'Oh, no. I don't need to be in it.'

Gareth laughed. 'We can't print a picture of an empty chair, love! If you don't want to be in it, is there anyone else who could do it?'

Patsy was torn. She could see that Oliver and Matt were standing on the circle balcony deep in conversation. She'd feel like an idiot if she interrupted them for Oliver to have his photo taken. She'd told him she could handle it and that's what she'd have to do.

'It's okay,' she sighed. 'Where do you want me?'

Pete asked Patsy to sit in the front row where there were a couple of rows of chairs still standing. He wanted her to perch on the back of the chair with her feet on the seat, which felt a bit wrong, her elbows on her knees and her chin leaning on her fists. Then he asked her to smile the biggest grin she could manage. It felt cheesy but when he showed her the image on the screen of his digital camera, Patsy was pleased with how it looked. You couldn't tell that most of the chairs had been dismantled and she looked pretty cool with a big smile, her hardhat on and her hair around her shoulders.

Happy to go with that?' asked Pete.

'Actually, I am. It's not a bad photo of me.'

'That's my job,' he said with a shy smile.

'We'll run it in this Friday's issue,' Gareth said.

'Great, thanks. I appreciate it.'

'No problem. Stories like this are our bread and butter.'

Patsy showed them to the door and then went in search of Oliver.

'We're talking about the layout up here,' Oliver said as she walked onto the balcony. 'I was thinking that we probably want to stick to serving food downstairs. It'll be a nightmare running up and down the stairs and it makes this a bit quieter for people who don't want to eat.'

'That sounds good,' said Patsy.

'Right, I'll get the lads to get rid of these chairs as well then,' said Matt.

'If you could have them taken down to the stalls that would be perfect. We're selling them all,' she said by way of explanation when Matt looked confused.

'Is there much of a market for threadbare, manky old seats like these?'

Patsy felt affronted on behalf of each and every chair and she could see Oliver suppressing a smile as he noticed her indignation. 'They go for a small fortune, actually. They're vintage and full of nostalgia.'

Matt turned to Oliver with an impatient look on his face. 'If these aren't gone in the next couple of weeks we're going to run into delays. We need the auditorium clear.'

'I've already listed them and we have plenty of enquiries so it won't take long,' said Patsy, wishing that Matt wasn't such a dick.

'If they're not out of here in two weeks, we'll chuck them out. You have my word,' said Oliver, nodding at Matt.

'Okay, no problem,' he said, flashing a smile in Oliver's

direction and completely ignoring Patsy.

'Right, are you ready to go or shall I wait for you?' Patsy asked.

'I think we're done here, right?'

Matt nodded and Patsy narrowed her eyes at the back of his head as he turned and led the way back downstairs.

'I don't know what it is about that man but he's so irritating sometimes,' she said to Oliver when they were on their way back to the coffee house.

'Hmm. I think he'd say the same about you, Pats,' Oliver said, looking highly amused.

'I am very easy to get along with. Most people love me. The problem is with him.'

'Well, he's doing a good job so let's try and keep him on side. How about I make it up to you and do the training session with Jack this afternoon?'

Patsy gave him a grateful look. 'Thanks, that's very lovely of you but I don't mind showing him the ropes. We don't want to scare him off, do we?'

Oliver gave her a gentle shove towards a nearby rhododendron bush. 'I think you forget who taught you everything a good barista should know.'

'That's true, you did and I'll be forever grateful but I think I've honed my skills to be a bit better than that. Still, as long as he's as good as you, that'll do for now.' She grinned and ran away from Oliver who pretended to chase her. 'Why can't it be like this with other blokes?' she said, stopping in front of him.

'I'm not sure I follow.'

'Like with us. We have such a good time together, have loads of fun but throw a tiny bit of attraction into the mix and all of this stuff is gone and it's all hard and game-playing and second-guessing. The minute anything looks like a relationship it's all weird.'

Oliver looked thoughtful as he offered her his arm to link with. 'I think Pats, that when it's the right person, it doesn't feel hard or weird. And if it is hard, you'd at least be thinking it was worth it, right? Maybe it's not like us being nutters together but it has to be fun, otherwise what's the point?'

'That's good advice, Ollie. Thanks.' She failed to keep the surprise out of her voice but he looked pleased that he might have helped. 'And obviously I mention it because it does seem a bit too hard with Ed at the moment. Maybe we're only meant to be friends.'

'You'll figure it out. You're just a bit out of practice.' He stopped walking and took her hand. 'Have a good time and maybe don't think too hard about it.'

They were wise words. Perhaps being out of practice with romance meant that she was missing obvious cues from Ed, and maybe it was only a bit of fun and she was reading too much into it.

'And if it doesn't work out with Ed, there's always Matt. He's single.'

'Sorry, I thought you said it was important to have fun.'

Oliver laughed, 'You two are hilarious. If you stopped winding each other up you'd probably get on.'

'No way,' Patsy said shaking her head. 'For all your excellent relationship advice, your matchmaking radar is way off.'

'We'll see.'

# 12

On Friday lunchtime, Patsy and Oliver were both working. Her phone buzzed in her apron pocket and she pulled it out to check the message while she waited for some milk to steam. It was a text from Ed to say that he was at the cinema to carry on with his work. Despite her reservations about their fledging relationship, if that's even what it was, her heart flipped in the same way it did every time she had any kind of contact with him. She finished serving her customer but had already started wondering whether to take a little picnic over to the cinema to share with Ed on her break.

'That text was from Ed, judging by the look on your face,' Oliver said, laughing as he swept past her on his way to deliver a panini to one of the tables.

Patsy rolled her eyes. 'He's texting to say he's working at the cinema this afternoon,' she said when he came back to the counter.

'Well, that's handy. It's your turn for a break. Why don't you make some toasties and take some coffee and cake, make it a feast on the house. I know I said I'd pay him in beer but coffee will have to do for now.'

'Thanks Ollie.'

'I hope you're taking a copy of the Gazette to show him.'

Patsy flicked him with her tea towel. The cinema story had made the front page of the Croftwood Gazette. Oliver had been thrilled at the publicity she'd managed to pull off but he also hadn't stopped ribbing her about how it must have been a slow news week in Croftwood for her to have made the front page.

'He's already bought a copy.' He had texted her a selfie of him next to it in the newsagents. Whether he had bought it or not, she didn't know.

'I bet he has. It's not every day your girlfriend makes the front page of a tabloid.'

'I'm not his girlfriend and you're just jealous because you were too busy chatting to Matt to get in on the action.'

Oliver laughed good-naturedly. 'Seriously, you look amazing in that picture. I hope he realises what a good thing he's got with you.'

Patsy gathered up her food and coffee and headed over to the cinema. The blossom on the trees was in full bloom and her favourite tree in the park, the handkerchief tree, was putting on quite a display.

There were some builders around the outside of the cinema, still working on the back wall. Oliver had said it needed to be finished in one go to keep the building secure so they were working into the weekend. The front door was propped open so she went upstairs to the projection box and found Ed with his head in the projector, cleaning again.

'Afternoon,' he said, smiling at her as he put his cloth down and pulled out some wipes to clean his hands.

'I've brought lunch. Shall we sit outside? It's such a nice day.'

'You're a terrible distraction,' he said, giving her a smile that made her blush. 'I've only just got here.'

'I know but I've got to get back to work in half an hour and then you can clean to your heart's content.'

'Well, I do want to be seen in public with the woman of the moment.'

'Shut up!' she said, secretly pleased that he'd acknowledged her brief media success.

They went out to the park and walked a little way away from the cinema where there was a sunny spot near a blossoming cherry tree.

'I bought you a cheese and chutney toastie,' said Patsy, with a questioning look as she realised she had no idea what Ed liked or didn't like. 'Was that a safe bet? You're not lactose intolerant or anything are you?'

'Not lactose, gluten.'

'Oh god.'

Ed laughed. 'No, I'm joking. But if I was I'd probably eat it anyway now I know you're not sympathetic.'

'I would be, but I hadn't thought about it,' she said, full of relief.

'No intolerances or allergies, for future reference.'

'Okay, that's good to know. It's a very lactose-heavy lunch.'

'And a very nice surprise. Thank you.' He lay down on his side, leaning on one elbow as he ate.

'It was Oliver's idea, a bit of a thank you from him. And obviously I wanted to come and have lunch with you.'

It was the first time she'd felt brave enough to say something indicating that she liked him and he answered by looking her straight in the eye as he said, 'If you hadn't come over for lunch, I was planning to ask you out for dinner.'

'We could still do that.'

'It's either or and now we're having lunch so…'

'Ed!' She hadn't seen this playful, teasing side to him before and she liked it. She also liked the fact that he seemed to have found his brave pants and finally made a move.

He grinned. 'I could come and meet you after work and we could get the bus back to Worcester and go out somewhere?'

'I'd really like that.'

Patsy and Ed caught the bus from Croftwood into Worcester. Once they'd got off at the stop by Worcester Cathedral, Ed turned to her and said, 'Where do you want to go?'

Her heart sank a tiny bit. She'd hoped he'd planned the evening, or at least had decided where he was taking her for dinner.

'Um, I don't know. Where's your favourite place?'

Ed took her hand as they strolled down the High Street.

'I was thinking of the Burger Shop?'

'Cool. I'm starving.' It was a good choice. Great food but casual. She preferred somewhere relaxing where they could be themselves and not feel like they were on their best behaviour because that wouldn't help anything.

'Sorry I was late meeting you. I lost track of time. I should have set an alarm or something.' He smiled sheepishly. 'Apart from making sure I'm not late for lectures, I don't normally have anything I need to be on time for.'

'That doesn't bode well for us,' said Patsy. 'I'm always on time. It drives me mad when people are late.'

'Maybe it's a case of opposites attract?'

'Hmm, I think you're going to have to up your game in the time-keeping area.' She grinned at him and he squeezed her hand.

'I'll make every effort to do that.'

Patsy loved that he said it so sincerely because she'd take his erratic time-keeping any day over some of the things she'd put up with from Dan.

'In the spirit of fairness, is there anything you want to say to me?'

'Aside from the fact that you're a constant distraction? I don't think so.'

'You love it,' said Patsy.

'I do.' He stopped and turned towards her.

He was so close, she thought this might be the moment that he was going to kiss her.

'You make me happy,' he said, simply.

Patsy thought her heart might explode. She closed her eyes, taking a second to enjoy the feeling. To savour the moment that Ed had finally told her how he felt. Before she could open her eyes again, she felt his lips on hers. She leant in towards him and kissed him, more definitely, hoping to convey the depth of her feelings through her lips.

'Come on,' he said, once they'd pulled apart, his eyes bright and smiling. 'The burgers are calling me.'

They sat at a cosy table for two in the restaurant which was situated underneath a railway arch near the University library. They ordered a bottle of wine to share and sipped it while they waited for their food.

'Have you thought about what films you'll show at the cinema when it opens?' Ed asked.

The conversations she'd had with Oliver hadn't extended past the plan to get the projector working and the next steps after that were a complete unknown.

'No, we have no plan at all. There's no point trying to compete with the big chains by showing recent stuff so it'll be classics, I suppose.'

'It's good that you're not bothered about having new films because it's hard to get hold of copies on 35mm now that it's digital everywhere. Classics are the way to go.'

'You know last week when we watched Jaws, I realised I hadn't seen it properly, all the way through, even though it's an absolute classic. There must be loads of films like that, ones that people kind of feel like they know but haven't actually seen. Maybe we should show those kinds of films?'

'Like The Breakfast Club. I hadn't seen that until I projected it a few months ago. When I was at school, I felt like the only person who hadn't seen it.'

'It's overrated,' said Patsy, thinking that if Ed agreed, they really were on the same wavelength.

'Absolutely, but still a film you have to have seen, like a rite of passage or whatever.'

'Even though you're thirty?'

'Five. Thirty-five. But if you want to think of me as thirty, that's fine. How old are you? And don't make me guess, it won't work out well for either of us.'

'Thirty-two.'

'Longest relationship?'

Oh god. It was inevitable that it would come up but Patsy had been hoping that she could have avoided it for a bit longer. It felt like it was their first proper date and the last thing she wanted was to started getting into her past.

'Um, I suppose about eight years. How about you?'

'Eight years is a long time. I managed a three year relationship while I was at university and then it took us a year to realise we were staying together out of habit. It wasn't me that pointed it out, to be honest. Self-awareness isn't really my strong point.'

Patsy smiled, grateful that he hadn't asked her anything else and also because she loved how honest he was. She owed him a little bit in return.

The food arrived and gave her a brief respite from the conversation but once she'd finished her falafel burger, she'd decided to tell Ed at least something about her past.

'I was married.' She looked at him but didn't see the shocked expression she'd been expecting.

'What happened?'

'We'd grown apart. We weren't the same people who had

fallen for each other in the first place and I couldn't see why we were together anymore.'

That was the bare truth of it, without any of the unpleasantness. She'd taken a long time to get over how her marriage had tainted her life and how she saw herself and she wasn't going to let it touch her. Especially not now that she had finally managed to move on and make a decent life for herself and was seeing a man who she hoped would never put her in that kind of situation again.

'I guess that's what happened with me and Sarah. Not many people are the same in their thirties as they are in their teens and twenties.'

'Mmm.' Patsy wanted to get off the subject of past relationships. 'Where did you go to university?'

'Lancaster. Good times,' he said with a nostalgic smile. 'That's where I got involved in the Film Society and tried to replicate that in Worcester when I got the job here.'

'So you didn't fancy being a projectionist as a career? You seem to love doing it.'

'No, it's terrible money and terrible hours and even back in the day, in the big cinemas things were very automated compared to the Film Society set-up. Takes all the fun out of it. I prefer it as a hobby, then I get the best of both worlds.'

They finished off the bottle of wine and then ordered coffee. Patsy suddenly noticed that they were the only ones left in the restaurant and pulled out her phone to check the time.

'Shit, I've missed the last bus.'

'Don't worry, we can sort out a taxi.'

A taxi back to Croftwood would be at least thirty pounds. Thirty pounds that Patsy didn't have to spare, especially once she'd split the bill for dinner with Ed.

'I might see if I can crash at Oliver's.' That was the last thing she wanted to do, rock up at his and Amy's late on a

Friday night but she might not have any choice.

'If you don't want to get a taxi, you can stay at mine. Not like that,' he added hurriedly. 'I mean, I can sleep on the sofa.'

'It's a tight time of the month, that's all, so a taxi isn't in my budget. I'm happy to sleep on your sofa, if you're sure you don't mind?'

'Look, just so you know my intentions are completely honourable, I can pay for you to get home. And for dinner, I was going to pay for that anyway, obviously.'

'No way. Splits on the dinner and thanks for the offer of the taxi but I'd rather not waste anyone's thirty quid on a taxi when I should have been keeping an eye on the time.'

'I take it as a compliment that you didn't notice the time,' said Ed softly, taking her hand across the table.

She smiled coquettishly at him, the wine weaving its magic and making her feel bolder than she would normally. 'It hasn't happened to me before, so take that as you wish.'

Ed asked for the bill and handed over his card before Patsy could object.

'Please. Let me,' he said.

'Thanks.'

They left the restaurant and walked, holding hands, both hardly able to take their eyes off each other. Patsy loved the way he looked at her. His face was so open and friendly but she could see more than that in his eyes. She could see that he felt exactly the same way as her and that was why she'd agreed to spending the night, even if it was on the sofa.

'Where do you live?'

'Barbourne. I should warn you I have a housemate.'

'A housemate that comes with a warning is interesting.'

'Hmm. Well, you'll see.'

They walked down Castle Street towards the racecourse and then along Severn Terrace. It made for a nicer walk home than along the main roads.

'I don't think I've ever walked along here before,' said Patsy. 'I bet it's gorgeous in the summer.'

'It is,' agreed Ed. 'Less so when it's flooded. It was pretty bad this winter. It takes me ages to walk through town to get to work if these paths are closed.'

Ed's house backed onto the river where the racecourse met Gheluvelt Park. It was fairly elevated so probably a safe distance from any flood risk.

'Blimey, this is lovely,' said Patsy, looking out of the window at the terrace which led down to the river. She could see a string of lights on the fence at the bottom which were reflected in the water. It was modern and furnished as if it were an Ikea showroom. Not at all what she'd expected for a man living alone. She spotted sage green subway tiles in the kitchen which made her the tiniest bit jealous.

'Thanks. My sister-in-law insisted on taking me to Ikea. Obviously if it was left to me I'd have skipped on the cushions and rugs and stuff.'

'That's the only thing that saves it from being a total man cave.'

'Oh, don't worry. Andy, my housemate does the best he can to keep up the man cave side of things. Do you fancy a nightcap?' he asked as he took her coat, hanging it on a hook in the hallway.

'That'd be lovely,' she said, wandering over to the sofa, a deep-seated affair which was begging her to grab a throw off the back and snuggle herself into it's roomy corner.

Ed poured the drinks and joined her on the sofa. 'Do you fancy watching a film?'

'Yes, why not? As long as it's a classic.'

'Oh, the pressure.' He frowned and moved to sit on the floor next to the television where he opened a wide drawer that was crammed with DVD's.

Patsy stifled a gasp. She didn't think she'd seen so many

DVD's all in the same place since HMV closed.

'Don't judge me, I'm single with a passion for films.'

'I didn't say anything!'

'I felt the wave of shock. What about this?' He held up a copy of Sleepless in Seattle, one of Patsy's favourite movies.

'Great choice but you don't have to choose a romcom on my behalf.'

'Don't flatter yourself,' he said with a grin. 'This is in my top ten.'

'Really?'

'No, not really. But it's easy to watch and I'm guessing you've seen it before so we can chat around the good bits.'

He put the film on, settled himself into the corner of the sofa and then pulled Patsy into his side where she leant happily against him. Reaching behind her, he pulled a throw off the back of the sofa and laid it across them both.

It had been a long time since she'd ever felt so content.

# 13

Sunday was Oliver's day off and Patsy was working until 4 pm. It had been raining all day and the flow of customers was slow, even the Sunday morning crowd who came in to read the papers over a coffee had mostly stayed away.

Patsy sighed, pulling her phone out of her pocket and mindlessly scrolling through Instagram only seeing things she'd already seen the last time she looked, ten minutes ago. If she'd been thinking straight she would have brought her knitting with her and stashed it under the counter in case of extreme boredom but she hadn't remembered.

She'd spent most of Saturday with Ed. He'd insisted on accompanying her back to Croftwood once they'd had a lazy breakfast at his and although Patsy was nervous about showing him where she lived because it was nowhere near as fancy as his place, he professed it cosy and charming, setting her at ease straight away. They'd spent the day sitting in the park, had a pub lunch and wandered on the footpaths at the edge of the woods before he reluctantly caught a bus back to Worcester so that Patsy could get a good night's sleep before her early start at the coffee house.

Friday night had ended with both of them sleeping on Ed's sofa after they drifted off sometime after the film finished. Patsy woke just before 7am to find herself in Ed's arms with an extra blanket over her and spent the half an hour before he'd woken up revelling in the wonderfulness of it all. It was also pretty amusing how relieved Ed was that his housemate had stayed at his girlfriend's place.

What she wanted now was to be texting back and forth with him instead of staring out of the window wishing for a new customer to serve, but he was busy setting assignments for his students and she'd promised not to distract him.

Idly, she checked her emails and found one from a buyer that had seen the newspaper article. They were interested in taking ten of the chairs for an office refurbishment and wanted to arrange collection that week. Ten in one go for their first sale was more than Patsy could have hoped for and she replied straight away to make arrangements to meet Marian, the designer, at the cinema the following afternoon. Marian had almost finished her project but thought the chairs would be the final touch.

'Guess what,' she said when Oliver called to check in. 'I've sold ten of the chairs!'

'Nice one Pats!'

'This office designer, Marian, saw the article in the paper and she's coming to pick them up tomorrow. Are you okay if I finish early so I can go and meet her?'

'Yes, of course. That's a brilliant start, well done.'

It was the boost she'd needed to get her through the rest of the day with a spring in her step. Aside from finding Ed to help them out she hadn't had much opportunity to do anything yet while the building work was still going on. The chairs were her thing.

She pulled her phone out again to text Ed but decided against it, remembering what he'd said about her being a distraction. It could wait.

The following afternoon Patsy made sure she was at the cinema in plenty of time to meet Marian. She was excited because that morning there had also been a sale via eBay that she would need to pack and arrange to courier to a buyer.

There were a handful of builders working behind the cinema screen, renovating the huge sliding door that was covering the gaping hole in the back wall now that the brickwork that had blocked it up so long ago had been removed. Although the massive wooden door was still solid and would do its job, it was a long time since anyone had slid it across the rails that it wheeled along, top and bottom and it was taking some painstaking cleaning and oiling to wake all the moving parts from their prolonged hibernation. It was much the same as the projector, although on a larger scale.

Ed had been working on the projector that morning while she'd been working her shift at the coffee house. In fact, he could still be up there now. Knowing he was close by but not actually seeing him was so tantalising. She wasn't going to see him until Wednesday evening, when they'd arranged to meet up and do some work on the projector. He was going to collect a Chinese takeaway on his way over from the bus stop and Patsy was looking forward to that.

While she waited for Marian, she checked over the chairs which had been in the back row and were now laid flat on the floor in pieces, the seats and backs separated now that the columns in between them had been unbolted from the floor. It was good that Marian wanted ten because every seat needed two sides and if they sold them one at a time, they would be left with lots of seats. The more someone bought in one go, the more they could sell because if there were two seats, they shared the middle armrest so that was three sides rather than four. If Marian had more projects like the one she was finishing now, that would be great for rehoming as many of the seats as possible.

Patsy heard the door to the auditorium open behind her and looked round, expecting to find Marian but was instead faced with a man she had hoped she'd never have to see again.

'Cleo. Fancy finding you here,' he said with a self-satisfied smile.

The room shrank away as she looked at him. The builders that were just a stone's throw away seemed to disappear and she felt a ball of anxiety lodge itself in her chest as panic began to set in and she suddenly had to fight to take a breath.

'How did you find me?' She wanted to know and yet she didn't. She'd been so careful to cover her tracks. In the beginning she'd expected him to walk through the door of the coffee house on a daily basis but she'd become complacent and now it was a shock.

'Saw you with your little venture in the paper.' He took a step towards her and she stumbled backwards, catching her foot on a chair that was on the floor.

'Stay away from me, Dan.' Despite the way her heart was pounding in her chest, making her feel as if her whole body was vibrating, she tried to sound strong. She was strong now. That's what she was willing herself to feel but the moment she'd seen him it had whipped her straight back to three years ago.

'It's not Dan, Cleo. It's Marian.'

Patsy felt her chest constrict. She couldn't breathe. He'd not only found her, but he'd duped her into meeting him. She'd let her guard down. It was her fault she was back in this situation.

'I know what you took and I want it back.'

'Everything alright, Patsy?'

She turned, reluctant to look away from Dan in case he came towards her, to see Matt marching up towards her from the front of the stalls. He was looking straight at Dan and from his expression, it was clear he'd heard at least part of the exchange.

'Don't worry,' Dan said, backing towards the door. 'Now I know where you are, I'll leave you to it.'

She slumped to the floor as Matt glanced down at her in concern but carried on towards Dan.

'I'll see you out,' he said, squaring up to Dan and forcing him to turn and leave without further comment. A moment later her was back. He crouched down on the floor next to her, waiting with her while she tried to regulate her breathing.

'Thank you,' she managed after a minute or so. She went to pull herself up and he stood and helped her to her feet, steadying her by taking her hand and supporting her with a gentle arm across her back. 'I'm a bit light-headed.' She allowed herself to lean into him for a few seconds.

'Okay?' His voice was full of concern.

'Yes, thank you.' She was feeling better enough to find the close proximity between them awkward, and moved back slightly.

'Who was that guy?'

She shot a look over to the door.

'Don't worry. He's gone and I've locked the door.'

'He's my ex. It didn't end well.' She attempted a rueful smile but knew she hadn't managed it.

'On the basis of that short interaction, I'd say you're better off without him.'

Patsy picked up her bag and pulled it purposefully onto her shoulder, trying to gather herself ready to leave. But she was terrified that Dan would be waiting outside.

'I'll walk with you. Are you going home?'

She nodded. 'That'd be great, thank you.' Normally she'd have worried about putting him out.

They left together, Matt scanning the park before he locked the door.

'Lead the way,' he said and they strolled in silence for a few minutes. 'So, did I hear him call you Cleo?'

Patsy looked at him. It was hard to reconcile this person who had just saved her from the worst thing that had happened to her in three years with the mostly grumpy, pernickety Matt. This Matt was listening and concerned and somehow, she wanted to tell him.

'He's more than my ex, he's my husband.'

Matt didn't look surprised at that revelation but then, he didn't know anything about her. If she'd told Oliver that, he would have had a different reaction.

'I left him. I haven't seen him for three years. I didn't think he knew where I was.'

'Well, I can understand the shock then. So my first impression that he's not a nice guy was right?'

'Yes. He'd always been controlling and over time, it became worse. I don't think I noticed it to begin with, maybe he hadn't been like it to start with, I can't remember. And when things didn't go his way… I didn't know what he'd do so I waited and took my chance. I left everything, just took what I could fit into a bag.'

'He must have had an inkling you were in this area to have seen the newspaper though.'

'Maybe, I don't know. It was bound to happen one day. When I first left, I expected him to walk into Oliver's every time the door opened. I thought I was still expecting it on some level but then when I saw him today, I realised that I'd got complacent and let my guard down.'

Matt gently took her hand and stopped walking. 'Do you know what he was asking about?'

She shook her head. 'I can't remember what he said.'

'Something like, he knows what you've got and he wants it back.'

'I don't have anything of his. I left with barely anything of my own.'

'Perhaps I mis-heard. I only caught the end of what he was saying.'

Patsy covered her face with her hands. 'I can't believe I led him here with that stupid article. I've been so careful.'

Matt moved her hands away gently until she was looking at him. 'It is not your fault. I agree it was probably always going to happen, but it wasn't because you have tried to move on with your life instead of waiting for that piece of shit to walk through the door.'

Patsy shrugged, a rogue tear rolling down her cheek. 'I should have been ready. I didn't want him to see that he can still make me feel like that.'

Matt pulled her very slightly towards him and looked into her eyes, searching for an objection before he pulled her into his arms.

'None of this is your fault, Patsy.'

Being in his arms made her feel safe. The terror that she'd felt at seeing Dan again had gone and she was left with the grim reality that he knew where she was and she was going to have to decide what to do about that.

When he pulled away, she looked up at him and smiled. 'Thank you. I don't know what I'd have done if you weren't there.'

'I think if you'd screamed loudly enough a builder would have come to your rescue.'

They carried on walking.

'You haven't told me why he called you Cleo.'

'Short for Cleopatra.' She expected ridicule but she saw surprise and who could blame him for that.

'God, that's quite a bold name. I'm not surprised you go by Patsy. Or Cleo.'

'My mum was a massive fan of Elizabeth Taylor and Richard Burton and the love affair that started when they were filming Antony and Cleopatra and she felt the need to celebrate that through me.' It was years since anyone had known that was her real name. 'Dan's the only person who calls me that now. Are you surprised, about all of this?'

He shrugged. 'I don't know much about you except that I can't even imagine anyone messing with you.'

Patsy smiled. 'Well, you do a good job of winding me up on occasion.'

He grinned at her. 'Ditto.'

They'd arrived outside Patsy's house. 'Do you mind not mentioning this to Oliver?' she said. 'He doesn't know but I need to tell him.' Now that Dan knew where she was, she needed the people around her to know what she was up against. That was her best defence because they knew her as the confident woman she'd tried hard to rebuild over the past three years and hopefully, the next time she saw Dan — because she was sure there would be a next time — she would be ready to face him knowing that the people in her life knew what was going on and would be ready to support her. The fact that Matt had been that for her today was a surprise, but a good one.

'No problem. It's your business, not mine. But if you need anything, even if it's someone on the end of a phone so that he knows you're talking to someone who knows where you are, please don't hesitate. I mean it.'

'Thank you, Matt, thank you. I just need to get my head round it and make sure I'm ready when I see him again.'

'Take care. I'll see you soon.' He did a weird kind of salute, smiling as he waited for Patsy to let herself in before he turned back the way they'd come.

She went up to her flat, locked the door and exhaled. There was such a lot to think about. So many things had changed in one afternoon.

# 14

Once Patsy had explained the whole story to Oliver the next morning, he suggested Patsy stay at the flat above the coffee house so that she wouldn't have to walk home from the coffee house at night.

'Just for a few days until you're feeling more solid. Surely if he's going to turn up again it'll be fairly soon and at least it's safer here, in the middle of town.' If Oliver was shocked at her revelations, he didn't say. All he had asked was for the details of what had happened at the cinema.

'Thanks Ollie. I think that would be good.' She took his hand and concentrated hard on fiddling with his fingers before she spoke. 'I'm sorry I didn't tell you. You're the only reason that I managed to get back on my feet and you deserved to know.'

He pulled her into a tight hug. 'I knew there was something,' he said gently, 'but I knew you'd tell me when you were ready. But now I know, I can help. For starters, we'll be more vigilant about making sure there's someone with you when you're at the cinema.'

Patsy went back to making sandwiches while they chatted.

'Okay, thanks. But just for now. Seeing Dan has spooked me but actually, it's no different to what it was like when I first left, thinking he'd be around every corner. I can't live like that again.'

'Give yourself time though, Pats.'

He was also on at her to tell Ed what had happened and was all for asking him to come over and stay with her but that was a step too far. She and Ed were still getting to know each other and landing this kind of drama on him would frighten him off. Besides, she couldn't get over the fact that Ed had been in the building at the same time and if it wasn't for him insisting on not being disturbed unless they'd arranged to see each other in advance, he might have been there when Dan appeared. She knew it wasn't fair of her to think that but she couldn't help it.

In the end Oliver had shrugged and said it was up to her but that if it was Amy in a similar situation, he'd want to know. Well, of course he would but Oliver and Ed were very different and Patsy wasn't sure how Ed would cope with a potential ex-husband stalker problem. And the other slight problem was that it would mean her having to tell Ed that technically, she was still married.

The next morning, still in bed at the flat above the coffee house, she heard the door unlock downstairs. It made her jump, her body instantly on high alert, even though she knew it would be Oliver. She pulled the duvet up to her chin and waited. The next thing she heard was the coffee machine whirring so she relaxed back into the pillow and closed her eyes again until she heard a soft tap at the door.

'Hey, Pats. Are you awake?'

'Yes, come in.' She pushed herself up to sitting as Oliver came in with coffee for both of them.

'Did you sleep okay?'

'Yes, I did once I got off.'

'So how do you feel this morning?'

She sighed. 'It was better only having to come up here last night instead of walking home. I don't know. Now I'm over the shock of seeing him, it's made me realise what a mess I left behind. I mean, I have no idea how to go about getting divorced from someone you don't want to see again or if that's even possible.'

'I don't know either. Maybe you could talk to Toby?'

Patsy nodded.

'You've been living hand to mouth in that crappy little flat and all the time he could have been supporting you, financially.'

'He doesn't have to do that and I don't want anything from him.'

'Legally or morally, you should have been able to come away with something, Pats.

'He's been in prison.'

'Christ, has he? What for?'

'It was for fraud. He was an accountant and the company we worked for had this charity thing where if you paid for something on their website, you could round up and the difference would go to their charity of the month.'

'Right, I've seen that loads of times online.'

'Well, he was in charge of the admin of that and diverted a tiny amount of each transaction into his own account. It was a while before anyone noticed and he'd taken thousands. They froze all of our assets because everything was in his name in the end.' She still hadn't told Oliver exactly how Dan had slowly engineered everything so that she had nothing but it was the first time she'd told anyone even a tiny part of what had happened and it felt cathartic to share the story.

'So, you had nothing?'

She nodded. 'I had to take my chance and leave. I didn't care about the house or anything else, it didn't matter. But now that I've met Ed, I suppose Dan turning up has reminded me that we're still married and you can't run away from that.'

'Are you going to tell Ed about that?'

'I don't honestly know. I mean, it might come to nothing with him.' She hoped that wasn't true but it was the only thing that justified not telling him.

'But it might not and if he finds out later on, well it could be worse than telling him now.'

'He's going to think it's awful that I'm still married. And I don't feel married, not in my heart, that's the worst part. It really is just a technicality.'

Oliver stood up and took her empty coffee cup. 'I'm going to open up. If you don't feel up to it, have the day off. I'm not going anywhere today.'

'Thanks Ollie, but I can't hide up here forever. I need to face him if he turns up again and I think it'll be fine now I've had a chance to prepare myself.'

'Okay, good for you.' He smiled. 'Talk to him like you do to me and he'll soon know you're not going to take any nonsense.'

'Thanks for that stunning piece of advice.'

'You're welcome. I'll put a breakfast panini on for you in half an hour.'

Feeling more herself after the coffee and with the tempting thought of the panini, Patsy had a shower and made herself presentable.

The first customer through the door was Toby. He had his laptop bag slung over his shoulder as usual with what looked like a wool blazer tucked over the top.

'Good morning, Patsy. Bit too warm for a jacket this morning once I got going,' he smiled.

'The usual?'

'Lovely, thanks. And one of those croissants, please.'

'No problem. Do you do any lawyering in real-life? Not online, I mean.'

'Not normally, but I'm happy to give you advice if you need it.'

'Obviously, I'm asking for a friend.'

He smiled, his eyes crinkling at the corners which Patsy found oddly reassuring. 'You should know that anything we discuss, if you wanted to that is, would be strictly confidential.'

Patsy finished making his coffee and placed it on the counter, then pulled out a plate for his croissant. She glanced at him and saw that he was looking at her quite intently, waiting for her to say something else.

'Look, I'm going to be here all day but if you're not ready or you'd like to talk somewhere more private…' He fished in the pocket on the outside of his laptop bag, pulled out a business card and slid it across the counter. 'Call anytime.' He smiled and then took his coffee and croissant and headed over to his usual table.

She wanted to ask him whether it was possible to get a divorce without having to confront Dan. She still didn't know him that well but maybe that was an advantage in this kind of situation. The main thing was that she knew she could trust him.

Patsy took the card and put it in her apron pocket. It felt comforting. As if she had taken the first step in trying to defend herself against whatever Dan decided to do next.

Oliver had popped out but turned up again in time for the lunch rush.

'I'm not doing anything so I might as well be here,' he'd said. Patsy knew he was worried about her and now that she had got through the first couple of hours of the day she was feeling better.

'Thanks for last night, Ollie. I really appreciate it.'

He shook his head. 'No need to do that, Pats. You'd do the same for me. I do worry about you wandering around on your own now. Maybe you should stay in the flat for a few more days?'

It would have been so easy to accept his offer, to take the sanctuary, but it wasn't a solution. She knew Dan would be back and she had to prepare herself for that. She couldn't hide away until he got fed up with trying to find her because how long would that take? Past experience meant she knew how persistent he could be.

'Thanks but I'll be fine. Now that I know he's around I'll be more careful but I'm not going to be frightened into hiding away.' She sounded a lot braver than she felt but it was important to her that she didn't burden Oliver with feeling like he had to look after her.

'Okay, well the offer's there. Right, let's crack on. These sandwiches aren't going to make themselves.'

Patsy smiled to herself and started buttering rounds of bread, grateful to have something to keep her busy.

When it was time to go home, it was still daylight which was reassuring.

'See you tomorrow, Ollie.'

'At the risk of sounding like your parents, can you text me when you get in?'

'You got it.' She pulled the door open as someone was coming in. 'Oh, hi Matt.'

He held the door open for her to come out, then pushed it to slightly before he went in. 'How are you?'

'I'm okay, thanks. Have we got a meeting I've forgotten about?'

'No, it's a purely recreational visit. I've dropped the twins back to their mum and I need a coffee. Have you got time to join me?'

He was inviting her for a coffee. That was different and actually it would be nice to talk to him. Patsy looked outside. It was heading towards dusk. 'I think I'll get home while it's still light tonight. Maybe another time?'

'Sure. Take care.' He looked earnestly at her and she knew that their days of antagonising each other were over.

'Hey, Matt. Thanks for looking out for Patsy the yesterday.' Oliver reached across the counter to shake his hand.

'I'm glad I was there. I don't think I've ever seen someone look so terrified.'

'It certainly shook her. Coffee?' Matt nodded and Oliver began making his usual latte. 'Sounds like a nasty piece of work. Pats said he's just got out of prison.'

'Really? What for? I'm guessing some sort of violent crime judging by how bloody sinister he was.'

'Some kind of embezzlement, but that might be the tip of the iceberg. It's hard to imagine the type of person that could frighten Patsy. He's got to be pretty bad.' Oliver passed the coffee to Matt and followed him over to a table so they could carry on chatting while it was quiet.

'Any idea what he's after?' Matt asked.

'No, by the sounds of it, there's nothing left. They lost everything, I mean Patsy came here with nothing. She stayed with me until she'd saved up enough for the deposit and a month's rent for the flat. She hasn't got anything to give him, he must know that.'

'She mentioned that he was controlling, maybe he's trying to pick up where he left off? That's almost worse than if he was after something like money, it might be harder to get rid of him.'

'She's adamant that next time she sees him she'll be ready to stand her ground but I'm not sure it's as easy as that.'

'If you'd seen her the other day, Oliver, she's a world away from being able to do that, whatever she might think. It's good that she feels strong enough to face him again but I'm not sure things are going to be dramatically different, not while she's so frightened of him. You can't change that overnight.'

Oliver sighed and stood up as a new customer came through the door. 'No, but at least now we know, we can be there for her, be on the lookout.'

Matt nodded. He'd been hoping to speak to Oliver and was glad that Patsy had told him what had happened. He was still stunned that the confidence Patsy exuded on the outside wasn't imbued into every part of her, that there was a pocket of fear which had exploded, totally out of her control when she'd seen that man. Knowing that there was this vulnerable side to her had made him think very differently about her and he was interested to see how it was going to translate into their working relationship going forward.

# 15

Patsy had suggested that Ed call into the coffee house to meet her on his way to the cinema on Wednesday evening. Although there had been no sign of Dan over the past few days, she was still anxious that he would turn up again and given that he'd tracked her down through the cinema, she thought that was the most likely place for him to show up if he was going to. Despite feeling more strongly, now that she'd had time to reflect, that she wasn't going to allow him to interfere in the new life she'd made for herself, she worried that her instincts would overwhelm her determination and she would find herself an emotional wreck again. Most of all, she didn't want that to happen in front of Ed and given that it was not impossible that he would be there if and when Dan turned up again, she knew she had to say something to him about what had happened.

'Hi,' Ed said warmly when he came into Oliver's.

Patsy felt the familiar spark of attraction flood through her as it did every time she saw him. She walked round to the other side of the counter and took his fingers in hers. 'It's good to see you.'

In return, he pulled her into a hug and then drew back to kiss her. 'It's great to see you.'

'Give me ten minutes and we can be out of here. Do you want a coffee while you wait?'

'No, I'll hang on until the meal.' He opened his backpack and showed her a four-pack of beers. 'As we're only cleaning parts tonight, nothing taxing, I thought this might take the edge off the monotony.'

'That works for me.'

Once Patsy had locked up, they headed to the cinema via the Chinese takeaway then walked through the park.

'Are you alright?' Ed asked.

Patsy realised she was clinging to his arm and instead, changed to holding his hand with a bright smile. 'I'm fine.' She scanned the park for any sign of Dan, even though logically she knew that he was hardly hanging out there twenty-four-seven, lying in wait for her.

Ed unlocked the door and when it was shut behind them, Patsy made sure to lock it.

They headed up to the projection box because at the moment it was the cleanest place in the building, and unpacked the food onto some paper napkins that Patsy spread out on the floor between them. Ed popped the tops on two beers and they tucked in.

'How did it go with the chair buyer? Was she keen to order extra like you'd hoped?' Ed asked through a mouthful of noodles.

It seemed like a good 'in' to a conversation about Dan, and Patsy took it. 'No, it wasn't the person I was expecting.'

Ed looked puzzled and stopped eating.

'It was Dan, my ex. I didn't tell you everything about our relationship.' And in fact she realised as she spoke that she was still going to hold back the truth, at least until she'd spoken to Toby about what her next steps might be. 'I sort of ran away from him. I know that sounds dramatic and it's hard to explain how I got to that point but at the time it seemed like the only option. He ended up in prison after that and I thought he was still there.'

'He just turned up here out of the blue? And duped you into meeting him by pretending to be a woman interested in buying the chairs? Christ, Patsy. You ought to tell the police.'

'He scared me but he didn't actually do anything.'

'It's clearly threatening behaviour. If you had to run away in the first place, that tells me everything I need to know about him. Shouldn't someone have told you he was out of prison?'

Patsy shrugged. She'd thought about that. 'The authorities wouldn't have known where to find me, as far as they know I still live at my old address and I started using a different name.'

'You changed your name? You're not really Patsy?'

'No, I am but I used to go by Cleo James. I kind of reinvented myself in my teens. Patsy seemed a bit old-fashioned and Cleo was the obvious abbreviation of Cleopatra. So when I moved back to Croftwood, I switched to Patsy and my maiden name, Clements. I needed a fresh start and having a slightly different name made me feel like I wasn't that person anymore.' She wasn't quite sure why she didn't want to share the fact that she was, technically, still married. Holding back with Ed when she'd told Matt and Oliver already was odd, but something was stopping her.

'Your name's Cleopatra?' Ed looked like he was about to burst out laughing.

'Well, we're not all lucky enough to have a name as ordinary as Edward,' she said defensively.

'My name's not Edward.' He looked less amused all of a sudden. 'It's Edwin.'

'Edwin? In that case I think we're both in the same boat.'

He grinned. 'I used to get the piss ripped out of me for it at school. My mum and dad met at an Edwin Starr concert,' he said by way of an explanation.

'My mum was an Elizabeth Taylor fan but Cleo or Patsy are both okay. As is Ed,' she smiled. 'Imagine if you had a name that made you cringe but you couldn't shorten it.'

'Like…I can't think of any.'

'Me either.'

Ed took her hand. 'Do you think he'll turn up again? Do you know what he wants?'

'I don't know. He'll definitely have an agenda, I just don't know what it is yet. But it'll be something to do with money, I expect.'

'What was he in prison for?'

Patsy explained without going into detail about their relationship because it wasn't necessary.

'You can't go home alone tonight.'

'I'll be okay.' Oliver was still keen for her to stay at the flat but a couple of days in, she knew she was doing the right thing by trying to get back to normal.

'I'll walk you home after we finish here.' He sounded insistent and she was moved by his chivalry, especially when it meant he would be walking the opposite way to where he needed to catch the bus home.

'Do you want to stay at mine?' It seemed the least she could do and she barely thought about it before blurting out the offer.

Ed blushed slightly. 'I'd love to,' he said with a shy smile. 'If you're sure.'

'I'm sure,' she said, taking his hand and squeezing it. He was reading something into the offer that perhaps she hadn't intended but maybe that was okay. Maybe she did need to let herself have some fun, especially now when her life was weighing on her more than usual. It might be exactly what she needed.

They spent the next couple of hours cleaning sprockets and other things which had been taken out of the projector. Ed had finished cleaning the inside and was ready to start re-assembling the mechanism once all the parts were similarly sparkling.

They locked up, Patsy feeling a lot safer now that she'd told Ed what was going on and they were both half expecting Dan to leap out of a bush at them. Physically, Ed was no match for Dan but Patsy knew that Dan wouldn't dare show his true colours in front of anyone else. That had been the biggest problem. On the couple of rare occasions she'd confided in someone, they'd dismissed her worries, sure that they had the measure of him and that he couldn't possibly be any different behind closed doors. Matt at least had seen something of it, and telling Oliver and Ed made her realise that this time she had people on her side who believed her without needing anything more than her word. That alone made her feel stronger.

Patsy let herself and Ed into her flat. She dead-bolted the door, put the chain on and turned to go into the lounge.

Ed's gaze flicked from her to the door, concern on his face at the locking ritual he'd just witnessed. 'You're scared of him,' he said quietly.

Patsy nodded. 'But now that you, Matt and Oliver know… that helps. You believe me.'

He took her in his arms and held her head against his chest. 'I do believe you,' he said, bending his head to kiss her.

She took his hand and led him into the lounge where they began kissing again, more urgently. She pushed him onto the sofa so that he was half lying in the corner. His hands were in her hair which fell out of its constraints into waves which he gently pushed out of her face as he brought her closer to him. They were both gasping for breath between the kisses.

'Come on.' Patsy stood up and pulled Ed after her, into the bedroom.

Later that evening, they had pulled the duvet, along with a couple of crocheted blankets, out onto the roof terrace and were cocooned together while they sipped steaming cups of tea and looked out over the lights of the town.

'This is the life,' said Ed with a lazy smile.

'It's nice in the summer with a gin and tonic in my hand but tonight might beat that.'

'It's so secluded. This is like a secret no-one knows about. I love it. You've made the place so cosy, it feels like yours.'

'Your place is nice.'

'My place is okay but would be even nicer without a housemate to ruin my feng shui,' he grinned. 'This has you written all over it.'

'I could crochet you a blanket to help you get with the shabby chic vibe?' Patsy offered, half joking.

'Really? That'd be amazing. Thanks.'

It was the first time anyone had been enthusiastic about her crocheted things and Patsy took it as a sign that Ed was one of the good ones, as if she didn't already know.

The next morning he woke her with a cup of tea and he was already up and dressed.

'I have to go,' he said, looking as reluctant to leave as she was to see him go. 'I've got a nine o'clock lecture. Will you be alright getting to work?'

'Yes, I'm fine. I honestly don't think he'd do anything to me in broad daylight and I'm sure he only knows about my connection with the cinema, not where I live.' She hoped that was true but wanted to reassure Ed.

'Okay. I'll come and meet you after work. Are you finishing at five?'

'You don't have to do that.'

'I want to. I would want to even if you didn't have a

stalker ex-husband.' He leant towards her and gave her a lingering kiss. She put her hand on his neck and tried to persuade him back down onto the bed. 'Oh god,' he groaned. 'Don't send me off to work feeling like this.'

'Five minutes?'

'Okay,' he said, already taking off his t-shirt. 'But I'm going to have to run for the bus.'

# 16

'The outside is signed off,' said Oliver, coming through the door of the coffee house with the biggest grin on his face. 'They're taking the scaffolding down this week.'

'Brilliant, so what's next?' Patsy was concentrating on cutting a traybaked flapjack into equal portions.

'Well, we'll revel in the progress for five minutes first,' he said, looking a bit crestfallen that Patsy hadn't been as excited about the milestone as he was. 'Coffee to celebrate?'

'Okay. I'll make it. Go on then, tell me what happened at the site meeting.'

'They showed me the back door and my god, Pats, it's going to be amazing.' His eyes were shining with excitement. 'It slides back and the light turns the whole place into something different. It's better than I could have imagined. I know I'm getting ahead of myself but I think we should have a party when it's finished for our friends in the town, you know, the other traders and anyone else we can think of.'

'That's a great idea. Like a soft-launch thing?'

'Exactly. So we can see how it functions as a space for events before we start marketing it. I mean, the cinema stuff is easy but the rest of it, it's hard to know how it'll work.'

'The more I talk to Ed about it, the more I realise how naive we are about the cinema stuff.' Patsy finished making the coffees and they sat down at a table near the counter. It was quiet and although there were customers in there, they were all happily enjoying their own coffees, so they could take advantage of the lull.

'What do you mean?'

'Well, for one thing, they stopped making actual films for projectors like ours a few years ago. There's only been the odd one since then and that was only because the directors insisted, so you can get a recent Quentin Tarantino on 35mm film but not much else.'

'Oh, right. I didn't know that.'

'Me neither. But you can get classics. We probably need to pitch ourselves as a cinema that shows retro films, which is good because it means we're not competing with the big cinemas in Worcester.'

'That could work. How classic are we talking?'

Patsy shrugged. 'I think maybe seventies and eighties could be a draw but they were still producing plenty of 35mm films in the nineties too.'

'I wonder whether we ought to think about retro as a more general theme for the place as a whole?' They'd talked about this before when they were deciding on the finishes for the interior with Matt. There were a lot of original features from the 1920s but even more from the 1980s so they were going to try and strip it back to whatever they could that was truly original.

'Hmm, I'm not sure the seventies or eighties have design aesthetics that are going to lend themselves to a cinema, and tempting food offerings from either decade are probably limited, if we're going down that road. I think we should stick to the plan we had of decorating it with a nod to the twenties, when it was built. You know, make the most of the original features that are left and food-wise, come up with a very simple, strong menu. We don't want to restrict ourselves by being too themey.'

'Okay, agreed. I don't like the idea of a theme either but I wondered if we should go all in to make ourselves stand out.'

'Didn't Matt say something about how the building shouldn't be the thing that defines the place? It should be remarkable in an understated way that let's everything else we do shine.' It was hard to believe that not only was she quoting Matt as the font of all knowledge on building design, but she must have been listening to him at some point and remembered what he'd said.

'That makes sense. I do remember that conversation now you mention it. Actually, I was thinking of taking Amy to a cinema in Birmingham which does something similar to what we're trying to do. Why don't you and Ed come too? We can make a night of it, stay over somewhere.'

It was ages since Patsy had been anywhere like that and the thought of going with Ed was exciting. A night out together in Birmingham would be a nice break from the norm. She hoped he'd be up for going as a foursome and as he already knew Oliver was easy to get along with, she didn't think he'd object. Hopefully Amy would manage to join in and relax as well.

'That sounds like a great idea. A research trip! Has Amy come round to the idea of the cinema now?'

'Well, not exactly. I'm hoping a jaunt to Birmingham might soften her up so there will have to be quite a lot of non-research mixed in,' Oliver grinned. 'Check with Ed and I'll book something up. If we could do a Saturday night that'd be easiest. We could leave right after we close and I'll see if Jack's around to work the Sunday here.'

'Perfect. I'll ask Ed tonight.'

Since Ed had spent the night at her flat, they'd spent almost every night together, at hers or his, depending on what they were doing. To start with, Patsy had worried that they were taking things too quickly but she soon came to realise that she wanted to see Ed as much as she could and it was daft to worry about abstract ideas of how much was too much time to spend together. The fact was that she'd spent so long being alone, that it felt very different now to hardly be by herself at all, and she loved it. Getting away for a night in a hotel together would be a wonderful treat. She was sure that Amy and Oliver would want some time to themselves as well and she would enjoy sharing her favourite places in Birmingham with Ed. She hadn't been back there since she'd left her job three years ago and despite everything, it held some good memories for her. It could be like a little test to see how it felt to mingle her new life with a bit of the old.

She put her hand in her apron pocket and fingered Toby's business card. He hadn't been in the coffee house for a few days which was unusual and so she hadn't called him in case he was away or something. But it was weighing more heavily on her, especially because she hadn't told Ed she was still married. She needed to find out what her options were before she created a huge drama about something when it might not be necessary. Maybe it was possible to get a very easy, quiet divorce. She had no idea, and until she did she was best keeping all of that to herself.

That evening, Patsy was in her flat alone. She'd expected Ed to come over after work but after their conversation about the trip to Birmingham, she'd told him in the nicest way possible, not to bother.

She had texted him at lunchtime to ask if he'd be up for the Birmingham trip and he'd sent her a cryptic text saying that it was 'logistically tricky'. It had sounded like an excuse, but rather than let it balloon into something from nothing, she'd called him.

'Don't get me wrong,' he'd said, which straight away made her think that he was about to offend her, 'I love staying at yours and having you to stay at mine but I'm getting behind on work and I could do with the weekend to catch up.'

'I'm not going by myself and playing gooseberry, it's meant to be the four of us. And the cinema we're going to sounds amazing, I thought you'd love that.'

She heard him sigh and rolled her eyes as she waited for him to speak.

'That does sound good. Could I come perhaps for the Saturday evening and get the last train back to Worcester? You can stay the night though.'

'It's hardly worth coming if you're going to get the last train, Ed. Look, if you're struggling to keep up with work, you should have said. We don't have to spend every night together and even if we do, you can still get on and work, or whatever. I don't mind.'

'I'm just feeling a bit overwhelmed, I think.'

She was glad he was being honest with her and she appreciated that they had been living in each other's pockets over the past couple of weeks. Both of them had abandoned their regular routines for the sake of their fledgling romance, but for him not to have said anything about how he was feeling and not got on with what he needed to do was a bit odd.

'If we didn't see each other for the rest of the week, would that make any difference to your decision?'

He was quiet for a few seconds. 'That seems a bit drastic.'

'Christ Ed, you either need time to work or you don't and surely you can get the same amount done in four evenings that you can get done in a weekend?' She couldn't hide her exasperation.

'Okay, you're right,' he said, halfheartedly. 'Count me in for the weekend then. Sorry.'

They finished the call and Patsy turned on the television. It did feel nice to be by herself again. She'd been missing her own company, having been used to nothing else for so long. It was a chance to catch up with things that had been neglected while she and Ed had been spending so much time together. She picked up her knitting and felt the rhythm of the stitches soothe her as she got back into the pattern. It had only been a month since she'd started seeing Ed and already it was morphing from the easy, happy relationship that they'd begun, into something more. The conversation they'd had that afternoon was testament to that and gave Patsy an uneasy feeling that she might have embarked down a road where she was no longer excited about the destination. It was hard to know whether the baggage she was carrying from her marriage was always going to colour her view of future relationships or whether maybe the easy fling that Oliver had suggested she go for with Ed, was all there should ever be between them. Perhaps the weekend away together was a mistake. It might send a signal that she thought it was more serious between them than she was beginning to think was the case. Although going alone with Oliver and Amy was an even less tempting prospect.

She texted Oliver.

**Ed's in xx,**

**Great! I'll book somewhere. Double or twin?**

Patsy laughed.

**Get a double in case the non-research takes over xx**

**Lol. Will do. Night Pats x**

# 17

On Wednesday evening, it was Knit and Natter night. Patsy was excited because having finished her latest pair of socks, she was planning to buy some yarn for her next project. She arrived early so that she'd have time to shop before everyone else arrived and distracted her.

'What are you starting next?' asked Jess, as she began tidying the yarn, re-twisting skeins and stacking balls of wool that had been considered by customers, neatly back into colour order.

'I'm thinking about a Love Note jumper. It's knitted on big needles so I might get it finished before we go to Birmingham. We're going on a cinema research trip.'

'And by we…?' Jess raised an eyebrow.

'Oliver, Amy me and Ed.'

'Ed's the guy that I've seen meeting you from work every evening for the past two weeks?'

Jess didn't know about what had happened with Dan. Patsy was happy she'd told Oliver and Matt but she didn't want everyone to know and Jess was a knitting friend and a high street colleague but not someone she normally confided in, so Patsy shrugged and smiled. 'He's been working on the projector for us and I suppose we kind of hit it off.'

'It's nice, Patsy. You guys look good together.'

Patsy began browsing the shelves, deciding on yarn type and colour. The pattern called for using a strand of 4-ply yarn with a strand of lace-weight fluffy yarn and it was fun looking at different combinations. As she played with the yarn, she thought about what Jess had said, that she and Ed looked good together. Was it something she'd said because that's the kind of thing you say? Because Patsy didn't particularly feel like they exuded anything as a couple. Sometimes you saw a couple and they were lost in their own world, maybe they'd be laughing or talking intently, but they were in a bubble and you'd think, almost enviously, that there was something special going on, that they looked great together. That wasn't how she felt about Ed.

She pulled out her phone and saw the latest in the text exchange she'd been having with Ed all day, saying that he hoped she would have a nice time at knitting club. She sent back a ball of wool emoji and a cup of tea emoji along with the love-heart eyed one for good measure.

Since he'd got the heebie-jeebies about going to Birmingham, they'd had the start of a heart-to-heart about where their relationship was going. It turned out that what she had thought was the fun part of their fledgling relationship, where you spent nights at each others places, not caring about much else that was going on, was causing Ed quite a few problems. He had launched into a serious conversation about whether they should live together to solve his problem of having to commute from her house to work. His other idea was to buy a car. Both ideas had amused as well as shocked Patsy; he was using a sledgehammer to crack a nut. It was a classic case of overthinking everything. If they'd discussed it when he'd first started worrying about it, she could have reassured him and maybe he wouldn't have been the ball of anxiety he'd been by the time he'd brought it up with her.

By the time the others had arrived, Patsy had picked out her yarn and was sat at the table casting on.

'Oooh, you're starting something new!' said Penny. It was always a great source of inspiration for them all to see what each other was knitting. There were quite a few things that had gone viral amongst the group and Patsy predicted that this jumper was going to be the next big thing.

'It's for a weekend away,' Jess said with a wink at Patsy as she brought a tray of tea and biscuits in for them.

'With someone special?' Mary asked.

'It's a research trip for the cinema. We're going to Birmingham to see a cinema that does something similar to what we're planning. Oliver, Amy, me and the guy who's been helping us with the projector.'

'Oh, lovely,' Penny said. 'A bit of time away is always a treat.'

'True. So are you and Ed excited about the weekend?' Jess asked with a knowing look that told Patsy she'd dropped her in it on purpose .

'Ed? Who's Ed?' Sue was so keen to know that she'd put her knitting down.

Patsy explained. There was no point trying to keep anything secret from these women, up to a point.

'How romantic. There's something about Croftwood Cinema,' said Penny. 'Me and Jeff met there, you know. He was working in the box office and I used to go to every Saturday matinee with my friends, it didn't matter what the film was. It took him months to ask me out.'

'That's so lovely, Penny, and a great idea. We need to do that, have a Saturday matinee for kids. There's nothing for them to do in Croftwood when they're early teens and it always made me feel so grown up going to the cinema without my parents,' said Patsy, the idea forming as she spoke, knowing she must remember to tell Oliver.

'You have so much to do before you open, Patsy. A little break will do you the world of good,' said Mary.

'I am looking forward to having a change of scenery, it'll be a real treat.'

'It will,' agreed Jess. 'I'm sure it'll be good for Oliver to have a proper break from work for a couple of days as well.' She knew too well the pressures of owning your own business.

'I can't remember the last time I went to Birmingham. I used to love going to the museum and art gallery.'

'As well as the cinema, Oliver's planned a few other places to check out. There are some bars which he thinks we could take inspiration from.'

'Sounds like that's code for a bar crawl.'

'It could be.'

'I've met someone too.' Jess had waited until the other women were talking about something amongst themselves on the other side of the table.

'That's great,' Patsy said, knowing that Jess had had a series of unsuccessful Tinder dates. 'From Tinder?'

'Yes, is there any other way?'

'Honestly, I have no idea but I didn't think Tinder was coming up with the goods for you.'

'Neither did I! But he messaged me and was very flattering and very persistent but good-looking enough to get away with it so…'

'Have you seen him yet?'

'Not yet but we've been talking. I really like him.' Jess had a slightly dreamy look on her face.

'Well I hope it works out.'

Patsy waited until the very last minute to leave the shop

that night, putting off the moment she would have to walk home alone. When Jess began locking the door, it seemed weird to still be hanging around.

'Thanks for waiting around to lock up with me,' Jess said. 'It gives me the willies having to do it when it's dark and so quiet out here.'

'Oh, that's okay. Where are you parked?'

'The other side of the church.'

'I'll walk with you.' It sounded benevolent but it meant that she'd have someone to walk with almost half of the way home. And she highly doubted that even if Dan was watching her, he would have hung around for hours waiting for Knit and Natter to finish. So although it was the first walk home alone in the dark since it had happened, she felt okay about it.

When she got in, she locked the door behind her and realised that despite the reality that it was unlikely Dan would have followed her, she'd been almost holding her breath since she'd left Jess at her car. But at least she'd done the walk home alone and that was a step back to normality. Ed wasn't going to be there every night and she wasn't sure she wanted him to be. She could do this. She was ready to navigate her life knowing that Dan could play some kind of part in it at any time. It wasn't what she wanted but she could accept that she couldn't move on without dealing with it.

The next morning at the coffee house, Toby was back. It seemed like fate that Patsy had resolved to move on and face her past just as he was back to hopefully help her do it.

'Morning, Toby,' she said as he walked in with his bag slung across his shoulder as usual, looking a little more relaxed than he normally did. He'd probably been on holiday.

'Morning guys, I'll have a latte, please and one of these

pain au chocolats. They look huge and very tempting.'

Jack was sharing the shift with Patsy to give him a bit more confidence before they left him by himself on Sunday while they went to Birmingham, so he busied himself making Toby's coffee.

'Have you got a minute to chat?' The perfect opportunity to talk to Toby was being handed to her and she was going to take it. It might help to settle things in her own mind before the weekend. She was acutely aware that being involved with Ed meant she owed him a better explanation that he'd had so far.

'Of course. Come over when you're ready.'

Once there were no customers left to serve, she left Jack to it and headed over to Toby.

'I won't be a sec,' he said, 'I'm finishing up a live chat with a client.'

He typed furiously for a minute or so and then closed the lid on his laptop.

'So, what can I do for you?' He smiled, making his eyes crinkle at the corners and Patsy felt like she could tell him anything and he would understand.

'I need to get divorced, ideally without having to have anything to do with... my husband.' It was a long time since she'd said those words and it felt uncomfortable.

'How long have you been separated?'

Patsy gave him a look of surprise but realised, of course he could easily make that assumption. He lived in Croftwood and everyone knew that Patsy had been single until Ed.

'Three years. I left and he didn't know where I was. Until recently.'

'So, I'm guessing that something happened to make you think you needed to sort out the divorce?'

She nodded. His gentle, understanding tone was making her feel a little bit emotional.

'Can you tell me what happened?'

'He turned up at the cinema a couple of weeks ago. He posed as a buyer for the chairs and arranged to meet me.'

'Right. So can I assume that the relationship was controlling, abusive in some way?'

Patsy looked at him in surprise.

'If he had to dupe you into meeting him after three years of him not knowing where you were, it's fairly obvious.'

She nodded. 'He seemed normal when I met him. It happened so slowly that I don't think I noticed it was happening until when I did notice there was nothing I could do to stop it.'

Toby nodded as if he understood.

'It started when I got my first decent job. He was an accountant there. He seemed respectable but he always had some side hustle going on which I'd assumed was harmless, for a bit of extra money. We got together quite quickly, I suppose and that whole time, you'd never have known that anything was off. As soon as we got married, he started getting jealous if I mentioned anyone from work, men mainly. The department I worked in used to go out for drinks sometimes after work and he started coming along even though he wasn't invited. He used to loiter, saying he had come to walk me home so that I felt obliged to leave early and go with him instead. That turned into him escorting me to and from work almost every day. I just… I lost everything else in my life.'

'I know how easy it is to get into that situation, I've seen it so many times and you're not the only one to not realise what's happening, not by a long chalk.'

'Thanks, that's nice to know because looking back, it seems so obvious and stupid not to have realised. Anyway, it got to the point where all I could do was go to work. My friends had started to get fed up that I wasn't going out with them anymore and drifted away. Everyone at work thought it was weird that he met me at the door every day so I didn't have anyone. My parents live up in Cumbria and I didn't want to worry them. Then I did get up the courage to tell one of my old friends. I bumped into her in Birmingham one lunch time when I'd popped out for a sandwich and we went for a coffee. She laughed when I told her what was happening. She thought I was having a bit of a moan about my husband and told me some story about how her husband got annoyed if she didn't text him when she's on a night out, as if that was the same.'

Now that she'd started telling the story, it spilled out with an ease she hadn't thought would be possible. And reliving it with Toby next to her made it a little bit easier.

'So you feel you're ready to start proceedings?' Toby asked.

'I'm hoping he'll see it as an indication that it's not worth messing with me. I need to take back control of the situation so that I can move on.'

Toby nodded. 'What do you think his motive is for seeking you out now?'

'His motivation is always money. He saw me in the paper with the cinema chairs so maybe he thinks he can get in on the cinema action, when in fact it's nothing to do with me financially.'

'Has he got a track record of anything to do with extortion or blackmail?'

'Well, he's been in prison for fraud.'

'Right. A tricky customer then. Although divorce-wise that could work in your favour because we can clearly claim unreasonable behaviour.'

'Great, so we can get things started?'

Toby explained what the next steps would be and asked her to think it through and let him know when she was ready to go ahead.

'Thank you, Toby. Even talking about it has made me feel like I've done something. It's a relief, actually.'

Patsy went back to the counter, the lunchtime rush was about to be upon them, but she felt lighter and happier than she had for a while. Telling Toby, him taking her instruction and embarking on the divorce process with her, it was exactly what she needed. And at least now, she could tell Ed that she was getting a divorce which was a marginal improvement on having to tell him she was still married.

# 18

Patsy had stayed over at Ed's on Friday night so that they could get a head start on Oliver and Amy and get to Birmingham early to enjoy an extra few hours on their own before they were due to meet. Amy and Oliver were travelling as soon as the lunch rush was over and they had all arranged to meet at the hotel before they headed out that evening.

The holdall that Patsy had packed looked shabby on the floor in the hallway of Ed's house next to his smart, compact, wheeled suitcase. She was slightly worried that the hotel that Oliver had arranged would be quite posh and would make her feel uncomfortable but she felt she had an ally when Ed appeared after his shower wearing his usual hoodie and jeans combo. At least they'd look out of place together.

'Ready to go?' he asked, lacing his converse boots then swiping his damp hair out of his eyes as he stood up.

'Yes, ready.' Patsy was wearing her favourite dress, it was navy blue with a scooped neckline, full skirt and a floral print that became more dense towards the hem. As it was still not reliably warm, she had worn a tight-fitting black long-sleeved t-shirt underneath and a cardigan over the top. Teamed with her best coat, a mustard wool boucle affair, she felt a million dollars and once she'd caught sight of herself in the hall mirror, she stopped worrying about whether she was going to look the part staying in a fancy hotel. This was a weekend away with her man, who looked sexy as anything straight from the shower and they were going to have a damn good time.

Ed laid Patsy's holdall on top of his case so there was no need to for her to carry anything, he pulled the door shut behind them and they set off for the station.

'I'm so excited,' Patsy said, squeezing Ed's hand. 'I can't even remember the last time I stayed in a hotel.'

'Neither can I. The only places I go to are other universities and you get put up in halls of residence. It's fine, but not quite as sumptuous as I imagine tonight's room will be.'

'Did you google it?'

'Yep. It's pretty cool,' he grinned. 'The kind of place I wish I had thought of taking you without Oliver having to organise it for us.'

'It doesn't matter,' said Patsy happily. 'You can organise it next time.'

'Okay. Come on, we need to hurry. I can see the train pulling in.' He nodded to the railway bridge that spanned Foregate Street where there was a train slowly making its way in the direction of the station.

They broke into a gentle jog, took the stairs two at a time which impressed Patsy given that Ed managed to do that and carry the luggage, and made it onto the train with a minute or two to spare.

'Sorry. We probably didn't need to run,' said Ed. 'I have a pathological fear of missing trains.'

'It's okay.' Patsy smoothed a rogue hair back into place. She had begun to realise that Ed liked to stick to a plan, if there was one. And he had one for today, or at least until Oliver's took over later on.

'Shall we drop the bags at the hotel first?' he asked when they had arrived at Birmingham New Street station.

'Yep, good idea. Do you know the way?'

Ed nodded and took Patsy's hand. 'It's close to the Cathedral.'

The hotel was in a Victorian building and was in an area that Patsy didn't know. Back in the day, she'd worked in Brindley Place and most of the places she'd socialised in were around there, on the canal side. This part of the city was equally well-served by pubs, bars and restaurants housed in old banks and commercial buildings and there was a relaxed feel despite it being only a couple of streets away from the heart of the city centre.

'This is lovely,' said Patsy, taking in the lobby with its frescoed ceiling, marble pillars and centrepiece staircase which swept to the left and right and was framed by a pair of Art Deco lights at its foot. 'It's already the nicest hotel I've ever stayed in and I haven't even seen the room yet.'

They were lucky enough to be offered an early check in and made their way to their room on the third floor. It did not disappoint. The room had high ceilings and three huge sash windows which overlooked the inner courtyard of the building where there were tables set out amongst trees and plants galore. The bathroom housed a huge bath which made Ed's eyes light up when he saw it. Neither of them had baths in their places, only showers.

'So what're we doing first?' asked Patsy as she took the dress she was planning to wear that evening out of her holdall and shook the creases out before hanging it in the wardrobe.

'I had thought it would be nice to stroll along the canals, grab some lunch by the water... but it seems a shame not to make the most of this room, doesn't it?' He sidled over to Patsy, took her wash bag out of her hand and laid it on the bed before kissing her and nuzzling into her neck in the way he knew she loved. 'I mean, the bath is begging for us to use it.'

Patsy had no objection at all to whiling away the day in their room while they waited for Oliver and Amy to catch them up. 'Come on then,' she said, taking Ed's hand and leading him into the bathroom with a wicked grin. 'Oh my god, they've got L'Occitane bath stuff!'

They ran the bath and kissed between stripping each other of their clothes before they abandoned the bathroom briefly in favour of the bed, Ed having the foresight to turn off the taps first.

'This is enough for me,' said Patsy afterwards as she lay with her back against Ed's chest in the most gorgeous bubble bath she'd ever experienced. She absentmindedly made mounds of bubbles on his knee which was not as submerged as the rest of him. 'If this is all we did for the whole two days, I'd be happy.'

'You're very easy to please Miss Cleopatra.'

Patsy grimaced. 'It's so weird when you call me that. It doesn't feel like it's my name. My mum is the only person who's ever called me that.'

'It's so exotic though and appropriate for the bath, even though it's water and not milk.'

Patsy turned around to face Ed while trying to keep herself under the water. She deposited some bubbles on his nose. 'So I'll call you Edwin from now on, okay?'

Ed grinned. 'Not if you value our friendship.' He swiped the bubbles from his nose and kissed her. 'Point taken, we'll stick to Patsy and Ed, shall we?'

'Yes, let's.'

There was a knock on the door and Ed leapt out of the

bath, sending a small tidal wave over the edge. 'Shit!' But he was laughing as he grabbed a towel.

'Who is that?'

'It's a surprise.'

While he was in the bedroom, Patsy took the opportunity to top the bath up with hot water.

Ed came back into the bathroom, having dropped his towel in favour of holding a bottle of Prosecco and two glasses.

'Oooh, Mr Edwin! What a nice surprise and I don't mean the Prosecco.'

Ed laughed and climbed back into the bath, this time at the opposite end to Patsy. 'Okay, let's stop full-naming each other.' He poured a glass and handed it to Patsy then poured one for himself. 'Here's to us.'

'To us,' she said.


Once Patsy and Ed finally got out of the bath, it was almost time to meet Oliver and Amy.

'Where has the day gone?' Patsy said, trying to tame her hair into a low, loose chignon and miserably failing.

'Time flies when you're having fun,' said Ed, coming up behind her and putting his arms around her waist. He was wearing smarter, darker jeans and a shirt; the first time Patsy had seen him wear anything other than a hoodie. And his aftershave made her knees weak. She looped her arm around the back of his head and pulled him towards her.

'Oh my god, Ed. How do you expect me to get ready when you're looking like that? And smelling so sexy?'

'You don't look too shabby yourself,' he said, kissing the back of her neck.

'Enough of that,' she said, sticking a couple of pins in her hair and hoping it would stay. 'We'll be late.'

'We're on holiday,' Ed said, turning her towards him and

gently kissing her again.

'Tonight I'm working. It's a recce, don't forget.'

'I have no problem mixing business and pleasure.'

'Neither do I. But mess up my lips and it's a different story.' She smiled and pressed a finger to Ed's lips which were making their way towards hers again. 'Come on, let's go.'

They made their way downstairs and found Oliver waiting for them in the bar with a bottle of Prosecco in a bucket on the table.

'Sorry, I've already made inroads into this,' said Oliver standing up to shake Ed's hand and kiss Patsy's cheek.

'Where's Amy?' There was no sign of her but perhaps she was still getting ready.

'She couldn't come,' Oliver said, giving Patsy a look which told her that Amy hadn't wanted to come but he didn't want to talk about it. 'Anyway,' he said, pouring them each a glass of Prosecco, even though Patsy knew Ed would have preferred a beer, 'I've managed to find a last-minute substitute.'

Right on cue, Matt walked into the bar. A few weeks ago, this would have appalled Patsy but now, she felt immediately pleased that he was going to join them.

'Hi guys, hope you don't mind me gate-crashing your weekend,' he said. He looked relaxed and different somehow, out of his usual uniform of jeans and a sports jacket. Tonight he was wearing navy chinos and a soft grey sweater with a white t-shirt peeking out from the neckline.

'Not at all,' said Patsy, introducing him to Ed and shifting along the banquette seat to make room for him. 'It makes sense for you to see this other cinema too, so we're all on the same page.'

'Actually, I think I'll have a beer,' he said when Oliver offered him a glass of Prosecco. 'Anyone else want anything from the bar?'

Patsy looked at Ed, expecting him to ask for a beer too but he said nothing. Well, it wasn't her job to babysit him through the evening.

Oliver topped Patsy's glass up, Ed's was almost untouched. 'Come on Pats, you two need to catch up. I had a head start.'

'We've had a head start too,' Patsy said, shooting Ed a cheeky grin which made him blush because Oliver picked up on her meaning straight away.

'Ah, taking advantage of the room service menu? Well, why not. I was about to ask how you'd spent the day but I guess that question's been answered.'

'What's the plan for tonight?' asked Ed in an attempt to veer the conversation away from the afternoon's events.

'We're eating at the cinema at seven. They have one sitting and then the film starts at eight. I'm not sure exactly how it works but that's what we're here to see,' said Oliver as Matt came back to the table. 'Here's to Croftwood Cinema.'

'Croftwood Cinema,' they all chorused.

'Is that the name it'll have in the end?' Matt asked.

'I haven't really thought about it. That's what it used to be called but we can change it if we want to.'

'It's probably useful that its location is in the name,' Ed said.

'That's true. I wonder if whatever we decide to call it, everyone will refer to it as Croftwood Cinema anyway,' Patsy said.

'You could go for something like Cinema Paradiso, after the film,' Ed said.

Oliver raised his eyebrows. 'That's not a bad idea. It sounds exotic and we mustn't forget that although it's a cinema it's going to be so much more than that.'

'Well, we don't need to decide yet. I think we need to see

what it feels like once we get started on the inside,' Patsy said.

Matt nodded, thoughtfully. 'You're right. I think the right name will reveal itself when you start to see it come together.'

Patsy beamed at him, finding it ridiculously pleasing that he'd agreed with her.

'Right, we're going to be late, drink up,' Oliver said.

The evening at the cinema was good fun and highlighted a few things that they needed to consider when they opened themselves. The main thing was that even though there was no rush to finish your food before the movie started, once the lights went down it made eating more difficult. Also, because it was ingrained in everyone to be quiet for the film, it felt uncomfortable to carry on eating past the beginning. The cinema had made it clear that eating during the film was fine but clearly most people still liked to stick to convention. Anyway, it was something to take into account once they started to work out the timings of things even though that was some way off.

'The film's out of focus,' Ed whispered in Patsy's ear about a minute after it had started.

'Give them a chance, it's only just started.'

He shook his head. 'It should be okay by now. I'm going to speak to them.'

He got up before she could say anything else and disappeared.

Patsy sighed and then got engrossed in the film which she'd never seen before, The Firm with Tom Cruise. After a few minutes, Matt moved into Ed's chair.

'Where's he gone?' he whispered.

'He thinks it's out of focus. He's gone to tell them.'

Matt stifled a laugh. 'They'll love that.'

Patsy nudged him, a halfhearted gesture on Ed's behalf although she thought exactly the same.

Matt stayed where he was and Patsy stopped wondering whether Ed was going to come back.

'What's happened to Ed?' Oliver asked when the lights came up.

'He went to talk to the projectionist.'

'We'll find him then because I arranged with the manager to have a look up there after the film. Come on.'

The three of them headed up the stairs, against the flow of people coming down.

Oliver knocked on the door of the projection box and went in. There was no sign of Ed and none of them asked whether he'd been up there. Patsy tended to agree with Matt that Ed's interjection was probably not going to be welcome and by unspoken agreement it was better not to align themselves with him if they wanted to keep on the right side of the cinema. After all, they were far enough away from Croftwood to be useful allies rather than rivals.

Knowing now what she did about the projection system they had, Patsy was interested to see that this cinema had something close to the setup at Croftwood and even managed to ask a couple of questions about it, which their projectionist was delighted by. They also had a chat to the duty manager who explained a bit more about how they ran things, what they'd learned about which films tended to be popular, what timings worked for them and plenty of other useful information.

There was still no sign of Ed when they came out and by this time, the cinema had emptied with only the staff left inside.

'Do you want to give him a call Pats? Find out where he is?' suggested Oliver.

Patsy was fuming. What was he doing? She called him as they walked in the direction of the bar Oliver had planned to go to but he didn't answer so she left a message telling him where they were heading. She wasn't going to let him spoil her night out. She'd enjoyed the cinema and was happy to carry on having a nice time with Matt and Oliver.

The rest of the evening was a cocktail-fuelled affair, at least on Patsy and Oliver's part. Matt was sticking to beer and Patsy was managing to skip one cocktail for every two that Oliver drank. There was more to it than Amy not wanting to come and Patsy knew that Oliver was putting a brave face on things, only the amount he was drinking giving away his real feelings, and then only to her.

Matt was surprisingly good company, telling them funny work-related stories, talking about his children with plenty of love in his voice and smiling eyes, even though he admitted it was hard when he had them with him because of the hours he worked. By the time they left to go back to the hotel, Patsy had almost forgotten to wonder about where Ed was. If Matt and Oliver thought it was odd that he'd not come back, they didn't say anything, escorting Patsy back to the hotel with their arms linked through hers.

'Thanks guys, what a great evening,' she said when they got to the hotel.

'You going to be alright, Pats?'

'I'll be fine.' She kissed them both on the cheek and headed upstairs while they headed into the bar for a nightcap.

She let herself into the room and found Ed asleep in bed. She didn't want to talk to him now. It could wait until tomorrow.

# 19

Ed stood in the foyer of the cinema in Birmingham. There was nothing that annoyed him more than an out-of-focus film. So much so that he didn't consider what he'd think if someone knocked on the door of his projection box and pointed out the same to him. He was on edge, feeling out of his comfort zone, particularly now that Matt had turned up. He knew that Matt had been Patsy's knight in shining armour the day that her ex-husband had turned up and that didn't sit well with him, especially because he had been in the building at the time. It could so easily have been him that had come to her rescue, if only she'd screamed or something, he could have swept down the stairs and now Patsy would be looking at him the way she looked at Matt. He'd thought she hated Matt, although her complaints about him had stopped recently. Now that they had that shared experience, something had changed between them. Something that he had no chance of replicating and tonight was the first time he'd seen it for himself.

Quite rightly, now he thought about it, the projectionist gave him short shrift and Ed was annoyed with himself. And embarrassed because they were supposed to have a tour afterwards with the manager, then the others would find out that the bloke thought he was a dick. He couldn't face that.

He went back inside the auditorium, planning to feign a headache or something so that he could go back to the hotel at the end of the film but when he headed over to their seats, he saw that Matt had moved into his seat and was now sitting next to Patsy.

It was a knee-jerk reaction but he couldn't think straight and he immediately walked out of the cinema. He stood outside and exhaled, the fresh air clearing his head but making him feel no differently. It was as if the afternoon he'd spent with Patsy had never happened. An afternoon where he'd felt something shift between them. Had he imagined that?

He wandered through the streets, meandering around to avoid people who were spilling out of pubs, groups of hens in high spirits, and Deliveroo bikes, eventually finding himself back at the hotel. He checked his watch, a part of him wondering what Patsy would do when she realised he was gone. It was a test of sorts and he knew in his heart of hearts that she was going to fail it. Yes, it was unfair and if he was a better person, he would have gone back into the cinema, sat down next to Oliver and given Patsy a reassuring smile. But he wasn't that man. He was self-aware enough to know that he lacked the confidence to be sure that he would be chosen over Matt, or even Oliver. These two men were better than him. Confident, comfortable in their own skin and more accomplished at chatting and joking with Patsy than he was capable of.

The hotel bar was busy, with a low-level buzz of conversation, laughter and people having a good time within the socially-accepted limits of a posh hotel. Ed took a seat at the bar and ordered a double whisky on the rocks. He took a slug, the reality of the situation beginning to dawn on him. He'd basically abandoned his girlfriend without a word. She was with her friends and he never would have done this had she been by herself, but even so, he was starting to feel like it had been a monumental mistake. Now that she'd sat watching that film without him for a good hour, there were limited options as to how he could come out of this with their relationship intact. Because if there was a relationship worth having, why had he got himself into this ridiculous situation in the first place. It was self-sabotage; he'd seen Patsy with Matt and his subconscious told him to get out before she pushed him. Christ.

When Patsy woke up, she stayed still, trying to gauge whether Ed was in or out of bed, asleep or awake before she made a move. It was going to be awkward whatever happened because what reasonable explanation could there be as to why he walked out of the cinema and came back to the hotel without a word?

She'd actually had a pretty good time last night, despite Ed. Or maybe because he wasn't with her, she wasn't sure. The afternoon they'd spent together seemed almost other-worldly now, in the face of the weirdness and she wasn't sure which was the real Ed. Attentive, sexy, afternoon Ed or dismissive, aloof, dickhead, evening Ed. It was very confusing.

No longer able to stare at the glass of water on the bedside cabinet without wanted to gulp it down, she reached out, knowing that it would signal to Ed — who she was pretty sure was still in the bed — that she was awake.

'Morning,' he said, and she turned to face him once she'd put the glass down.

'Hi. Did you sleep well?' she asked with a heavy

undertone of sarcasm.

'I'm so sorry about last night. After I'd seen the projectionist, they wouldn't let me back in. I think you or Oliver must have had my ticket.'

Patsy frowned. That seemed unlikely. 'I did have your ticket but I'm sure Oliver nipped out to the loo with no problem.'

'Well, I don't know what to say. I tried to get back in and to be honest, I was so pissed off, I left and decided to wait in that bar that Oliver had mentioned we'd go to afterwards.'

'Okay… the Botanist?'

'Oh. I thought he'd said the Alchemist. I was in the wrong place.'

He grinned as if that was the explanation for all of it. If he thought that was a good excuse, in the age of mobile phones, he was wrong.

'And you didn't call me because…?'

He faltered. It was astounding that he hadn't thought of this before.

'I'm sorry, it didn't occur to me. I thought you'd decided to go somewhere else so I came back here and went to bed.'

'Honestly Ed. That whole explanation sounds so… weird. I don't know if it's the truth or not, but if it is it's only marginally better than me thinking you decided to ditch me. Either way, you missed the tour and I thought that's what you'd enjoy the most.' She shook her head in disbelief, not knowing what to think.

She climbed out of bed, glad that she'd worn the night-shirt she'd packed but thought she wouldn't need. 'I'm going to get dressed and go down to breakfast and then I'm leaving.'

He shot out of bed. 'Well, I'll come with you.'

'Whatever.'

She got dressed in record time but he was just as speedy

and they went down for breakfast together in silence. She was glad that neither Matt nor Oliver were in the restaurant. Forced jollity this early in the morning would have been too much. Oliver had offered her a lift back to Worcester and she texted him to confirm because forty minutes on the train with Ed wasn't something she wanted to put herself through.

'So you went to New Street station and then pretended to go to the loo and left him there?' Oliver said, laughing. 'Christ Pats, that's classic.' He had picked her up in front of the Mailbox where he'd parked his car overnight.

'He ditched me, I ditch him.' And he'd got the message that was what had happened because he'd texted her and said sorry again and that he'd hopefully see her soon.

'From a purely selfish point of view, do you think he'll finish the projector if you're not seeing him any more?'

'I don't know,' she said, laughing at his honesty at a time of personal crisis. 'I'm so out of practice with this kind of stuff, I don't know whether it's break-up-worthy or just a blip. We had a great afternoon yesterday, I thought things were good between us so perhaps it's too soon to say it's over. I do think it's a wake-up call and a sign to maybe slow things down a bit. I think I'll know when I see him again.'

'Mmm. Speaking of break-ups, I think Amy and I might be calling it a day.'

'Really? Because of the cinema?'

He shrugged, keeping his eyes on the road ahead. 'I think that was the beginning of the end. She's asked for her investment in the coffee house back.'

'But… can she do that?'

'We went into it as partners, and she's turned into a silent one over the past couple of years but it's her money. The thing is, she knows that I'd have to pull some of my investment out of the cinema if I have to pay her back.'

'She's playing games, Ollie.' Patsy was indignant, able to

see quite clearly what Amy's game was. 'She's trying to force you to give up on it.'

'Maybe, maybe not. But I think it's safe to say the love has gone.' He glanced at Patsy with a sad smile.

'Can you get a loan?' She wasn't going to start telling him she was sorry about Amy. He deserved someone better. Someone who loved him and supported him in whatever he wanted to do.

'I've already got one, that's how I paid for the building in the first place. The problem is that it comes in chunks and each chunk is contingent on something being finished. So I got one when the outside was done, and the next one will come when the kitchen's in. If I use any of that money to pay Amy back, we won't be able to afford to do the work to get the next chunk of money.'

'I wish I could help, somehow.'

'I appreciate the sentiment but I'll sort something out, Pats. It's not your problem to fix.'

'Bloody Amy.' Patsy wound her window down once they got off the motorway, enjoying the wind on her face.

'Maybe it's for the best. At least this way I'm not going to be beholden to her. I can't stay with her just to get through the project.'

'Can't you? I'm joking,' she added when he gave her a look of disbelief.

'In the long run, if she's not on my side, it's better to know now rather than down the line when our affairs are even more tangled together.'

Patsy agreed but quietly resolved to find some way of helping him.

When he'd dropped her off at her flat, she booted up the ancient laptop and dragged a chair out onto the roof terrace. She got changed into leggings and a sweatshirt which was warm enough to keep the late spring chill off, put some sunglasses on her head and stepped out of the window, laptop under her arm and a cup of tea in the other hand ready to do some serious research.

She had skills. She'd been a good software engineer three years ago and although things moved fast in that industry, she knew she had a sound, if rusty knowledge base. Could she take on a contract? Something she could work on in the evenings for a couple of months, maybe that would be enough money to see Oliver through.

There were a few websites she remembered where short-term software engineering contracts were posted but there was nothing that she thought would be doable at the right price in the tight timeframe they had. Then, when she went onto a Reddit thread which she thought might have some more leads, she struck gold.

Bug bounty hunting.

Ethical hackers could attempt to hack into a company's website and if they managed to, would flag up to that company how they did it, and potentially then be paid by an organisation grateful that an ethical hacker had got there first, highlighting a potential way for a real hacker to get in. It was perfect because she could do it in any spare time she had, there was no expectation from anyone because you could just dip in and out, start a new hunt if you hit a dead-end but the pay could be huge. It might take some time to hone her skills because being a software engineer didn't give her the same skills she would need to be a hacker, but she wasn't starting from scratch. She was excited. She'd finally, hopefully, found a way to help Oliver without having to disrupt her life and without anyone knowing what she was doing. It was the perfect solution.

# 20

Not long after their visit to Birmingham, Oliver announced that it was time to confirm their plans for the interior of the cinema so that everything they wanted to do could be incorporated into the design and they wouldn't waste money by changing their minds for lack of a definite idea.

Patsy and Oliver headed over to the cinema after work and sat on the floor at the front of the stalls with the plans before them and an array of paint, wood and flooring samples. Ed was upstairs working on the projector having complied with health and safety by texting her first. They hadn't talked properly since Birmingham and Patsy was hugely relieved that Ed was willing to put their problems aside for the good of the cinema. Early on in the process, she'd realised that the putting back together of the projector was something she wasn't going to be much help with and now he was at that stage, it was easy to feel released of the obligation to help him.

'I think we should go for wooden block worktops everywhere,' said Oliver, indicating a picture of a bar which looked like it could be a direct relation of the coffee house.

'I think we should have either polished concrete or resin. If we went for resin, we could embed some actual celluloid film into it, it could look really cool. And it'd be easier to keep clean than wood.

'I quite like that idea,' Oliver said thoughtfully. 'You're right, wooden top on a bar probably isn't great unless it's varnished to within an inch of its life. And resin would be cheaper than polished concrete.'

'And less industrial looking. We're not going for that are we?'

All they knew was that they weren't going for swirly patterned carpet and velvet curtains. It was a decision that had been made quite quickly after their night out in Birmingham. It had to look like more than an old-fashioned cinema. Both of them knew what it shouldn't look like but the vision of what it should was evading them at the moment; it was a wisp of an idea that neither of them could capture.

'No, I don't think so. But also, we need to steer clear of the traditional red velvet look that all cinemas had in the eighties. The cinema in Birmingham hadn't managed to shake off that image and I'm not sure it worked as retro, it just looked old-fashioned.' Oliver looked at Patsy, gauging her reaction.

'I know. I feel mean thinking that because I loved what they were doing in terms of the offer, but it looked like no-one had thought about how the place looked at all. If nothing else, that weekend made me realise what we shouldn't do.'

'I wonder whether we should settle on a colour scheme. That might help us make some decisions.'

'Well, definitely not black and white or anything like that. And I think we agree on nothing too cinema-ey and traditional,' she smiled. 'I like the idea of mustards, oranges, greens, like a seventies palette?'

Oliver raised his eyebrows in a manner that Patsy knew meant that hadn't occurred to him, but he thought it was a decent idea. 'Hmm. I quite like that. He swiped through the paint samples. 'This sort of thing?'

'More like this sort of thing.' Patsy toned down the brightness of his choices. 'And we could use this dark wood laminate for the counters and cupboards and shelves which would look really cool.'

Oliver started to look excited. 'And what about this flooring for the backstage bit behind the screen?'

'Hey, that's what we ought to call that space!' Patsy said, excitedly. 'Backstage at Croftwood Cinema!'

'That is perfect! Nice one Pats.'

After another hour of brainstorming, during which time they'd hopefully made enough decisions for Matt to be satisfied they wouldn't hold up the work, Ed appeared and offered to order pizza for them all.

'I need to get off, actually,' said Oliver, tactfully. 'I'll leave you to it. You okay to get home, Pats?'

She nodded, willing Ed not to offer to walk her.

After Oliver had left, they made small talk about the progress with the projector until the pizza arrived, then they sat cross-legged on the floor, across from each other with the open pizza box between them.

'So have you made any decisions yet?' Ed asked between mouthfuls. 'About the decor,' he clarified, gesturing towards the paint samples with his slice of pizza after seeing the look of panic cross her face when she thought he was referring to their relationship.

'We're getting there,' she said. 'I think Oliver's taste is basically what you see in the coffee house so veering him towards something that's not a carbon copy of that is a bit of a challenge.' She smiled.

'That wouldn't be the worst thing you could do,' said Ed with a shrug. 'I like the coffee house.'

'So do I,' said Patsy. 'But what makes it cool is because it's not like anywhere else in Croftwood, it's got its own vibe. That's what we need here, but a different vibe.'

'Hmm, I get you.'

'We did come up with a name for our behind-the-screen bar slash party area though. Backstage at Croftwood Cinema,' she said, feeling more at ease with Ed again. As long as she didn't think about that night in Birmingham, it was okay.

'Yeah, that's cool. Makes me think of an old Hollywood film set or something.'

'We could theme it like that,' Patsy said thoughtfully. 'We'd decided to stay away from themes but that could be perfect for the backstage area. What says Hollywood glamour, you know in the thirties and forties?'

Ed looked at her with a panic-stricken expression, much like the one she'd given him earlier. 'I'm not sure how much help I can be with that. You probably need to talk it over with Oliver. It's a good idea,' he said, encouragingly.

They managed to avoid any talk of their relationship until they were on the way to Patsy's house after Ed had insisted on walking with her. It was easier to talk as they walked side by side. Less scrutiny perhaps.

'Where are we, Patsy?'

She resisted the temptation to deflect by naming the road and instead answered as honestly as she could. 'I'm not sure. I struggled to understand how we went from an amazing afternoon together to…'

'To me leaving you in the cinema.'

'Yes. It's like you were a different person that night and I suppose it made me wonder whether I know you well enough to know that it's out of character. I wanted it to be out of character and for you to give me some explanation that didn't sound like a rubbish excuse and you couldn't. So I don't know what to think. I like you, Ed, but maybe it's a sign.'

'Maybe. I wanted to be able to explain but all I have are crap excuses. And I can't tell you whether it was out of character because…it seemed like the only option at the time.'

Patsy felt like she was beginning to come to a conclusion. Ed wasn't someone she could fully understand. She'd lived with Dan, who she also didn't understand but in an entirely different way. With Dan she had seen everything about him, he hadn't held anything of himself back. She didn't understand how he could behave like he did but there was no mystery there. Ed, on the other hand, was like a fog. She thought she saw glimpses of a man she could grow to love, like the afternoon they'd spent in Birmingham, the time they'd spent together in her flat, cocooned on the roof terrace, talking about everything and anything. But there was so much she couldn't see and didn't know. Perhaps he would always be an enigma. The problem was that it was as difficult to live with that as it was with Dan because the one thing they had in common was unpredictability and that was something Patsy didn't want to have in her life. She'd so carefully curated the perfect existence, with little or nothing she wasn't in control of and that meant everything to her.

'I think for me, I'd be happier if we could be friends?' She looked at him for any sign of what he thought about her suggestion and saw a brief wave of relief.

'I'd really like that. Thank you. I appreciate that you're willing to put it behind us, Patsy. Helping with the projector means a lot to me and if we can still work together as friends, that's great.'

And that told Patsy everything she needed to know.


The following morning it was Patsy's turn to open up the coffee house. She was desperate to talk to Oliver about her idea of a golden age of Hollywood theme for the backstage area. Normally, he wouldn't come in until late morning, just before the lunch rush, but now he was back in the flat upstairs while he sorted things out — or not — with Amy, Patsy was hoping he might venture down in search of coffee a lot earlier.

Not long after she'd served her first wave of customers, Matt came in. He was wearing a suit which was quite unusual for him and he was clean-shaven and had done his hair. He looked very smart.

'Job interview or court?' she joked, starting to make his usual latte.

'Court.'

She laughed but then looked at his face and realised he wasn't joking.

'Oh, god. Sorry. Is it to do with the divorce?'

'Yes. It's a formality to do with access to the twins. Well, I hope it's a formality.'

Patsy didn't know what to say. She knew he was a great dad but had seen first-hand how hard it was to manage when his work schedule wasn't always nine to five.

'I'd offer you a croissant but I don't want you to get crumbs on your tie.'

He smiled. 'That's okay, the coffee will be fine. Is Oliver about?'

'He's upstairs, not due in until later.'

'Upstairs, like living up there again?' Matt looked a little more relaxed now there was someone else's drama to focus on.

'For now. I don't think things are great with him and Amy. Whether it's a break or the end, I'm not sure.' In fact, she was pretty sure, but didn't want to sound gloomy since Matt was probably already having a bad day.

'It's a shame she didn't want in on the cinema project. She was pretty keen when they did this place up together. I guess a big project either draws you together or drives you apart,' he said, looking wistful.

'I suppose you see a lot of that, people embarking on massive projects together and what it does to their relationships.' Patsy leant her elbow on the counter, resting her chin in her hand, while Matt stirred his coffee, in no rush to take a seat.

'So how is your relationship?' His eyes darted to look her in the eye very briefly as if he knew he might be on dangerous ground.

'You mean after the cinema ditching?'

'At least you were with me and Oliver. It could have been worse.'

'It could. We've decided to be friends.'

'I did wonder whether there was any coming back from that, frankly.'

'It was a mutual decision but he seemed more worried about losing the projector makeover than me, so it's probably for the best.'

Matt laughed. 'As long as you're alright, that's the main thing.'

'I am, thank you.' She grinned and began to tidy the counter just as Oliver appeared.

'Morning, Pats. Any chance of a coffee?' he asked, before sitting at the table nearest the counter, where Matt joined him.

'No problem. I'll come and join you while it's quiet because I've had a great idea.'

Patsy made a coffee for herself and Oliver, Matt declining the offer of a refill, then she sat down. All the excitement of the idea began to bubble inside her again as she began to explain her concept of a 1930s Hollywood theme for the backstage area.

'Perhaps we can get away with that area being a bit more themed because it's separate from the rest of the space,'

Oliver said.

'Remember it needs to work when the doors are open too. You don't want the transition from inside to outside to be too...' Matt stopped, trying to think of the right word.

'Abrupt,' said Oliver.

'Exactly. Thanks. Anyway, that's something to bear in mind. That reminds me.' He rifled through his case and pulled out a sheaf of paper. 'I've been meaning to drop this off with you but it slipped my mind. It's a list of everything we need to decide on for the interior. I've made a start on the decisions I know about but I think it's probably time for you to take it on.' He handed Patsy a document which was a long list of every element that needed consideration from the colour of the walls to the taps in the toilets.

Patsy took it from him trying not to feel overwhelmed. This felt like a lot more responsibility than she thought she'd agreed to. 'Yes, that's fine. We'll get it as far as we can and then perhaps we can go through it?'

'Don't worry, Pats.' Oliver could read her like a book. 'It's listed in order of priority so we'll start at the beginning and work through. As long as the first few things are sorted out, they can get on.'

She looked at Matt, widening her eyes to convey her fear but he just gave her a reassuring smile. She exhaled loudly. 'Okay. One thing at a time. We can do that.'

'Of course we can.' Oliver squeezed her hand.

'I need to get off,' said Matt, looking at his watch and then downing the last of his coffee. 'Look, if you have any questions, give me a call, or we can meet at the cinema to go over anything you're not sure about.'

'I hope it goes well,' Patsy said.

'Thank you.' He seemed to look at her for a long time, then turned and left.

'He's got a court thing, to do with the kids,' she said to

Oliver.

'Ah, I'd forgotten that was coming up.'

'Have you ever met his wife?'

'Yes, when we were doing this place, he invited me and Amy round for dinner. The twins were only little so I suppose Nicole had a lot on her plate but she was so uptight, making nasty digs at Matt the whole time, saying things like they were a joke but none of it was funny. The whole thing was a bit awkward, to be honest, so we obviously said they must come round to ours sometime but it never happened. I wasn't that surprised when he said they were getting divorced, and aside from the impact on the children, I didn't think he'd be that gutted about it and to be fair, I don't think he has been but being apart from the kids has been hard for him.'

'I can imagine. It's not the same having them a couple of nights a week, it's probably unsettling for all of them. Maybe you should give him a call later, make sure it went okay.'

Oliver raised an eyebrow. 'Are you worried about him, Pats?'

'Well, yes. He's a colleague at the moment.' She batted away Oliver's comment but wondered why she was so concerned about someone she could barely be civil to a few weeks before. In fact, she struggled to remember exactly what it was about him that she hadn't liked.

# 21

Patsy was sat on the sofa in Oliver's flat with the huge spec document on the table in front of her. They had been working on it sporadically for days, each of them taking turns to come up to the flat and work on it, leaving it covered in Post-It notes with questions for the other. They'd made good progress on the basics, anything that wasn't related to what the place was going to feel like and look like in the end. Things like the bathroom fixtures and fittings, the kitchen, boring things like plug sockets and light switches, all of that had been decided but until they knew what they wanted it to look like, they'd hit a stumbling block.

'I think we should go for the Hollywood glamour thing for the whole place,' Patsy said, when Oliver appeared after locking up for the night. 'It's sleek but understated and if we can get the bare minimum done, it'll still look okay because twenties and thirties was minimalist, it was the Great Depression. Like the hotel in Birmingham,' she was on a roll now. 'It was so beautiful but the foyer, you would say that was totally Art Deco and actually it was only those lamps and the stair balustrade. The rest was just paint choices and clever lighting. We can so do it, Ollie!'

'Look Pats, I don't hate that idea,' he said, sitting down next to her with a weary sigh. 'I did love that hotel, it was cool and much more my style than the mustards or whatever you want to call the scheme we decided on the other night, but I've got a meeting with Matt to finalise everything tomorrow afternoon. I don't think we've got time to change everything and get this spec document finished before then.'

Quickly trying to come up with a solution that didn't involve another evening of sitting in the cinema stalls and gazing around them for inspiration, Patsy said, 'If you're willing to give me tomorrow morning off I can come up with a proper scheme and have everything ready for Matt by lunchtime tomorrow.' As Oliver's mouth opened to most probably object, she continued. 'I'll stay here tonight, we'll get as much done as we can, then an hour before the meeting with Matt I'll pitch it to you so we can make sure we've covered everything and if we don't love it, we'll go with the idea we had the other night.'

Oliver shrugged. 'Okay, seems fair enough. Are you sure you have time? That'll be a lot of work.'

'Definitely.'

They brainstormed for a while, fuelled, perhaps unwisely at that time of day, with coffee and leftover pastries from the coffee house.

'So if we go for the muddy purple on the walls with pewter beading and woodwork, the marble-effect ball light sconces along the walls and the Art Deco fan lights for the tables, what are we going to do about the chairs and tables? When we were going for the seventies type theme we were going for faux leather in those kind of muted colours. I don't know what would work now.'

Oliver was busy printing out the ideas they'd already settled on for a mood board which he had said would be just as good if they set it up on Pinterest but which Patsy insisted needed to be a physical thing. 'What about dark brown buttoned sofas and chairs?'

Patsy sighed. Bless Oliver, they'd be the perfect suggestion for the coffee house. He had no idea but was trying his best. 'Hmm, I'm not sure that would work with the colour palette.' She kneaded her eyes with her knuckles. 'I don't know if we can pull together the whole scheme by tomorrow. There's such a lot to think about.'

'Well what about velvet chairs? Like an actual old-fashioned cinema?'

Ready to shoot down the idea for its lack of taste, Patsy paused. 'If they were purple velvet and a deep pewter grey and maybe a lighter grey and maybe even a colour pop of something else on the very odd few. You know what? That could look classy.' She started googling for images.

'And for the tables, maybe lots of small bistro tables in that dark pewter or even glossy black? If they're small, that'll make them easier to move around when we need to.'

Patsy stared at Oliver who had gone from tasteless to brilliant in a couple of minutes. 'Oliver! You're a genius, that'll look amazing.'

At 2 am, Oliver began dozing off over his laptop so Patsy sent him to bed. Aside from a power nap at about 3 am, she worked through, enjoying seeing their vision come together. Now that they'd made the big decisions, it was easy to fill in Matt's spec document with details like paint colours, flooring choices and light fittings.

As promised, Patsy had everything ready to show Oliver an hour before the meeting with Matt. He'd got Jack to cover the coffee house and came upstairs to see the results of her all-nighter.

'Okay, so here it is.' Patsy pulled out the boards that she had finished filling with their ideas. If Oliver'd had any doubt as to the depth of her vision, he could see now that he had no need to worry.

'Blimey, Pats. This looks amazing.'

'Really? Do you like it more than what we planned the other night?'

'Yes! I love it, it's perfect. It's… I can't believe it, Pats. It's exactly what I wanted although I didn't know it. And you've definitely elevated it since I went to bed last night.'

Patsy threw her arms around him. 'Thanks Ollie! What relief! And you did come up with some great ideas last night, it wasn't only me.'

They sat on the sofa and spread Patsy's work over the coffee table. She explained to Oliver her thoughts behind the overall design and how that translated into the details. She'd even made a comprehensive list of suppliers for some of the things she felt were must-have items to pull the scheme together and had added quite a few things onto the spec that weren't even on there before.

'You know what, you're wasted being a barista.'

'Well, no offence but being a barista wasn't a life-long ambition.'

Oliver grinned. 'I know. Far be it from me to encourage you to do anything which might make you leave the Oliver's empire but you're brilliant at this stuff. How you pulled this together so quickly, I have no idea.'

'I think it was the Matt effect. We have to be ready, otherwise he'll be stressed out and grumpy with us. And I'm guessing that if there are any hold-ups, it'll end up costing more.'

Oliver nodded, gravely. 'That's absolutely true.'

'So Amy's not snapping at your heels for the money?'

'Not exactly but I know there will be a deadline at some

point. I think it's helped that I could move back here, it's taken the pressure off.' Oliver leant back into the sofa and looked at Patsy. 'Seriously, Pats. You should be project managing this. I know I'm going to regret this because I don't know if the coffee house can cope without you but hopefully Jack can fill at least one of your shoes. Do this. It's easily a full-time job now that we're getting nearer to the end, especially with the catering things you were going to do anyway later down the line. I honestly think if we stand any chance of being ready before the end of the summer, you need to take this on.'

The thought of not working at the coffee house anymore was scary. It was all she'd known for three years and all she'd expected to know for the only future she'd allowed herself to envisage. It was overwhelming. 'I don't know, Ollie. I don't know anything about doing something like this. It's one thing putting ideas together but I have no idea how to put it into practice.'

'We'll go through it with Matt. He'll be able to explain what he needs and how it fits in with the rest of the team. Don't decide now, wait until after that and see what you think. If you like the sound of it, we can make a firm plan.'

'Okay. Thanks, Ollie. I really appreciate you having faith in me like this.'

'I don't need faith, Pats. I know what you're capable of, you're the one that needs the faith, in yourself.' He squeezed her hand.

'Well, I'm relieved we're sorted. It feels good to have the plan in place.'

'And Ed's still okay to carry on like he was?'

Patsy had told Oliver that they'd ended things and he had done a good job of being sorry, managing to wait a good couple of minutes before he asked about the projector situation.

'Yes, I think so.'

'It's okay being friends?'

'To be honest it'd be easier to never have to see him again but then that seems like a shame.'

He raised an eyebrow, questioningly.

'He's the first man I've been out with since Dan and I'd expected more, somehow. I suppose I thought he might grow on me and end up being the one.'

'Does he need to be the one? He's the first guy you've been out with, the odds were unlikely. I thought you'd decided just to have fun?'

'I don't know if I know how to do that, relationship-wise. I feel like it has to be all or nothing. Is that weird? The more time we spent together the more I realised that we weren't compatible. He was quite self-centred, in the nicest possible way.' She cringed as she said it, feeling massively disloyal to Ed. 'Maybe not self-centred, but inflexible. I get the feeling that he was trying to force me to fit into his life as if he doesn't want anything to change.'

'If I'm being completely honest, I think most relationships are based on compromise. I'm not saying you should compromise, but you need to make sure that you're only making reasonable compromises and that that's all someone expects from you. It can't be all one way and you shouldn't be settling for anything if it doesn't make you happy.'

'That's what it was like with Dan, everything was on his terms and I don't want to fall into that again.'

'Good, knowing what you want is half the battle.'

Above everything else, she knew that not telling Ed the whole truth about Dan was the main thing that bothered her because she knew if he was someone she was taking seriously, if she thought they had a future, she would have told him.

# 22

Patsy went down to wait in the coffee house for Matt to arrive for their meeting while Oliver stayed upstairs to make some phone calls.

'Are you sure you're okay for another hour?' she asked Jack. He'd looked slightly shell-shocked when she'd first come down. Judging by the number of full tables, he'd had a very busy spell, but from watching him serve the couple of customers who had been in since, she had no worries about his competence. He was friendly and chatty and that was the main thing anyway. If he made a rubbish coffee for someone, they'd be more forgiving about it if they liked him.

'Yes, I think it's going okay?'

He was looking for reassurance so Patsy gave him a big smile and said, 'I think so too. It's a bit scary doing it on your own the first few times, especially if you get a busy patch but you're fine. We haven't had any complaints about you,' she grinned, 'and if you're really stuck, we're only going to be upstairs. Just shout.'

'Thanks, Patsy. I'll go and clear that table.'

Patsy started making coffee for herself and Oliver.

'Help yourself to a coffee when you have a lull,' she told Jack when he came back behind the counter.

'Thanks. What can I get you?' He asked his next customer.

'Cappuccino, please.'

'Hey, I can do that one,' said Patsy, recognising Matt's voice although she had her back to the counter. 'Hi Matt, won't be a sec. Go on up, I'll bring the coffee.'

'Thank you,' Matt said, smiling at her before heading through the door to the flat.

Patsy took the coffees upstairs. Matt was sat where she'd been on the sofa and was looking optimistically at everything that was laid out on the coffee table ready.

'Latte, cappuccino,' she said, handing Oliver and Matt their coffees.

'Thanks,' said Matt. 'It looks like you two have been busy.'

Patsy grabbed a chair from the nearby dining table and sat across from Matt and Oliver, the coffee table between them.

'Patsy's done most of the work and I've asked her to take on the role of project manager.' He handed Matt the master document. 'She's already done most of the research and I think as she's got such an eye for it she ought to be involved in all the decisions from now on. We've got cover for her here so she's free to be on site as much as she needs to be.'

Matt put his coffee down and sat back, grinning. 'That works for me. Hopefully you'll be much easier to pin down than Oliver.'

'Thanks, mate,' said Oliver in mock outrage, 'I thought you of all people would know you don't have a minute to yourself when you're your own boss.'

'I can be sympathetic until I need a decision making and then it's annoying when I can't get hold of you.'

'I'm sure Pats will be a huge improvement then,' said Oliver. 'Look at this, it's all her work.' He pulled some of the key elements to the top of the pile of pictures and plans that were strewn across the table. 'This is her vision and I want her to make sure it comes to life.'

Patsy sat there watching Matt as he wordlessly sifted through her painstakingly prepared design boards. For some reason this made her feel a bit uncomfortable. She felt like he was judging her and it reminded her of what he'd been like in the beginning.

'It's a very coherent vision,' he said, finally. Patsy softened a little. 'But do you have any experience of project managing? Any procurement experience? Knowledge of commercial building standards and regulations?'

'To be fair, we're paying you for that,' said Oliver. 'And I don't know much more than Patsy about procurement and project managing.'

'Buying stuff isn't rocket science,' Patsy said, defensively. 'I'm a very organised person and... and I have no idea why I'm justifying myself to you.' She aimed this at Matt but looked at Oliver as she said it, hoping he would put a stop to Matt's doubts.

'Come on Matt, you've got to get on board with Patsy. Give her a chance.'

'Look, don't get me wrong, I'm only making sure you know what you're getting into. It's a lot of work.'

Patsy could see in his eyes that he genuinely wasn't trying to be a dick about it. He looked concerned, if anything.

'It's okay. I've got the time, and I would like to see it through and be involved in the whole thing from start to finish, now that we've decided what we want,' she said.

Matt smiled and gave a small nod. 'Let's get started then.'

'Right. So what do we need to look at first?' Oliver asked.

After an hour of having to justify every inch of her design but holding her nerve and doing just that to prove she could be business-like and calm, Patsy was relieved when Jack called up the stairs for help.

'I'll go,' she said.

'Thanks, I think we're almost done anyway,' said Oliver.

Matt nodded in agreement and Patsy skipped down the stairs. She felt like she'd won Matt over, not that he'd admit it, but he'd asked her questions that she knew the answers to, asked her reasons for various choices and hadn't come back with any negative comments. She was exhausted but felt like she'd made a good job of pitching her vision. Surprisingly, she found herself respecting the fact that Matt was so thorough in checking that she knew what was what. It showed that he was good at his job, even in the face of his client calling the shots. And it was right that he checked those shots. He was the kind of person they needed on their side.

The coffee house had developed a little queue which she and Oliver would take in their stride but which, completely understandably had freaked Jack out.

'I'm sorry to interrupt your meeting, Patsy.'

'Don't worry, we'd pretty much finished. I was glad to get out of there.'

'How did it go?'

'Really well. We might be needing a bit more help from you in here.'

'No problem,' said Jack, grinning. 'I totally nailed drawing a heart on someone's latte this morning and she gave me a tip.'

'Wow, that's great. Did you fancy her?'

Jack looked at Patsy in shock.

'I just wondered if that's why you did a heart?'

'No, it's the easiest one. Shit, do you think that's what she thought?'

Patsy laughed. 'Maybe learn the ferny leaf one and save the heart for someone special. It can be a useful hint.'

'Cheers, Patsy. I'll get some other patterns sorted out. I think I ought to have my own one, like a graffiti artist tag.'

'Good idea. Go for it.'

She was going to miss working regularly in the coffee house but she had to admit, she was excited about putting more time into the cinema. Bringing her own design to life was going to be incredible.

The most glorious early summer's day had turned into a balmy evening and Patsy was heading over to the cinema to meet Ed. It was the first time they'd worked together since their break-up but Oliver was keen to find out what progress was being made so when Ed had texted to say that he was going to work there that night, she arranged to meet him.

Ed was in the projection box with his head inside the projector, fitting the shiny parts back inside. He popped up to say hello but then went back to what he was doing as they chatted.

'So you're the boss now?' Ed said with a smile after Patsy told him the new arrangement. 'Congratulations.'

'Thanks, but it doesn't feel like a new job.'

'Come on, it could be the start of a new career. With the cinema in your portfolio of work, you'll be able to start selling yourself as a designer.'

'It's one thing helping out a friend when, to be honest, they'd think anything you did was brilliant but a completely different thing to do that for anyone else.'

'Why? It seems like an amazing jumping off point to me.' He finished fitting something inside the projector and turned to pick up the next part from where they were still laid out, labelled on the paper on the floor.

How could Patsy explain to Ed how important her comfort zone was? That it wasn't about being a barista versus being a designer or project manager, it was about having a life that made her feel safe.

'It is an amazing opportunity and I'm looking forward to working on the cinema but I've never wanted to be a designer.'

'What do you want to do?'

'I'm happy doing what I do.'

'But being a barista, it's not forever for anyone is it?' He passed her an Allen key that he'd finished with.

'Well no-one sets out to work in a coffee house, but some things are more important than money.'

'No, I get that. The most important thing is to be happy but what about your dreams, Patsy? I know you're content with your life but what about your ambitions?'

All of these things were mixed up so tightly with the life she'd had with Dan, she wasn't sure she could explain herself properly to Ed without telling him everything. 'I don't know, Ed. I think being happy with what you have, well, there's a lot to be said for that.'

Warming to his argument, he stopped what he was doing and turned to her. 'Well, I think you're wasting a talent if you go back to the coffee house after this.'

'But what about loyalty? Oliver's giving me this chance. I can't just do the job and then leave, it would feel like I'd used him.'

'I think he would want you to take advantage of the situation. He's a good guy, he knows this could be a chance for you to move on.'

'And what if I don't want to move on?' Patsy was starting to fume. She didn't want to take it out on Ed but he didn't understand. That was her fault. 'I'm happy, Ed. Not everyone has ambitions or dreams of changing their life. You're hardly the example of taking risks and seizing opportunities. Isn't your job the only one you've had, ever?'

'Yes, but—'

'Exactly. You don't know what I did before, Ed. You don't

know that this isn't better or that this isn't already my dream.'

'You're right,' he said in a soothing tone which made her think he was trying to placate her.

'Don't try to talk me down. You don't know, Ed!'

'I know that, Patsy, but you're not telling me so I have to piece together all these things I know about you, which isn't very much, to come up with what the actual picture is. I know you've been holding back about your past but I wanted to know, Patsy, I wanted to be part of your life but I know that you feel you can't trust me with everything, and aside from what happened in Birmingham, that's why there's no future for us.'

'I wanted to tell you…'

'That's not the same as telling me though,' he said. 'Can you tell me now?'

Patsy shrugged. 'What's the point?'

'Is it because you thought it'd change how I feel about you?'

'No. I don't know whether it would or not. I try not to think about it most of the time. There's no need to and that's why I didn't tell you.'

Ed stood up. 'It's affecting you, whatever it is. You can't move on until you deal with it. I don't know if it's because your ex turned up the other week or what, but you need to confront whatever it is, Patsy. It's the only way forward for us.'

Patsy stared at Ed in disbelief. 'But we're just friends now, right? We don't need to find a way forward and friends don't need to share this kind of stuff if they don't want to.'

Ed looked confused for a second and began fiddling with something inside the projector. 'Right. Yes, of course, you're right.'

Patsy sat down and watched Ed as he immersed himself

again in the job at hand. The inside of the projector was spotless now, a far cry from how it had looked in the beginning. What was going on? Was he holding a grudge over this feeling that she hadn't told him everything? It hadn't occurred to her that he'd care that much once they'd split up but then, perhaps it was hard to switch into being friends so abruptly when they didn't know each other well enough to navigate anything other than the brief relationship they'd had.

On some level she understood that it could be frustrating to have been shut out of someone's past. If they didn't trust you with that, was there any trust at all? But she did think that Ed was right in saying that she needed to put it behind her if she was going to move on, so it was time to talk to Toby again.

After she'd spoken to him at the coffee house, he'd outlined what the next steps would be and sent her away to think about what she wanted to do next. With the cinema project ramping up, it hadn't seemed like a priority but perhaps Ed was right and now that her life seemed to be moving at a much faster pace than it had in the past three years, it was time to get everything aligned for whatever might happen next.

# 23

Patsy had called Toby and arranged to meet him at his home office to discuss the divorce. He'd told her his address, and it wasn't that far from where her flat was, only Toby owned the whole house. But he was a lawyer, so maybe it shouldn't have been surprising.

Toby's house was detached, a three-storey villa built in local granite, quarried over a century ago from the nearby hills. It had been restored, with new sash windows, new mortar between the stonework and a smart blue brick laid driveway

She walked up the driveway, rang the bell and the door was opened a few seconds later by Toby wearing more casual clothes than normal, a t-shirt rather than a shirt, but still looking well-groomed and business-like.

'Patsy, come in.' He smiled and stood back to let her in. The hallway was beautiful with the original Victorian floor tiles and a wide, sweeping staircase.

'Wow, this is amazing,' she said.

'Thanks. Bit crazy as it's only me most of the time, but I fell in love with the original features.'

'It's lovely in this part of town. I've got a flat on Churchdown Avenue.'

'This is definitely the best part of Croftwood.'

They stood in silence for a minute while Patsy gazed around and then took her coat off.

'I want to offer you a coffee but I'm not sure it will be up to your standards,' he said with a grin as they headed into the most enormous, yet cosy kitchen Patsy had ever seen. It had oak cabinets, huge dark granite slabs on the floor and the whole back wall was windows, that looked out over a well-kept lawn. The back of the house was on the first floor because it was built on a slope. There were a couple of comfy looking sofas in one corner where Patsy could imagine herself lounging while someone else cooked dinner.

'I'm always happy to waive my standards if someone else makes me a coffee.'

'Okay.' He went over to a cupboard door which disappeared somewhere when he'd opened it to reveal a very swanky coffee machine. 'Latte?'

'Yes, great. So how long have you lived here?'

'Not that long, only a few months. I moved here from London.'

'Croftwood's not too quiet for you?'

He smiled. 'Access to London nightlife didn't seem like a priority anymore, it suddenly seemed more important to have a different pace of life, so here I am.'

'Where there is no nightlife.'

'Oh, come on. Haven't you been to quiz night at the Three Nuns?' He finished making a coffee for each of them. 'Right, shall we take this down to the office?'

They went back into the hallway and down a staircase into the basement. Surprisingly, it was bright and modern, furnished with a huge desk, bookshelves on every wall which were groaning with legal books and other titles which Patsy couldn't believe anyone actually read. There were two comfortable swivel chairs either side of the desk but the best thing was that it opened out onto the garden. The doors were open and a warm breeze was drifting through.

'I'm not surprised you come to the coffee house to work, this is more distraction than workplace,' she said.

'It's so quiet though,' Toby said. 'If I'm doing webchats with clients, it ends up feeling a bit isolating being down here all day by myself. Take a seat,' he said, gesturing to one of the chairs and then sitting down behind the desk.

She was a client. She'd almost forgotten that.

'I just need to take a few details. Can we start with your husband's name and address.'

'I'm not sure where he's living. I suppose it could be his parent's.' She gave Toby the details he needed but had no idea what Dan had done since he left prison.

'Once I've prepared the papers, we'll try serving him at that address. If that's not correct, we'll have to make reasonable efforts to find out where he is before we can apply to the court to dispense with service but we'll cross that bridge when we come to it. Leave it with me for now and I'll let you know when we're going to serve.'

'You mean when you're going to post the papers? How will we know if he's got them?'

'I think in this instance we'll employ a process server who will physically go to the address with the intention of handing them to him. That way we know if he has them or not and can get evidence of him receiving them in case he's not forthcoming with acknowledging receipt in the proper way.'

It all seemed overwhelming suddenly and much to her mortification, Patsy began to cry.

'Hey, hey,' Toby leapt up from his chair and rushed round to her, twirling her chair until she was facing him. He knelt in front of her and took her hand.

'Sorry,' she mumbled.

'It's okay. I understand how difficult this is.'

She began fishing in her bag for a tissue but Toby beat her to it, offering her his handkerchief which was unused and neatly folded.

'Thanks. Aren't you a bit young to be using proper hankies?'

'Call it a hangover from my days in chambers,' he said with a smile, leaning back onto his heels.

'I don't know why I'm crying. This is what I've wanted for years. I think there's more to it than I realised. I mean, I'd never thought about the fact that I don't know where he lives or what he's doing. When did he get out of prison even?'

'I can help you find out some of that if you want. And as for the divorce process, once we get it going, there's not much more to it than we've covered today, I can take care of it for you and only involve you if necessary, if that helps?'

'I can't ask you to do that. You're already doing so much more than giving me advice. I'm happy to pay you,' she added, knowing that there was no way she could afford this kind of legal help. If Toby wasn't helping her she'd have been googling how to do the whole thing herself and would have no idea what any of it meant.

'No,' he said softly. 'I'm happy to help. It's hardly more than a paperwork exercise.'

'Thank you. And don't worry about finding out about Dan. I don't need to know.'

'Okay. Can I get you another drink? Maybe a brandy would be more appropriate now.'

'I'd better not. I've already given myself a throbbing headache from crying. I should go. I can't tell you how grateful I am, Toby. I wouldn't know where to start with this, which is maybe why I haven't done anything about it before.

Coffee's on me next time you're in.'

They headed back upstairs.

'I guess working online means you don't have to deal with crying women normally,' Patsy said, stuffing the hanky into her pocket after Toby gestured that she should keep it when she offered it back.

'There is that,' he smiled. 'But you've reminded me how disconnected I've become. It's easy to forget that there are real people on the other end of the internet connection sometimes.'

'That's the best thing about my job. The people.'

'Even when Rosemary's waiting on the doorstep insisting to be let in half an hour before you open?'

Patsy laughed. 'You must have been early once to even know that happens.'

'You've got me.'

'Thanks Toby. I'll see you tomorrow?'

He nodded and smiled, giving her a wave before he closed the door.

She'd finally done it.

# 24

Patsy stood on the circle balcony to watch the first boards of the new flooring go down and breathed a sigh of relief. Until she saw it in the building she hadn't been completely convinced that she'd made the right choice. There was so much to consider aside from how it looked: how the sound carried, whether it was too reflective, whether it was too slippery to be safe given the gentle slope of the floor from the back of the stalls towards the screen. The local flooring shop had been really helpful, pulling in samples from suppliers and advising her on the things to consider and in the end she'd chosen what looked like dark mahogany floorboards that were actually made of some kind of composite, an upgrade from a vinyl floor but the same idea.

Now she could see how beautiful it was going to look, she couldn't wait to see the colour start to go on the walls. Then it would start coming together and she was pretty confident that they'd be on track to open before the end of the summer.

She'd managed to find a company who made the chairs she wanted and would upholster them with whatever fabric she decided. They'd sent a sample which was now in Oliver's flat at the coffee house and she had forced Jack, Oliver, Jess and anyone else who had a few minutes to spare to sit in it and let her know their honest opinion on whether it would be comfortable. They all insisted that it was more comfortable than normal cinema chairs and Jack had come up with the idea of having a few two-seater versions that couples could specially request.

'Patsy, are we running the floor into that area behind the screen?' The boss of the flooring guys shouted up to her. It was annoying that he didn't know that, but Patsy supposed that was the whole point of her being the project manager; to make sure that there was always someone who knew.

'Yep, all over the ground floor!'

The balcony where she stood would be for viewing and drinks rather than dining so they had decided to go for a sumptuous carpet in a dark sooty colour. The chairs up there were going to be a slightly upgraded version of the chairs they had just sold but wider and more comfortable. Basically it was a more traditional experience which would suit anyone who wasn't interested in eating.

She headed downstairs to the foyer which had been stripped back but would be rebuilt as soon as the floor was laid, with the original ticket booth, a bar and cloakroom. The sound engineer that Ed had organised was coming for a preliminary survey and was due any minute. While she waited, she stepped outside into the sunshine and sat on a nearby park bench, briefly closing her eyes as she raised her face to the warmth.

'Good morning, Patsy.'

'Rosemary, hi!' Patsy shaded her eyes to look at the older woman who ran the library.

'I hear from Oliver that you're planning a launch party?' Nothing got past Rosemary. 'I must say, it doesn't look as if it will be finished in time.' And optimism wasn't in her vocabulary.

'I know it looks like there's still a lot to do but it's starting to come together quickly now.'

'Hmm. It's hard to tell from out here.'

'Do you want to have a quick look inside? They're laying the floor but we can look from the door.'

Rosemary's face lit up, as Patsy had known it would. This would win her brownie points for a long time.

'That would be wonderful, if you're sure.'

'Come on.'

Patsy led the way into the cinema.

'Oh, the ticket booth is gone,' Rosemary said with a disappointed tone.

'We've taken it down temporarily. It'll be back better than it was before.

'I am pleased to hear that. I doubt I'm the only one who would appreciate these nostalgic details. Of course, a lot of it has gone since its heyday.'

Patsy had a brainwave mixed with a touch of trepidation.

'Do you remember what it was like, back in the day?' Okay, that was a vague approximation of time, but she didn't want to offend Rosemary by getting her age wrong.

'We used to come here when I was a girl. I suppose it was the late 1950s. It was shabby then, but had all the original features. When they finally spent some money on it, it never felt the same again. It lost its character, I suppose,' she said wistfully.

It was too good an opportunity to miss.

'I'd love to hear about what it was like. Would you be willing to meet me at Oliver's tomorrow? I could show you my plans. It's not too late to add in a few elements that would make it more authentic.'

'Oh, I'd love to, Patsy. Shall we say ten o'clock?'

Patsy let Rosemary have a look at the auditorium. There

wasn't much to see but she was thrilled nevertheless and they confirmed their plans to meet the next day just as the sound engineer arrived.

After hearing that they'd need some new speakers and that the control system was basically rubbish but useable, Patsy headed to the coffee house to grab some lunch before she had to be back at the cinema to take delivery of the new bulb for the projector. Ed had insisted she check it before signing for the delivery which she thought was overkill but as it was so expensive, she hadn't argued.

'You're a glutton for punishment,' Oliver said when she walked in.

'You need to be more specific. There are so many things you could be referring to.' She perched on a stool at the end of the counter realising that it was the first time she'd sat down for hours.

'Rosemary's been in,' he said with a knowing look.

'Well, yes, you might be right but she was so enthusiastic about seeing it and I think she could help me put a few original features back into the scheme. It doesn't do any harm to have a chat.'

'Come and tell me that when she's dissed all your ideas and is trying to take over.'

Patsy laughed. She knew how difficult Rosemary could be and it did annoy her when she knocked on the door of the coffee house before opening time, but she suspected Rosemary had a heart of gold and could be very helpful once you knew how to handle her.

'Any chance of a toastie and a coffee or do I have to make it myself?'

'You have to make it yourself.'

'Thanks. I'll have cheese and chutney.'

Once she'd finished her lunch, Patsy waited until Oliver was free and gave him an update on what the sound engineer said.

'Can you ask Ed if he thinks that tallies with what he'd thought?'

'Yes, he said he'd come back when we've tested the projector. We probably need to make sure Ed's available for that. I'll speak to him about whether he can arrange to have some time off during a weekday.'

'Make sure you tell him we're happy to pay for his time. It's turned into a lot more for him than just cleaning the projector up.'

'But he loves it.'

'Mmm hmm,' Oliver said, grinning. 'I'm not sure it's his love of cinema projection that's the driving force here.'

'Oh, shut up,' she said, because it definitely was. 'See you later.'

She headed back to the cinema with a spring in her step.

'Let me open this to check it's okay,' she said to the courier when he turned up right at the beginning of the delivery slot.

He tutted and held out his machine for her to sign. 'I haven't got all day.'

'Sorry, it won't take a minute.'

She opened the outer box and saw the inner box advising not to remove the packaging until you were ready to install. She gave it a tentative shake, figuring that if it was smashed to smithereens she'd be able to hear it.

'Thanks for waiting.' She signed on the screen then took the lamp straight up to the projection box. Ed was going to meet her after work so they could install it and have a go at running some film through, which they were both pretty excited about. She had wondered whether to tell Oliver so that he could come and watch the big moment but Ed had said there was no guarantee that they'd get as far as that tonight.

The flooring was across most of the stalls by the end of the day. The backstage flooring was finished so there was only the back of the stalls and the foyer to go. Patsy was amazed that it had gone down so quickly. Once the guys had left, she spent a while walking around, getting a feel for the place. It was better than she could have imagined, especially the backstage area which looked pretty much there apart from needing a coat of paint and some light fittings. The huge wooden door that dominated the room had been completely finished as part of the first phase and reminded Patsy of a sound-stage entrance in a Hollywood film studio, which was perfect for the theme they were planning.

Ed arrived at five o'clock, triumphantly pulling a small reel of film from his bag. 'I borrowed a trailer from the Film Society.'

'Oh my god, I hope it works!' Patsy said with a little squeal of excitement.

'Did you check the bulb?'

'I don't think it's broken but it said not to open the packaging until you're ready to install it.'

'That makes sense. To be honest, I've never fitted one before, I watched a YouTube video and they had it in some special container so that you're not handling it. They could explode when you light it otherwise.'

'Christ, Ed. Are you sure we're going to be able to do this ourselves? That bulb cost almost two grand, we don't want to have to buy another one.'

'I think if we're careful it'll be fine,' he said confidently. 'Right, let's do it!'

Patsy stood nervously behind Ed with his phone paused on the YouTube video until he was ready for the next instruction. Once the bulb was in he gently took the packaging out of the lamp housing.

'Okay.' He closed the side of the lamp housing and screwed it into place. 'Let's fire her up.'

Patsy retreated a bit further away and put her fingers in her ears, just in case.

Ed screwed his face up as his finger hovered over the button. 'Actually, let's lace up first. We don't want to have to fire it up twice tonight.'

Patsy exhaled loudly. 'I don't think I can take this kind of pressure, Ed.'

He laced the trailer film through the projector with the deft hands of experience. He briefly pressed the button to run the projector to feed enough film through to reach the reel that was ready to wind the film onto the tower. 'That's a good start,' he said as the projector whirred into life with the pleasing flicking sound that Patsy remembered from the Film Society.

Ed wound the end of the film onto the reel and switched the tower on to tension the film.

'Okay, this time it's the real thing. Ready?'

Patsy resumed her position. Ed faced away from the projector as he pressed the button to light the lamp. It gave a loud buzz and sprang into life, the light showing through the tiny darkened glass window on the lamp housing and leaking through any gap it could find.

'I think we're in business,' Ed said, grinning. 'You switch on the projector, Patsy.'

She moved to stand next to him, pressed the button and watched as the film began to move through the mechanism, gaining speed until it was at full pelt after a few seconds and Ed flicked the handle to let the lamp shine through the gate. They squeezed together to look through the window and sure enough, they could see the trailer for Star Wars Episode 1 playing on the screen.

Ed pulled her into a fierce hug. 'We did it!'

'You did it. You're amazing!'

He pulled away to watch through the window again.

He fiddled with the lens until the picture was much sharper. 'The picture's a bit off centre and the screen needs a good clean and that corner mending but it's not a bad start. Better than I'd expected to be honest.'

The trailer ran out, Ed closed the lamp off and switched off the projector and the tower.

'Shall we run it again?'

'Yes, go for it!'

It felt like a real milestone and she wished she'd asked Oliver to come. There had been some tangible progress today, not only with the projector but with the whole place and Patsy was buzzing. It was nice to see Ed so excited and she was pleased they were navigating their friendship well enough for him to have been able to see the project through. He deserved it.

# 25

Rosemary was already waiting at Oliver's when Patsy arrived ten minutes early for their meeting the next morning. She had wanted to tell Oliver that Ed had got the projector working but that would have to wait until later now.

'Morning, Rosemary. Can I get you a coffee?' Patsy took her coat off and put it behind the door, automatically grabbing an apron and then realising she wasn't coming to work.

'I'm fine thank you. Oliver is making me a latte.'

'Great. I'll grab a drink too and we'll go upstairs.'

Patsy laid her mood boards out on the table and explained to Rosemary what her vision was. 'But it'd be great if we could add some things which speak to its past, before it was stripped out in the eighties.'

'The one thing I remember is the magnificent chandeliers. They were similar to these,' she said, pointing at one of the lights Patsy had dismissed as too traditional.

'So we're going for these lights, as a kind of nod to that type of thing but with a modern twist.'

Rosemary pursed her lips. 'I am simply telling you what it

was like.'

'Of course, sorry Rosemary.' Patsy knew it was all too easy to get on the wrong side of Rosemary and that she should just accept all the information and then do with it what she could rather than cheese Rosemary off by telling her that her ideas were too old-fashioned.

'There used to be beautiful balustrades up the stairs. I don't know whether they were removed or covered up but they were painted gold and black and were very ornate.'

Well, that was exciting. Patsy was fairly sure they'd not thought to tear down the boxed wooden balustrade which ran up the stairs. Maybe the original was still underneath?

'And there were, I suppose they must have been plaster mouldings, around the chandeliers and around the top and sides of the screen, and heavy red velvet curtains, like in the theatre.'

'I don't think there were any curtains when we took over but that might be a good idea to keep dust off the screen and it would be quite theatrical for the curtains to open when the film starts. And you don't perhaps want the screen out when it's being a function space. Sorry, I'm rambling.' Patsy said as she saw Rosemary's face pinch again.

'In the foyer, next to the dear little ticket booth which you're reinstating,' Rosemary paused with an eyebrow raised and Patsy nodded. As if she would dare not. 'There was a confectionary booth. None of the tack they sell in cinemas these days. This was like a miniature sweet shop where you could buy a quarter of sherbet lemons or toffee bonbons. Not an expansive choice but most people are happy with sweets or a box of Maltesers.'

'Now, I do love that idea. We are planning to have a bar in the foyer but we could definitely incorporate the sweet booth idea.' Patsy jotted that down on her notepad.

Rosemary reminisced a little more and Patsy's imagination

whirred with the possibilities. Some of her memories had sparked ideas which would enhance the decor but some of them were best left in the past in Patsy's opinion.

'I don't know if I will be lucky enough to be invited to the launch party but I would very much like to see how the cinema looks when it's finished.'

'Consider yourself invited, Rosemary. Thank you so much for sparing the time to talk to me today, I really appreciate it. There are some things you've told me that we'll definitely try to incorporate.'

'Well, Oliver is very dear to me,' she said. 'It's important that it's successful for him.'

'I couldn't agree with you more.'

That evening, Oliver met Patsy at the cinema as soon as he'd closed up. He'd asked Matt as well and Ed was due any minute. Oliver produced a bottle of champagne and some plastic glasses.

'I can't believe we're going to see the cinema in action,' he said. 'It's all coming together.'

'The floor looks great,' said Matt, running his hand across it as he sat on the floor with his arms resting on his bent knees, looking fairly uncomfortable in the middle of the stalls area.

'Thanks, it's turned out better than I'd hoped,' said Patsy proudly.

'Sorry I'm late!' called Ed from the door to the foyer. 'I'll head straight up, give me five minutes. I'll flash the working lights on and off so you know when it's going to start.' He came back a moment later. 'Don't forget there won't be any sound. It's not set up properly yet.'

'What are we watching anyway?' Oliver asked, as Ed disappeared upstairs.

'Star Wars trailer.'

'Cool. Do you know what? I'm going up there to see the action.' Oliver leapt up and ran to the door, leaving Matt and Patsy alone in the stalls.

'So how's things?' Matt asked. 'Any more trouble with the ex?'

'No, thank god. It's a huge relief but at the same time I still think he'll surface sometime.' Patsy remembered Toby's advice. 'Toby said I ought to speak to the probation service and see what the situation is but I haven't tried to find anything out yet.'

'You don't think it'd give you peace of mind to know what he's up to?'

Patsy shrugged. 'It might do but it wouldn't stop me looking over my shoulder all the time. Although, I don't feel like that at the moment. I wonder whether it's because I'm so busy with this, it's full on and so different to my normal life, it's made me feel a little bit invincible.'

'That's good. You're making a great job of it.' He looked at her in a way she hadn't seen before. There was respect but something else too that she wasn't sure of.

'Thanks. I meant to ask how the court thing went?'

'We've got joint custody of the twins but I can only have them one night a week and every other weekend. I'm hoping it'll be more in the school holidays but I think it's the best outcome I could have got, according to my lawyer.'

'That's less than you have them now, though.'

'Yes, I mean, I usually have them a couple of nights in the week and then I let their mum decide on the weekend arrangements because they have so much going on. You know, parties and things like that.' Basically his ex-wife arranged their visits to him based on what suited her but it was nice that he didn't speak badly of her. 'Anyway, it's better for all of us to have a firm arrangement from week to week.' He rubbed a hand over his face and shifted position slightly.

'We should have brought some camping chairs with us,' Patsy said.

He grinned, the weariness that had come over him during their conversation about his children, ebbing away. 'Or we could drag that roll of carpet in from the foyer?'

They went to the foyer where the plastic wrapped roll of carpet was waiting to be moved upstairs to the circle.

'Put your back into it,' he said as they tried to pick up an end each. Patsy started laughing and went all weak, collapsing onto the floor.

'Hang on, hang on,' she said, trying to compose herself. She stood up. 'Okay, ready.'

They somehow managed to shift the carpet into the stalls with Matt carrying the front and Patsy barely managing to keep the other end off the ground. Positioning it across the stalls so that they'd be able to sit on it to watch the film, they both sat down to catch their breath. Then Matt pushed his foot to the floor which made it roll backwards and Patsy squealed as she lost her balance, laughing again when she saw the mischievous look on his face.

'Oi! I could have fallen off!' She was trying to be stern but couldn't stop laughing.

'Like this?' he said, tipping it again but catching her firmly as she lost her balance.

They both stopped laughing as they looked into each other's eyes, Matt's hand loosening its grip on her arm. She'd never noticed that his eyes were the darkest blue and it was difficult to look away.

The lights dipped off and on again, signalling that the film was about to start. Matt dropped his hand but held her gaze until the lights went down and they watched the silent Star Wars trailer, joined a few minutes later by an ecstatic Oliver and a modest Ed.

'How amazing was that?' Oliver sat down next to Patsy and popped the champagne.

'Pretty cool. It really is a proper cinema now,' she said.

'Okay, tonight we christen it.' Oliver poured the champagne into the plastic cups and they each took one. 'Here's to the first of many more film showings at Croftwood Cinema. Cheers!'

'Cheers!' they all chorused.

'Oh my god,' said Patsy, suddenly remembering that she'd meant to check the stairs. 'Rosemary told me something that might be quite exciting. Come with me!'

Patsy led the way into the foyer. 'She reckons the original balustrade is gorgeous and she thinks it was boxed in.'

Oliver tapped the boxed balustrade. It was hollow. 'Could be true. Who's up for a bit of late-night excavation?'

'Me!' Patsy said, and they all laughed.

'Okay, let's find something we can make a hole in with.'

'Hang on a sec,' said Ed and went sprinting off up the stairs, returning with a large screwdriver.

'Go on, you do the honours,' Oliver said, gesturing to the stairs.

'Here goes.' Ed flashed a look of excitement at Patsy before he stabbed the screwdriver into what turned out to be fairly soft hardboard. He wiggled it around until there was a hole around an inch in diameter.

Oliver took out his phone and shone the torch into the hole, then with a grin on his face, held the lens up to the hole and took a picture.

'Look! It's still there, just like Rosemary said!'

They huddled into a four-way hug and jumped for a few seconds before breaking apart and heading back into the stalls to top up their cups.

'Here's to Rosemary! God bless her interfering!'

'To Rosemary!'

When they'd run out of champagne, and Ed had shut everything off in the projection box, it was time to leave.

'I can walk you back,' Ed said to Patsy as they waited for Oliver to lock the door.

'Oh—' Before she could politely object, Matt had stepped in.

'That's okay, it's out of your way, Ed. I can walk her home.'

They said goodbye to Ed and Oliver who began walking back towards town together.

'It isn't on your way, is it?'

'Not really,' he said, turning to grin at her as they began walking. 'But for some reason I wasn't ready to say goodnight.'

Patsy's eyes widened as she stared ahead. 'To me?'

'Mmm. It was fun tonight, mainly because of you.'

He was right, it had been fun. Even when she'd half expected him to produce a fistful of safety goggles once they'd started hacking at the banister, he'd looked like that was the last thing on his mind and it was refreshing to see him outside of a work situation again. Very much like the last time he'd walked her home, in fact.

'I do enjoy larking around on a roll of carpet,' she said, laughing.

'You constantly surprise me, Patsy.'

Again, his words hit her unexpectedly. This time she waited quietly to see what he said next.

'The cinema is going to be incredible. Your vision is beginning to shine.'

Patsy began to say that it was Oliver as much as it was her, even Ed was playing a fairly major part in it but Matt held up his hand to stop her.

'No, you have to take the credit for how it's coming together. That's all you.'

'And you didn't think I could do it?'

He was looking straight ahead, walking with his hands in his pockets and she liked the way his eyes crinkled at his temple as he smiled.

'Perhaps I under-estimated you.'

'Perhaps you did.' She tucked her hand into the crook of his arm because at the very least, they were friends now.

# 26

Patsy and Oliver decided to head to the cinema with coffee and cakes to plan the programme for the cinema opening. Now that Jack was a master barista, they felt comfortable leaving him to it and able to relocate somewhere other than the flat upstairs.

They sat in Patsy's favourite spot, on the circle balcony which still wasn't furnished so the appeal was a little lost on Oliver as he didn't find the smell of new carpet as delicious as Patsy did.

'Comfy?' he asked, leaning against the back wall with his laptop resting on his stretched-out legs.

'Yes, thanks.' Patsy was lying on her back, reading a list of films which were available from the British Film Institute. 'What do you think we should do? Run the same film for a week at a time?'

'Well, that's what everyone else does, isn't it? I wonder if it makes more sense from a technical point of view.'

Patsy rolled onto her stomach to look at Oliver. 'Maybe. I know the film comes in reels and has to be put together so I guess that takes time and you probably don't want to be doing that every day.'

'Okay, so let's assume a film a week. We're opening four nights a week, agreed? Thursday to Sunday,' said Oliver.

'Agreed. And I guess we close the cinema on nights when we have a function booked. As long as we advertise it properly and far enough in advance, it shouldn't be a problem. Maybe we could do reduced rates for booking a function on a Monday to Wednesday?'

'Good idea. Right. So what else?'

Patsy took a cake from the paper bag of goodies that they'd brought with them. 'I've had some ideas about what we can do during the day. It doesn't have to be every week, that might be too much, but what about a session for parents and their babies and toddlers? We can keep the lights up a bit, show a kiddies' film and have coffee and cakes for the mums and dads.'

'That's genius, Pats. I love it. I wonder if we can easily show one film in the day and another in the evening?'

'My limited technical skills suggest yes. I reckon you could have a film on one of those massive reels, put the other film onto another massive reel and you're sorted. You could just swap them over, with some help, I think it'd be pretty heavy. And we'd have to buy another massive reel because we've only got two.'

'Okay, well we can do that. Maybe once a fortnight?'

'I have another idea too which I'm personally invested in,' said Patsy, sitting up properly and leaning against the wall next to Oliver. 'Purl at the Pictures.' She spread her hands in the air in front of them as if she were showcasing an invisible sign.

Oliver looked at her, none the wiser.

'Okay, think the baby and toddler thing but with knitters. Or crocheters, or whoever wants to come. But the point is we leave the lights up a bit so people can knit while they watch the film.'

'Well, that will appeal to some people but do you think there'd be enough to make it worthwhile? And that's another film to deal with,' said Oliver, clearly with little enthusiasm for the idea.

'I think you'd be surprised and I don't think anyone would mind what film it was. Cheap and cheerful would be fine. Look at this list,' she said, waving it under Oliver's nose. 'There's a huge number of films which are so cheap, we could show them once and still make money.'

'Okay, we'll put the knitting on the list. Remember Matt suggesting the family film afternoons at the weekends with pizza? I loved that idea.'

'Oh, me too. We could show the same film Saturday and Sunday, something like Toy Story.'

'Madagascar!' Oliver was getting more enthusiastic now and had forgotten to be annoyed about sitting on the floor.

'Good one. Next thing, projectionists. I think we need to recruit two or three people to do a rota between them, and we should both be trained too. Then if there's an emergency at least between us we always have a projectionist to fall back on.'

'I suppose that does make sense. When you put it like that we should probably both learn. How hard can it be?' he said with a nervous laugh.

'I don't think it's hard but I think it takes nerves of steel. Imagine, everyone in this cinema is relying on you to do it right,' she said, making her eyes wide and scary.

'I might have changed my mind about getting trained. I'm not sure I can handle peril of that magnitude.'

'Oh, shut up,' said Patsy, giving him a friendly shove. 'It'll be fun. I'll see if Ed will give us a lesson.'

'Okay. Bring it on.'

'Oh, I meant to say, Jess wondered if she could run sewing

workshops here? They can only take six people at a time in the shop and here, well they could take as many as they can cope with. She thought it'd be perfect because they can bring a video projector to play tutorial videos on the screen.'

'That's brilliant too, basically a rental of the space?'

'Exactly. Right shall we choose some films then?'

They spent the next hour making three lists of films. One for the main shows, one for the family films and one for the knitters. Patsy was keen to fill that last list with romcoms and Oliver couldn't argue but he did have strong opinions on the kids' films. For the main shows they chose their favourite classics, ranging from thrillers like The Day After Tomorrow to comedies like Ferris Bueller's Day Off and total blockbusters like Back to the Future and the Indiana Jones films. It was pretty easy and Patsy had the job of booking them. As they were aiming to open properly within the next few weeks, they were probably going to have to take whatever was available to them but hopefully the lists would help with deciding what they could use when.

Once they'd finished, Oliver was heading back to the coffee shop while Patsy decided to go home and tackle booking the films from her roof terrace. It was a balmy late-June day and it was important to make the most of the sunshine while it lasted.

Patsy locked the door and pulled her sunglasses out of her bag, re-did her bun which had become saggy from lying on the floor in the circle, and walked the long way through the park.

The big pond that spanned the bottom of the park was fed by a natural spring that had been landscaped into a stream with lots of jungly plants around it and little bridges that delighted children as well as Patsy, and she liked wandering through that way if she had time. It felt like a secret part of the park that no-one knew about although since the council had put in a new play area right next to it, it was a bit less secret than it used to be.

She strolled along, enjoying the dappled shade of the trees and smiling at the squeals coming from the playground as she approached. It was after school time, so not as busy as a weekend would be but there were a few families who looked as if they'd decided to make the most of the lovely weather and were having picnics.

'Hello, Patsy!' A small girl ran up to her with a big grin on her face. Luckily, Patsy recognised her as Matt's daughter, Flo.

'Hi, Flo.' Patsy looked to see where Matt was and spotted him waving with one hand as he pushed Sammy on a swing with the other. He was wearing sunglasses which she had to admit she found surprisingly attractive.

'Daddy says I have to wait for a turn,' Flo said, sticking out her bottom lip. Patsy could see that the only other spare swing was on the other side of the row of swings and Matt would struggle to push both children at the same time.

'Shall we go and see if it's your turn yet?'

Flo nodded enthusiastically and ran over to Matt.

'Hi,' smiled Patsy. After the other night at the cinema when they'd larked around on the carpet, Patsy had been wondering how things would be between them when she saw him again.

'Don't you just love the park,' he said with a wry smile.

'I can see you do,' she grinned.

'Daddy, can Patsy push me on the swing?' Flo asked in a way that suggested no wasn't an option.

'If Patsy doesn't mind,' he said, raising his eyebrows and giving her a lop-sided smile.

'Come on then,' said Patsy.

Flo ran to the spare swing and Patsy held it as still as she could so that the little girl could clamber on.

'Higher, higher!' she shouted, as Patsy laughed and looked at Matt to see him laughing as well and shaking his head.

'She's so bossy,' he called over. 'Do you want to swap?'

She shook her head. 'We're okay.' She watched as Matt switched from standing behind Sammy to standing in front of him, pretending that he was getting kicked every time the swing came forwards which made Sammy laugh in the exuberant way only children did.

'Daddy!' Flo shouted, 'Do that to me!' And he ran over and pretended to be kicked by her as well, making her erupt into uncontrollable giggles.

Patsy was laughing too at the sheer joy of it all. Then the next minute, they both wanted to get off the swings and headed over to play in an igloo made out of willow.

'Do you want to sit down?' Matt gestured to a picnic blanket that was laid out nearby where he could sit but easily keep an eye on the twins.

'Sure.' Patsy followed him and kicked her sandals off before she sat cross-legged on the blanket, absent-mindedly reaching over and picking a piece of grass to fiddle with.

'How's things with the cinema?' he asked.

'We've had a massive planning session about films. We're going to go with your suggestion of the family film and pizza thing on a Saturday.'

'Really?' he said, grinning and sounding chuffed.

'We'd probably have thought of it ourselves anyway,' teased Patsy, 'but you can take the credit if you need to.'

He laughed. 'Thanks, it's nice to feel like a valued member of the team.'

'You are part of the team,' she said, sincerely. 'For all your obsession with hard hats, we couldn't have done it without you.'

'Thanks. That means a lot.'

A silence sat between them as they watched the children

skip from the igloo to play on some logs that were upended like stepping stones. Matt sat up straighter and called over, 'Be careful, take it in turns to help each other!'

They watched as the twins did exactly that, having come to an agreement that three stepping stones was a turn.

'Do you want to join us for a picnic tea?' he asked. 'We've got plenty.'

'That's a kind offer but I know it's your only time with them this week, so I won't stay.' She started to put her sandals on.

Matt put a hand on hers, stopping her in her tracks. His touch was so unexpected and at the same time so welcome. 'Really, the twins would love it if you did. They're still going on about the bloody chairs and the Post-It notes.'

She looked at him and he pushed his sunglasses up onto his head.

'Please,' he said. 'I wouldn't ask if I didn't mean it.'

'Thanks, I'd love that.'

He started unpacking packets of all sorts of things that he'd bought from Waitrose. Mini sausages, tortilla chips and hummus, Babybels, all the things that a kiddies picnic should have. He had a big bottle of Appletizer and some plastic cups. 'This is a huge treat,' he said solemnly before he called the children over.

After a lovely picnic, with plenty of scattered crumbs the only evidence that there had been any food, they said goodbye and Matt and the children headed home for the evening, Patsy carried on along the path she'd started to take a couple of hours earlier and marvelled at how it was possible to find a man more attractive because of his children. He was great with them, a world away from the harried father the night of the Post-It notes. Now that he had the routine set up with his ex-wife, he was clearly devoting himself to them when they were with him and she loved that about him. It shouldn't have been surprising because that was exactly how he approached work, and why he was so fastidious about everything. It was because he was giving his all to what was important to him, whether it be work or his children and that was something Patsy had only just begun to appreciate but something that all of a sudden, she really did appreciate very much.

# 27

It was a week until the launch party and the cinema was almost finished. In fact, most of what needed finishing was purely the special arrangements for the night itself rather than anything integral to the cinema being finished. But tomorrow, they were having a pre-launch dry run to make sure they'd thought of everything. It would be more low-key than the proper launch which would hopefully give Patsy and Oliver chance to enjoy it a bit more.

Ed had invited a couple of his classes — students were always willing guinea pigs — and they'd invited some of the local traders like Jess. Altogether there were going to be about fifty people which was plenty to provide them with enough people to make it feel real but only around half the number they were hoping to invite to the launch party and nowhere near as many as they hoped they would be dealing with on the busiest of nights.

The chairs and tables for the stalls had been delivered two days ago and Patsy was unpacking them as and when she had a minute to spare. They looked amazing, exactly as she had envisaged. In fact, everything was looking just as she'd hoped which she couldn't quite believe.

The muddy lilac walls looked fabulous against the floor and all the colours of the upholstery contrasted perfectly. They had sumptuous dark plum velvet curtains to cover the screen, which had been carefully cleaned and its tear repaired almost invisibly. The curtains helped to absorb the sound as well which the sound engineer had been pleased about.

After their 'christening the cinema' night, Oliver had called the builders back in to pull off the hardboard and reveal the beautiful original wrought iron balustrade that was hidden inside. It had to be sand-blasted as the paint had begun to peel so it was just as well they'd investigated it before the decorators had finished. It had created an awful mess but now, it was restored to its former gold and black glory and it made the foyer into a wow factor that they couldn't have imagined.

The dry run was going to be for the venue as a function space, so primarily it would be held in the backstage area which had been transformed into a Hollywood party space from the 1940s complete with huge shuttered lights on tripods, a bar with a mirrored back and glass shelves to hold the glasses. Round tables on tall pedestals were scattered so that guests could stand and mingle, and stools, small tables and some of the velvet chairs from the main auditorium made it into a space which felt intimate but perfectly spacious. Patsy was excited to see how it would feel with more than a handful of people in it.

They had converted a storage area which ran down the side of the stalls into the kitchen. There was access from the foyer as well as from the backstage area which made it perfect for functions or regular nights serving cinema goers. Oliver had taken Ed's suggestion and employed some catering students from Worcester University to work in the kitchen. They were full of brilliant ideas and he was pleased to be able to offer them valuable experience which formed part of their course as well as paying them a wage. One thing he and Patsy hadn't considered was that the food needed to be easy to eat in the dark and so not too messy. The students were all over it and came up with brilliant twists on classic dishes to make it work. Everyone's favourite was a steak pie which had the mash baked inside with the filling. It was delicious as well as practical with the mash soaking up some of the gravy so that it was less messy yet moist.

'Need a hand?' Matt came up behind Patsy while she was busy unpacking chairs, making her jump.

'Christ, Matt! Are you trying to give me a heart attack? But, yes. I do need a hand.'

'What else is left to do?'

'What isn't?'

'That's not a very helpful answer.'

She sighed. 'We need to string the fairy lights in the trees at the back. The weather forecast is great for tomorrow so we're going to have the doors open and maybe put some of the chairs and tables outside.'

'Have you got any security?'

Patsy laughed. 'Matt, this is Croftwood. I think we can manage to keep things civil.'

'No, not because of trouble. To make sure only people on the guest list get in. I mean, if everyone's out the back, what's stopping people from walking in the front? You can't keep it locked because of fire regs.'

'Thank you Fireman Sam. I've got it covered.' But she hadn't and was annoyed she hadn't thought about it. She didn't have any door staff, thinking that they didn't need them for the dry run but perhaps that was an oversight. It was another thing for her to-do-before-tomorrow list. Maybe she could ask Jack to man the front door because there would be enough people at the back to make sure there were no gate-crashers. She pulled out her phone and sent him quick text to see.

'Fine. Sorry. Do you want the fairy lights up tonight?'

'No, just in case they get nicked overnight. You never know. I think once the chairs and tables are unpacked we're done for tonight.' She sighed, realising how tired she was.

'Okay. I'll help you unpack and then how about I ring for a takeaway?'

'That sounds really good, thanks.'

She and Matt had ended up working closely together over the past two weeks. He'd been on site almost every day to make sure that everything was finished to exactly the right specification but tonight he was there as their friend, part of the gang helping to get everything finished in time. It had surprised Patsy how well they'd worked together, but something had changed between them since the night with the carpet. His tendency to second guess her had disappeared. He trusted her and they had developed a mutual respect for each other where work was concerned.

Where work wasn't concerned, it was slightly less clear what was happening. Matt had walked her home a few more times and they'd chatted easily about all sorts of things. Quite often, she found herself watching him. He was attractive and now that she actually liked his personality, it was hard to ignore the rest of him. She started to notice things like how his hair naturally swept to one side because of a cow-lick on the other. How he  absentmindedly rubbed the back of his neck if he was trying to make a decision about something. And now that it was high summer, he was wearing some very sexy tortoiseshell sunglasses that made him look like a 1940s film star, especially now that he'd taken to wearing linen shirts and chinos in the hotter weather. A couple of weeks ago he'd admitted he'd underestimated her and now she was beginning to think she'd done the same to him.

They unpacked the chairs and tables together, checking them over for defects before they moved them down towards the screen ready for some of them to go into the backstage area. 'We could do with Flo and Sammy to help us with this, I bet they'd love it,' she said, thinking back to how they'd enjoyed her fake chair testing exercise.

'I expect they'd be making a cardboard box fort by now,' Matt said, his voice full of affection.

'I'm fighting the urge to do that myself, to be honest.'

He laughed. 'If you can get all these unpacked you can eat your takeaway inside this one.' He pulled one of the biggest boxes to the side.

Oliver had been in the kitchen cleaning but he'd finished so came to offer a hand. 'I'll get all these boxes flattened,' he said, 'and then I'll start moving the furniture into the backstage area.'

Matt smacked his hand to his chest in a dramatic but silent gesture behind Oliver's back when he flattened the big box, and Patsy burst out laughing. She was so tired, she hardly had the energy to smile but he was really keeping her going.

'What's so funny?' Oliver asked them.

'We were saving that box to make a fort,' Matt said.

'Okay...'

'Who's left apart from us? I'm going to order a takeaway. Chinese?'

'It is just us now. I've sent everyone else off. A Chinese sounds great, thanks mate.'

'Any objections to getting a few dishes to share?' Matt headed towards the foyer to make the call since the reception was a bit dodgy in the middle of the building.

'Sounds great,' Patsy called after him. 'Can you make sure the front door's locked?'

He nodded and gave a thumbs up.

'You two are getting on well these days,' Oliver said with a glint in his eye.'

'He's been very nice to me lately so I don't think he's a misogynistic arse any more.'

'That's quite a change of heart.'

'What can I say? He's grown on me.'

'And what's going to happen when this is all finished?'

Patsy stopped scissoring a mass of bubblewrap and tape that covered the table she was unpacking and looked at Oliver. It hadn't even occurred to her that she would see less of Matt once they were up and running. It was obvious now Oliver had said because what reason would there be for their paths to cross? Before the cinema she had hardly ever seen him in the coffee house. Is that what it would be like again, or would it be different because they were friends now?

'Well, he'll still be around. He lives in Croftwood, doesn't he?'

'Yes, in the posh houses off the Worcester Road.'

He smirked, knowing that Patsy knew exactly where he meant. Everyone in Croftwood knew because there had been extensive opposition to the planning application for the exclusive development a few years ago, with the main complaint being that it was too close to the woods and would spoil the countryside. It was reminiscent of somewhere in America rather than semi-rural central England and actually, envy had been the main driver behind people's objections. It was very close to the woodland but the well-considered architecture made the houses seem as if they belonged there, as much a part of the landscape as the woods themselves.

'Blimey. Maybe that's why he didn't mention it,' she said to Oliver.

'He designed them so I wouldn't think he's ashamed, he likes to keep things low-key, that's all.'

And that was fair enough, although she was quietly impressed that Matt was behind those houses. She loved them and knowing Matt was the closest she'd ever come to having a chance of going inside one, or even having need to venture up that road. But she was getting ahead of herself.

It seemed like no time at all until Matt was back carrying a couple of white takeaway bags. They spread out some cardboard in the middle of them and laid out the takeaway dishes on the floor. Oliver grabbed plates and cutlery from the newly equipped kitchen and they dug in.

'I've never felt like I deserve a takeaway more,' Patsy said with a mouthful of noodles.

'Mmm. I know what you mean,' Oliver said. 'I haven't worked this hard since I was setting up the coffee house.'

'You two are lightweights, this is the pace I work at all the time.'

Patsy laughed and threw a prawn cracker at him. 'As if.'

'You bringing anyone along to the party, mate?' Oliver asked Matt, glancing at Patsy with a raised eyebrow when Matt wasn't looking.

'No. You? Is Amy coming?'

Oliver shook his head. 'No, that's as good as over. Just some business to sort out and then we can call it a day.'

'Ah, sorry to hear that.'

'It's for the best. I think we've both moved on, we want different things. No point resenting that.'

For all Oliver's reasonable assessment of the situation, Patsy knew him too well to think that he was as unscathed by the whole thing as he appeared to be. When they had more time, she'd make him talk to her properly about it, make sure he really was okay but for now she'd settle for not letting him feel like he was the only singleton.

'I'm planning on hanging out with you two for the evening, if that's okay. Me and you will be working, Ollie, Matt, you can keep us supplied with regular small amounts of alcohol to keep our stress levels down, everyone's a winner.'

'I'm looking forward to it already,' Matt said drily but with a grin on his face.

# 28

Patsy was nervous as soon as she woke up. Toby had texted her the day before to say that he was ready to serve the divorce papers on Dan. He'd needed her go-ahead, and she had given it. Dan would find out that she'd filed for divorce. She managed to sip a cup of tea but didn't have any breakfast and although she wasn't working a shift at the coffee house that day, she was there just as Oliver was opening up so that she could casually bump into Toby and find out what was going on.

'Aren't we meeting this afternoon for the projectionist training? I told Jack two o'clock.' Oliver was bemused; neither of them came to work at this time in the morning unless they were opening up.

'Yes, I know. I thought I'd give you a hand this morning and I need to go and see Jess about knitting.'

'Okay, well thanks. It's always nice to have you around.'

'I'm hoping Toby will be in soon. He's planning to have the divorce papers served on Dan today.'

'Ah, so you're a bit jittery,' said Oliver.

'No,' Patsy said defensively. 'I just want to know what's

going on.' She reached for a croissant then her stomach got the better of her and she drew her hand away again. 'Oh, alright. Yes, I'm bracing myself for some sort of reaction from him. He won't take it lying down.'

'Possibly not, but you're doing the right thing. You need a clean break.'

'I do, and it feels like the right time, so whatever happens, I'm not going to back down.'

Patsy made herself and Oliver a coffee while he carried on setting up for the day and then she took her laptop and sat at one of the tables near where Toby normally sat. The bug hunting had yielded precisely nothing towards the sum of money Oliver needed to hand over to Amy but Patsy wasn't going to give up. She was desperate to do something to help out and surely persistence was the key to successfully finding a bug that was going to solve the problem. He'd said Amy was being flexible about the deadline but Patsy knew she wouldn't wait forever.

'Morning.' Toby had come in while she was engrossed in looking for an issue with one of her bug bounty targets. 'Busy?'

'Just pottering at something,' she said, closing the laptop.

'Can I get you a coffee?' he asked.

'Thanks, that'd be lovely.'

He came back a couple of minutes later with two coffees and Patsy shifted over to sit at his table.

'So, is it too early for anything to have happened?'

'Yes. We can probably expect some news around lunchtime, if we're lucky. Try not to think about it. I know that's easier said than done,' he smiled.

'I'm keen to get on with it, that's all. I feel good about having made the decision, but I am nervous about his reaction.'

'I'm a lawyer and it was no easier with my own divorce.

Knowing all about the procedures and things didn't help me feel any better about it. It's always hard knowing how the other party will react.'

'I doubt your wife was quite as much of a loose cannon as my husband is,' said Patsy, smiling.

'Perhaps not but please, try not to worry. It's quite often the case that people are, if not expecting divorce papers to be served, not all that surprised when they are.'

She hung onto the fact that he had vast amounts of experience in this field to be able to say that, but he didn't know Dan. She'd bet the cinema on the likelihood of him doing something.

At around lunchtime, she checked her emails and found one from Toby. It was a confirmation that the serving of the papers had taken place with an attached video.

She looked across to him. He was in the middle of something, had his earbuds in and was typing furiously. She clicked on the file and watched the footage, which had presumably been filmed on a body camera, of the person knocking on the door of her in-law's house, the door being opened by a sleepy-looking Dan who accepted the papers, signed for them and then closed the door. It was that easy. What had she thought was going to happen?

She bounded over to the counter, feeling lighter than she had for ages.

'He's got the papers,' she said to Oliver while he was steaming some milk.

'Brilliant, that's good news. Not that I don't want to celebrate that now but we're absolutely slammed. Is there any chance you could clear some tables?'

'No problem, boss,' she grinned, picking up a tray and a cloth.

'Hey, thanks Toby,' she said to him as she cleared his back-log of coffee mugs and gave the small bit of table the wasn't taken up with his laptop, phone and current coffee mug a cursory wipe.

'No problem,' he said with a smile, taking out one of his earbuds. 'I'll file the evidence of service with the court and everything will go into motion. I'll keep you posted.'

'Great.' She stood there looking at him before she realised she'd been stood there smiling like a loon for what seemed like minutes. He was smiling too, with an amused twinkle in his eyes.

As soon as the rush died down, Patsy and Oliver left Jack to it and headed to the cinema to meet Hayley, one of Ed's colleagues from the Film Society, for their first lesson.

'I'm a bit nervous,' Oliver said, as they waited for Hayley by the front doors.

'Don't worry. It seems very methodical to me. I think I'm going to make a cheat sheet of steps so we can refer to it until we know what we're doing.'

'Okay, good idea.'

'Think of it as a slightly more complicated coffee machine, if that helps.'

'Now, that I can do, but if I mess up a cup of coffee I'm only disappointing one person, Pats, not a whole cinema full of people.'

'Make sure you're listening and you'll be fine. We're in this together.' She held up a fist for him to bump which he ignored, looking at her like she was from another planet.

Hayley went through the whole thing twice, using the Star Wars trailer which was still the only piece of film they had. Patsy made a thorough step-by-step guide. Or at least she hoped it was thorough.

'Okay, who's going first?'

'I'll go,' Patsy said, realising that Oliver was still looking like a rabbit in the headlights.

She laced the projector, checking that the frame was square in the gate — the most important thing — and that the tower was on so that the film didn't spew out of the projector all over the floor, which was another most important thing. She screwed her eyes up as she turned on the lamp, expecting it to choose that moment to explode but it didn't, then she turned on the projector and waited for it to get up to speed before she opened the shutter to let the light through. There were pictures but no sound and the picture was wibbly along one side.

'Oh. That doesn't look right,' said Oliver, peering through the tiny window at the screen.

'Do you know what you did wrong, Patsy?' asked Hayley, sounding like a teacher.

'Um, no.' Patsy was trying to control the frustration she had with herself for getting it wrong and would rather Hayley just came out and said what the problem was.

'I know!' said Oliver, looking as if he might start bouncing up and down with his hand up. 'It's back-to-front so the sound isn't being picked up by the light thingy.'

'Exactly,' Hayley said. 'Remember, the three lines on the edge of the film need to be towards you so that the sound optic can read them.'

'Right,' Patsy said gloomily as she turned everything off and rewound the film - something she had remembered how to do - before cheering up once she realised it was know-it-all Oliver's turn. 'Your go, Ollie.'

She watched him lace-up the projector, making a big show of checking the film was the right way around this time. But when he started it up, there was a snap. The film had broken and was churning up in the projector before Hayley stepped in and quickly switched everything off.

'Okay, so when you laced around the sprockets, Oliver, you

needed to leave a couple of fingers worth of a loop of film so that it has room to move. It was too tight and so that's why it snapped.'

'Oh my god,' said Oliver, as he took a length of damaged film out of the projector. The holes on the edges had broken and the sprockets had pierced and creased the frames of film. 'This is the only thing we have to practise with and I've ruined it.'

'No harm done,' Hayley said and proceeded to chop out the damaged section and tape it all back together again. 'Count how many I've taken out,' she said, handing the damaged film to Oliver.

'About twenty?'

'Okay, so one second of film is 24 frames so we've cut out less than a second. You'll barely notice the difference. Right, Patsy, your turn again.'

'Oh, man, this is stressful,' said Oliver.

'It's not, it's fun,' Hayley insisted, as they watched Patsy lace up again.

This time it was perfect.

'Come on Ollie, beat that.'

He gave her a dirty look and laced up for his second attempt which was also successful. Once he'd switched off, they shared a triumphant hug while they waited for the film to rewind.

'I think you guys have got it,' Hayley said, laughing at them as they jumped up and down like children.

'Brilliant, thank you.' Oliver said. 'We really appreciate it, Hayley. Let me come down with you to unlock the door.'

'So now all we need to do is find some other people we can teach to do that.' Patsy was laid out again on the new carpet in the circle while Oliver perched on the balustrade, checking his emails on his phone.

'We'll have to come up with a rota for the front of house as well as this. I think you and I need to be the back-ups but we'll be knackered if we're doing this as well as running the place. It's hard enough keeping on top of the coffee house and that's a drop in the ocean compared to all the things we need to cover here.'

He was starting to sound panicked. Patsy rolled onto her side and looked at him.

'We can't do it all ourselves, Ollie. How do you see it working?'

'I suppose I'd thought we'd run it between us but I don't think that's going to work. Running this place is a full-time job and we need a team of people, bar staff, box office, usherettes…'

'Luckily it's not the 1960s so I think we can skip that one.'

Oliver came and lay down next to her, exhaling as he closed his eyes.

'What do you want to do? Coffee house or cinema?'

He flicked his head around to look at her in surprise. 'Surely it's not either or?'

'I think it might be. Or at least you have to choose one that you're managing and I'll manage the other, I suppose?' She knew she could manage the coffee house in her sleep and now that she knew every tiny little thing about the cinema, she could probably do a decent job of managing that too. 'Is that what you thought? That we'd split it between us?'

'Of course, that's what I meant it to be right from the start. Only I didn't know what it would look like until now. I suppose what I want is the best of both worlds. I want to do it all, Pats. Not because I don't want to share it with you but because I don't want to miss any of it.'

Patsy reached for his hand and squeezed it. 'Well, we'll do it together then. We'll make plans together and both manage both businesses but you'll be the man on the ground in the coffee house and I'll be the woman on the ground here, when it comes to the day-to-day stuff like rotas and ordering stock. What do you think?'

'As long as I don't have to worry about finding usherettes I think it's a fabulous idea.'

'Everything's coming together, Ollie,' she said, closing her eyes and smiling until the lack of Oliver agreeing with her made her look up. 'What?'

'Amy wants the money. She's given me to the end of August. That's so close to when we're likely to open, it doesn't give us any time to start trading to build up some cash.' He dropped his phone down onto the carpet and ran his fingers through his hair. 'Shit.'

It seemed pointless to utter empty reassurances when they both knew what the situation was. Unless they could find some more cash, they might not get the cinema to the point of being able to open. They'd have to use the money they had put aside for the final purchases of fixtures and fittings, marketing, hiring and training of staff to pay Amy. It was terrible timing.

'Is there any chance she'd give you a bit more time?'

He shook his head. 'She needs it for something, apparently.'

'What?' Patsy asked, cross, although not with Oliver.

'I don't know, Pats. She doesn't have to tell me stuff like that any more and I have no right to ask. It's her money, that's all there is to it. And I will pay her at the end of August, no question.' He gave Patsy a determined look, daring her to fight him on the decision but she'd known him long enough to know that it wasn't a decision to be questioned.

'We'll have to do it then. Somehow, we'll do it.'

# 29

'I meant to say…' Patsy said as she buttered rounds of bread to prepare toasties ready for the lunch rush.

'Mmm?' Oliver said absentmindedly. He was sat on a stool on the other side of the counter doing the accounts on his laptop and sadly, too far away to be flicked with a tea towel.

'I've invited Rosemary to the dry run tonight.'

'Really?' Oliver gave her his full attention now. 'You really want to chance being brought down by Rosemary being judgmental about your choices, tonight of all nights?'

When he put it like that, she agreed with him but she had promised Rosemary in that moment of weakness after she'd been so helpful. It seemed safer to have her at the dry run than risk there being any actual customers around the first time she saw the place.

'I thought it'd be a nice gesture after her helping me out. And she did tip us off about the balustrade.'

Oliver raised an eyebrow. They were all in love with the balustrade. 'Okay, I suppose you're right. You're giving her the grand tour though, not me.'

'Alright. Now get your bloody apron on and start doing

some work. I'm doing you a favour filling in so Jack can have the day off.'

'A favour so he can work at the cinema tonight? For the person who didn't think gate-crashers could be a possibility,' he teased her.

'Oh shut up. Bet you a deep-clean of the coffee machine that we don't get any gate-crashers.' Patsy and Oliver both hated that job and sadly hadn't got around to teaching Jack how to do it yet.

'You're on.' Oliver slapped the laptop closed and stashed it under the counter before he donned his apron and started grating cheese. 'I'm looking forward to tonight.'

'Yeah, me too. I'd rather be enjoying the night than in charge of it but if it goes smoothly enough hopefully it'll be a bit of both.'

'I'm glad we're doing this. It would have been so stressful if the first thing we did was the launch event next week.'

'We need to see how the kitchen's going to run, that's the most important thing.'

'Fair play, Pats. I thought tonight would be a hard deadline to meet.'

Patsy blushed but was chuffed to bits. 'Once we got started it was just making sure everything got done in the right order and having a plan.'

'I know that, but some of the best project managers don't manage to hit deadlines as tight as that and it's your first project. It's a massive achievement.'

'Thanks, Ollie. That means a lot.'

'Once tonight is over we can start marketing and promoting. Oh, I meant to tell you, I'm paying that photographer from the paper to take some publicity shots at the launch. Hopefully we'll get into the paper again.'

Patsy shuddered. The last time she'd been in the paper it hadn't worked out that well for her but she recognised the huge value it would bring to the cinema to have the launch publicised.

'Look, you don't have to be in any photos, if you're worried,' said Oliver.

'It's okay, it makes no difference now. He knows where I am and I think if he turned up again, it'd be okay.'

'Well, as long as you're happy. Have a word with Pete at the start and let him know if you want him to avoid you in the shots.'

'I think I'm past being scared, Ollie. I'm not going to be forced into looking over my shoulder for the rest of my life. I don't know whether it's the cinema or what, but I feel strong.'

'I don't know what it is either but you've got stronger by yourself. You took on this massive challenge and it's been a triumph.'

'Okay, steady, we don't know whether it's a triumph yet, let's hold off on the self-congratulation for now.'

But Patsy was proud of what she'd done. And proud of how she felt. The cinema had seemed like a huge step outside her comfort zone when Oliver had first landed the idea on her but it had been the making of her and she could see how she had been hiding from life since she'd come back to Croftwood. And she still would be if it wasn't for Oliver encouraging her out of her comfort zone with the cinema.

'I'm just going to drop the lunch sandwiches round to Jess's.'

She packed the sandwiches in a large paper bag and without bothering to take her apron off, left the shop and ran straight into Toby.

'Patsy, good to see you,' he said with a smile. 'How are things?'

'Oh, good thanks. I'm sure Oliver will mention it but we're having a dry run at the cinema tonight. You're welcome to come along if you'd like to? It's a test night for friends and locals.'

'Thanks, I'd love that.'

'Cool. I'll see you later then.'

Patsy carried on to the Haberdashery, pleased that Toby was coming. Hopefully Oliver wouldn't mind; they needed plenty of friendly faces.

'Hi Jess, shall I pop the sandwiches in the kitchen?'

'Please!' she called from the counter where she was ringing up a sale for someone.

Patsy waited until she was free, accidentally becoming engrossed in looking at yarn until Jess came up behind her.

'Thanks for the sandwiches. How's it going, are you ready for tonight?'

'It seems a bit rash to say yes, but yes. I think we are. You are coming, right?'

'Definitely. I meant to ask, the launch party next week, is it okay if I bring a friend?'

'Is it a boy?' Patsy teased.

'It is. The guy I told you about from Tinder. We've seen each other a few times.'

'Of course, it's fine. I'm looking forward to meeting him. I'd better get back. See you later.'

Once the lunch rush was over she headed to the cinema to make sure everything was ready. Thankfully, the unpredictable English weather was on their side and had provided a perfect July day with the hint of a breeze to take the worst of the heat out of the air. When Patsy arrived, the caterers were already in the kitchen and the builders that Oliver had asked to help out with some of the last minute things were stringing the fairy lights in the trees outside and fitting the fire exit signs.

Patsy headed upstairs to the circle which wasn't quite finished yet as they hadn't installed the chairs. She lay down on the floor and inhaled the smell of the new carpet, one of her favourite smells in the world and one you didn't come across that often unless you frequented carpet shops. With her eyes closed, she took some deep breaths and tried to calm herself down. The anxiety had been building all morning but after a few more minutes of inhaling the beautiful fragrance of the carpet, she felt a renewed energy and a smidgeon of excitement for the evening.

After hauling herself up from the floor and brushing the bits of new carpet from her clothes, she leant her hands on the balcony and surveyed the space. It looked amazing. It felt odd to be so proud of something she'd achieved; it had happened so rarely in her life that she couldn't remember ever feeling like this before. Tears sprang to her eyes as she looked at the chandeliers which were perfectly understated, the flooring which set the beautiful colour of the walls off so sublimely, and the wonderful jewel coloured velvet chairs which would always remind her of the night at Oliver's flat when the whole thing had come together. She just had to hope that it all continued to come together tonight because that's what mattered.

Patsy and Oliver stood alone in the foyer, staring at each other. Patsy was wearing her second favourite frock — she was saving her absolute favourite for the launch next week, and Oliver looked smart and handsome in a suit with a floral shirt, open at the neck.

'We brush up well,' he said. Patsy could hear the nerves in his voice.

'You look very handsome.' She reached up to tuck a rogue lock of hair into his trademark quiff.

It was time to open the doors. They were deliberately not making a big deal of it because it wasn't really the opening night but as seven o'clock approached, the two of them were feeling like it was the start of everything.

'I might sit in the ticket booth and welcome everyone,' Patsy said, shaking her hands in front of her to try and dissipate the nerves.

'You bloody won't. We're both standing on the doorstep to welcome people and I told Jack not to open the back door until seven-thirty so we can make sure most people come in the front door.'

'Oh, god, I haven't checked that the fairy lights are on out the back.'

'They are. I saw Ed checking out there earlier on.' He smiled at her and took her hands in his. 'This is it, Pats. Are you ready to open the door?'

'No, the bloody bar person isn't here yet.' She took a step towards the kitchen just as a young girl emerged and took her place behind the bar, giving Patsy a wide smile as she did so. 'Okay. Ready now.'

Oliver opened the doors to find a couple of small groups of students, Ed's invitees no doubt, loitering a few metres away.

'We're open guys!' he called to them. They half-heartedly began to make their way towards the door. Oliver had a look of panic on his face.

'It'll be fine when they're mixed in with everyone else,' Patsy said reassuringly. 'They probably feel a bit out of their comfort zone.'

Oliver nodded and began greeting them enthusiastically. 'Thanks for coming. Please help yourself to a drink from the bar.'

That perked them up. Students love a free drink and Oliver was offering beer and wine on the house for the evening. They hadn't quite got the bar staff trained up for the cocktails yet but they would have to make sure they were ready before they opened properly.

'Can I have a drink from the bar?' Patsy asked once the

first flurry of people had gone in.

'Go on. Get me a glass of red while you're there, please. Probably could do with taking the edge off.'

Patsy laughed because it wasn't often she saw Oliver nervous and if she stopped to look at him, it made her feel better straight away. She helped herself to two glasses of red and went back to stand on the step with him.

'I can't wait to go in and see the backstage with everyone in there,' she said.

'And I can't wait to open the doors at the back. It might be time to get Jack manning this door and we can go and do that together.'

Oliver went ahead to send Jack back while Patsy waited to greet any latecomers. She stood on the step with her wine, enjoying the peace and quiet of the park before she joined the party.

'Hi.'

Patsy gasped and span around, her heart racing as she hadn't heard whoever had crept up behind her.

'I'm so sorry, I didn't mean to frighten you,' said Matt.

Patsy put a hand on her heart and laughed with relief. 'I was in a world of my own, don't worry.'

'The place looks great.' He leant towards her slightly before he paused, looking unsure, and then kissed her on the cheek.

'Oh, thanks.' That had been a surprise. A nice surprise that made her stomach flip a tiny bit and wish that he hadn't been so chaste in going for the cheek.

He was wearing dark jeans and a white shirt, open at the neck and a tweed jacket. His hair was in the usual waves it always was but he looked so polished that Patsy found herself staring at him for a few seconds too long before she remembered to speak.

'Come on, let's go in,' she said. 'We're about to open the

back door.'

Jack arrived to man the front door and Patsy led Matt inside.

'Help yourself to a drink and we'll go and join everyone backstage.'

Matt took a glass of red and followed Patsy into the auditorium. He hadn't seen it since yesterday and she could see he was clocking all the small things that had been finished since then. It was great to see someone noticing and appreciating what they'd achieved. In all the rush to be ready none of them had had time to do that.

They walked through the stalls and went through the door into the backstage area only to be immediately heckled by Oliver.

'Come on, Pats! Time for the grand opening of the door!'

She shot an apologetic smile at Matt and joined Oliver beside the door.

'Thanks to all of you for being our guinea pigs tonight,' Oliver said. 'Please enjoy the food and drink and if there's anything you think we can improve, please let one of us know. I also want to take a minute to thank Patsy without whom this place would be a carbon copy of the coffee house and would be nowhere near able to show an actual film. So let's raise a glass to Patsy.'

Patsy glared at Oliver, feeling her face redden in embarrassment but she was touched and smiled while everyone chanted her name as they raised their glasses to toast her.

'And by opening these doors, I now declare Backstage at Croftwood Cinema open!'

Oliver and Patsy grabbed the huge iron handle and heaved the door open, although once they'd begun to pull, it slid easily across on the rails, revealing the glammed-up corner of the park outside and inevitably, that's where everyone headed. Apart from Patsy who went to find Ed who seemed to have missed the whole thing.

'Ah, Patsy. There you are.' Rosemary was waiting in the doorway, blocking Patsy's exit into the stalls.

'Rosemary. Welcome.' Patsy gave her biggest smile and tried to make sure her eyes joined in. 'Have you had a drink?'

'I don't appreciate giving my time up for no reason. I can't see that you've taken any notice of the suggestions I made.'

Patsy smothered an eye roll and tried to avoid looking at Oliver who she knew would be making an 'I told you so' face. 'On the contrary, Rosemary.' Patsy took Rosemary gently by the elbow and led her into the stalls. 'Look. Those curtains are entirely due to your suggestion. There weren't any curtains before.'

'But they're…purple.' Rosemary almost spat. 'They should be red.'

'We have to consider the rest of the decor and you know, we need to have a modern twist on the traditional. Same with the chandeliers.'

Rosemary tutted but looked a little appeased.

'And this, you won't believe.' Patsy led her to the foyer and showed her the ornate balustrade. 'Look, we didn't even know that was there until you told me.'

Rosemary looked as pleased as punch. 'Do you know, I walked straight past that earlier on. How could I have missed it? It looks wonderful. Just as I remember.'

'Thank you, Rosemary. I really did appreciate you sharing your memories of the place.'

'It was my pleasure. We'd better get back to the party, hadn't we?'

Seeing the food beginning to come out, Patsy detoured from her route to the projection box to find Ed and instead went into the kitchen to make sure everyone was okay. One of the lecturers from the cookery school was supervising so there was nothing to worry about but Patsy wanted them to know they had support if they needed it. As the food began to come out and people began to look for a place to sit, it became obvious that there weren't quite enough chairs in the backstage area. Some of the students were sitting on the grass outside, seeming quite happy to do so but it was a good note for the next event they held that they needed to make sure that there was a chair for every guest to sit down to eat. The kitchen staff produced food from a limited menu, sending out enough meals for everyone in the space of an hour, which was quite a feat and something they hadn't been sure would be possible on their first try.

Patsy went to the bar and grabbed another glass of wine, forgetting where she'd left the first one and then went in search of Ed. He was standing outside, deep in conversation with Toby. Most people were outside under the fairy-light-strung trees which were also hung with big flouncy tissue paper flowers that Jess had made for them. It was a perfect evening for entertaining outside.

Ed greeted her with a smile. 'I was wondering where you'd got to. Do you know Toby?'

Toby jumped in before she could answer. 'Ah, yes. Oliver's has become my home from home over the past few weeks. A bit more lively than actually working from home.'

'Did you know Toby's a lawyer? Used to be a top barrister in London and gave it all up for a quieter life in Croftwood. I was saying it's the best thing he could have done.' Patsy realised she hadn't socialised with Ed and other people before, apart from Oliver and Matt. Where had Chatty Ed come from?

'It's a wonderful part of the country, I have to say,' said Toby.

'I bet you miss the buzz of London sometimes though?' She was feeling like being devil's advocate.

'Well, I still get up to London a fair bit, keep my hand in, you know,' he said diplomatically. 'But it's nice to have the best of both worlds.'

'You couldn't pay me to leave Worcester,' said Ed.

Patsy couldn't help but raise her eyebrows and she noticed Toby stifle a smile before he made his excuses and went inside.

'Matt,' she said, with some relief as he wandered over to join them. 'Have you had any food yet?'

'I've eaten,' said Ed. 'It was alright, actually.'

'I'm going to see if there's anything left. Matt?'

'Great, I'm starving,' he said, and followed her inside, leaving Ed to move on to a group of students.

'God,' she said. 'I think he's had too much to drink,' she said.

'There was no need to rescue me,' Matt said sounding surprised.

'Well, I feel responsible for him for some reason. I'm sure the last thing you want is to spend the evening talking to someone who you think is a bit of an idiot.'

'Is that what I think?' Amusement danced in his eyes.

'I assumed after the Birmingham thing…'

'Okay, well you assumed correctly. He treated you badly and I can't for the life of me think why anyone would.'

He leaned towards her but unlike earlier on, he paused much closer towards her, his lips so close to her ear that she could feel his breath, warm on her skin. Considering how much time they'd spent together lately she realised it was the first time she'd been close enough to notice how he smelt. And it was divine.

'You're a constant surprise,' he whispered in her ear before he gave her a much more considered, tender kiss on the cheek.

All she could do was close her eyes, feeling him linger

there, and imagine his kisses slowly making their way around to her mouth. She drew in a breath and quietly tried to exhale; it seemed important not to startle him for fear he'd move away and it would be over.

Whatever it was.

It was Matt and she hadn't felt as turned on by a kiss on the cheek in her life.

Of course, he did pull away, with a graze of his hand down her upper arm which almost undid her. Before she could gather herself, or think of anything to say, his phone began to ring and he excused himself and headed into the foyer.

Patsy exhaled, feeling briefly dizzy from the adrenaline. What was happening? Aside from work, they barely knew each other. She wouldn't even have said she found him attractive with his clean shaven, preppy look, wavy dark blonde hair and dark blue eyes. But there was something about him. And now she knew what a kiss from him could do, a kiss on the cheek no less, it was going to be difficult not to think about what a proper kiss from him might feel like. It was going to be a challenge to keep her mind on the job in hand for the rest of the evening.

She could hear music playing in the backstage area so she picked up her drink and headed back outside. The few people still there had started dancing while others mingled under the trees outside, the small corner of the park becoming all the more magical looking as dusk and then darkness fell.

Patsy took her drink outside, looking for Oliver. He was sat under a tree talking to Jess.

'Hey, you. Take a seat.' He gestured to the grass beside him and she collapsed with a sigh.

'It seems like a hit,' said Jess. 'I would love a party here.'

'It does look great, doesn't it?' Patsy looked into the backstage from her position opposite the back door and couldn't believe they'd pulled it off.

'It really works,' agreed Oliver. 'Was it worth us having a dry run?'

'Yes, I think so,' said Patsy. 'I've quite enjoyed it and there's not much to iron out before next week but I'd hate to have felt as nervous as I did tonight before the actual launch party. I'm hoping to enjoy that a bit more.'

'Hmm, I think Ed'll be the nervous one that night,' said Oliver.

They'd decided to show a film, a crowd-pleaser but something relatively short which Ed was sorting out for them with his contacts from the Film Society.

Matt had come back to join them and over-hearing Oliver's comment, said, 'If it goes down as well as tonight has I think you'll be onto a winner. I've enjoyed it.' He looked at Patsy when he said that, making her blush.

Unable to bear his gaze on her, memories of the kiss hurtling back, she looked around for her drink. 'I've had four glasses of wine tonight and not had more than a sip from any of them,' she said.

People were beginning to leave. There were a hardcore few who had begun dancing the night away in the middle of the room but the catering staff had already cleared everything up aside from a few glasses and had said their goodnights with Oliver making sure to thank each of them for making the night a success.

'Think it's time to turf out the stragglers and lock up,' he said.

The four of them began to take the chairs inside and then once the last few people had gone, Oliver pulled the doors across and locked up.

'I think we can leave it at that. Is everyone out, Jack?' Oliver called across the stalls.

Jack poked his head around the door. 'Yep, just checked the

loos. All clear.'

'Great. Everything else can wait. Let's go.'

Oliver locked the door.

'Our first night. Done,' Patsy said wearily.

Matt put an arm around each of them. 'The first of many. Well done you two.'

'Okay. Come on, let's get home.' Oliver and Jack offered to walk Jess to her car so they said their goodbyes, Oliver gave Patsy a big hug then, looking slightly emotional, he, Jack and Jess headed back towards town.

Patsy and Matt watched them walk away, then he turned to face her and took her hands in his.

'Do we need to talk?' he asked.

She nodded. It would have been more romantic to simply pick up where Matt had left off earlier but things for her were complicated and she knew his life was too. He knew most of it already, and was the only person she knew to have seen Dan with his own eyes, but Patsy wanted to share everything. And make sure he knew what he was getting into, if that's what they decided.

They headed arm in arm back to her flat in companionable silence. She tried not to think about the fact that Matt was coming back to her flat. Tried not to think about what might happen there and instead concentrated on how the evening had gone.

It was strange to think that the cinema was up and running because the sense of relief she thought she'd get after their dry run had gone so smoothly was non-existent. Perhaps that's because the launch party had more riding on it and had to be perfect or maybe that's what life was going to be like all the time now, going from one big night to the next. Either way, that was fine. She needed to turn her anxiety — not only about the cinema but about her love life too — into anticipation and channel that into making Croftwood Cinema amazing.

# 30

Matt followed Patsy into her flat. She'd left the windows open and now that the sun had set, the place was a lot cooler than it would have otherwise been; the Victorian eaves weren't as well-insulated as they would be nowadays.

Taking the idea from the cinema, Patsy had bought some solar-powered fairy lights and trailed them through the branches of the oak tree that grazed her roof terrace and she'd bought a couple of old deckchairs and given them an amateur makeover with some bright floral canvas from The Croftwood Haberdashery. Now that she was so busy with work, it seemed more important to have somewhere she could enjoy relaxing in when she got home.

'This is fantastic,' Matt said, climbing out of the window onto the roof terrace before Patsy could even suggest it.

'Is it too late to have a glass of wine?' Patsy suggested, hoping he wouldn't prefer a cup of tea.

'Never too late on an evening like this.' He hooked his jacket on the back of one of the deckchairs and eased himself down into it. Patsy watched in mild horror since her makeover had only been cosmetic, and might not have done anything to strengthen the ripe old fabric that still lay underneath but it seemed to be holding.

She grabbed a bottle of her favourite red wine, hoping that her taste for fairly cheap Australian Merlot would go down okay, and climbed out of the window with it under her arm and two glasses in her hand.

Matt pulled himself up to a sitting position and took the glasses from her while she sat down herself and then poured the wine. The fairy lights and the glow from the streetlights on the road below created the perfect ambience for what might be an awkward talk about navigating their possible relationship.

Patsy had positioned the deckchairs so that they were overlooking the direction of the park and it was nice to be sat there, in an easy silence, looking at the twinkling lights of Croftwood rather than each other. It took the pressure off a little bit.

'This is the first time I've planned a relationship before it's even started,' said Matt.

Now that he'd started the conversation, it was easy for Patsy to pick something to banter about with him. 'I think it might have started before tonight.' She raised her eyebrows and smiled.

'Okay, I'll give you that.'

She could see his eyes crinkling at his temples the way they had when they'd walked next to each other and she loved that she could tell his expression even when he wasn't looking at her.

'Once we'd got past the endless health and safety advice.'

Matt almost choked on his wine as he began to laugh before he'd managed to swallow.

'That's my job! And don't think I didn't see you rolling your eyes every time I handed you a hard hat.'

'Is that a euphemism?'

'For what?' He was still laughing.

'I don't know,' she said, laughing too. 'It just sounded like it could be.'

'I'll never look at a hard hat in the same way.'

They looked at each other and smiled, each taking a sip of wine.

'Between us, we have a few things to navigate if we're going to take things further.' Matt's practicality took over but Patsy didn't mind that side of him anymore. If anything, it was reassuring.

'Gone are the days of getting off with each other on a night out and then carrying on from there.'

'I think so.' He paused. 'Nicole and I promised each other that we'd be careful about who we introduce to the twins.'

'I can completely understand that. You need to be sure it's something serious before you let them get attached to someone new.'

She glanced at him and he was looking at her with that look she was starting to recognise. One that she loved.

'That's it exactly. I've been dreading having to navigate that when the time came. But with you…'

'It's not rocket science,' she said gently. 'Anyone should understand that your children will always be the most important thing, otherwise they're the wrong person.'

'The very fact that you think that tells me that you're the right person, Patsy. And as ridiculous as it sounds, I'm starting to feel as if things could be serious between us.'

It would be easy to shrug his comments off with a flippant remark, but Patsy knew the difference between someone telling you what you wanted to hear, to maybe get you into bed or something and someone speaking from their heart. What was the point of either of them dancing around any of this? He knew her biggest secret and he had treated that information as tenderly as the kiss he'd given her earlier. He had just told her what he needed from her if they were going to embark on anything more than a kiss and she would treat that just as carefully.

'Maybe they already are. A few weeks ago, I wouldn't have dreamed of feeling like this about you. In fact, I definitely fell for the charms of your children first.'

He threw his head back and laughed again, then held out his glass for a cheers which Patsy returned.

'But I feel the same way as you,' she said. 'I'm happy to fast forward from a kiss to fairly serious if that means we can be together.'

'And you feel ready for that? Given everything that's happened, that's maybe still happening. It's not terrible timing?'

'Whenever did love wait for the best time?' She gulped, realising what she'd said. But she did think she was on the cusp of loving him, only the fact that it felt too soon was stopping her from allowing herself to believe that's what was happening. But in fact, it had probably been burgeoning for many weeks without either of them noticing. 'I'm sorry. I didn't mean that.'

Matt put his glass down and pushed himself out of the chair. He knelt in front of Patsy and took her wine glass from her, placing that down too.

'Don't apologise. I've never felt like this before either. It's taken me by surprise but I've never been more sure of how I feel.'

Patsy reached up and touched his cheek.

'Matt, I know you rescued me that night and I will be forever grateful for but I don't need you to do that anymore.'

He mirrored her, stroking her cheek gently with his thumb before leaning towards her. 'I know, Patsy. You astound me more and more every day that I know you. You never needed rescuing, you needed the confidence to know that you could rescue yourself and that's what you've done.'

Finally, the kiss she'd been dreaming of for hours was hers. It was more than she had imagined. It was as if she could feel his soul in that kiss. Her heart was blossoming, reaching towards him, with everything she had wanting to be close to him, be at one with him.

They parted, looking into each other's eyes to wordlessly consent to what was inevitably going to happen next. Matt stood up and led Patsy over to the window where they climbed through, one after the other. They stood in front of each other, eyes locked. Matt gently turned her around and began, ever so slowly, to unzip her dress. It was sweet torture, he did it so slowly but she was aware of every single time his finger and thumb touched the skin on her back as if tiny electric shocks were passing between them. He gently lifted the dress from her shoulders and lowered it so that she could step out of it. It was a gesture which she loved, the respect he had for her second favourite dress was so much sexier than if he'd flung it carelessly aside in the throes of passion.

Stood before him in her best sage-green lacy underwear, Patsy, just as slowly, unbuttoned his shirt. Their eyes were again, locked on each other, both of them revelling in this unspoken agreement to tantalise each other as if there were no rush at all. He gasped as her fingers pushed into the space between his stomach and the button on his jeans so that he could undo them and he ran his fingers slowly down her spine while she unzipped his jeans and began pushing them over his hips, moving ever closer to him so that there was barely anything between them.

She pulled his shirt off and he stepped out of his jeans. Now, both in their underwear, she smiled at him and undid her bra herself, letting it fall to the floor. They moved together again, Matt grazing his lips against hers, with the lightest of touches that instantly drove her to want more. But he pulled away with a smile when she tried to go in harder and instead teased his finger into the waistband of her underwear, moving it from side to side as he watched her, desperate, on the verge of bursting as he forced her to wait for what was to come. Ever playful, she began to lightly run her fingers across the fabric of his underwear, knowing now that he was feeling just the same way as her. He broke first, lifting her up by her thighs and kissing her as she'd never been kissed, before he laid her down on the bed because neither of them could bear the sweet agony of waiting any longer.

Waking up next to Matt was wonderful. Patsy didn't think anything could top last night, but seeing him there before he woke, his eyelashes spread on his cheeks, his hair all over the place, even the small snoring noises he was making filled her heart with more joy than she would have thought possible.

She lay watching him, loving being able to see his body in daylight for the first time as the sun shone onto the bed, illuminating them both as if there was an after-glow from the amazing sex they'd had. His chest was covered in golden hair and she could see well-defined muscles in his shoulders and arms as he lay on his back, one arm lying above his head, with a sheet only just covering his bottom half.

He stirred enough to notice that the sun was up and gradually came to while Patsy watched him.

'Morning,' she said, lying on her side with her head propped on her hand.

He smiled. 'Not a dream, then.'

'That's so cheesy.'

He turned to face her and reached his arm around her waist, encouraging her to move towards him. 'There's nothing cheesy about it. You feel the same way, I can tell by your face.'

She grinned because he was absolutely right. 'I do. I'm not used to being romanced, that's all.'

'That amazes me.' He leant towards her and kissed her gently.

'I'm not used to romancing either,' she said, between kisses.

'I think you're doing alright on that score,' said Matt before he pulled her on top of him, starting the day as perfectly as the last one had ended.

# 31

Patsy's Knit and Natter friends were the first to arrive on the night of the launch party. Everything was ready and she was relieved to see some friendly faces.

'Come on in guys.' Patsy led Mary and Penny into the foyer as Carol and Sue followed.

'My goodness, this is marvellous!' Mary placed a hand on her chest, her eyes sparkling as she took in the cloakroom where one of the bar staff had been bribed to dress as a Flapper girl and had even managed to get Marcel waves in her hair. The ticket booth was manned by Jack who Patsy had persuaded to slick back his hair and dress like Gene Kelly while he handed out tickets to the guests as they arrived. The tickets were really programmes for the evening along with the menu choices in the form of an oversized cinema ticket for Where Love Lingers, the film that Ed had chosen. It was a 1950s black and white film set in the 1920s which fitted with their theme for the launch perfectly.

'You can have a complimentary drink,' said Patsy. 'Would you like one here or in the Backstage bar?'

'Oh, I think the backstage bar sounds wonderful,' said

Penny, looking round at the others, who nodded in agreement.

Patsy led them through the stalls where the furniture had been arranged so that the guests could dine and then stay seated to watch the film. As they reached the door to the backstage area, Patsy paused in the doorway so that they could go in first. 'Welcome to Backstage at Croftwood Cinema.'

'Oh my. It's perfect. Look at the film up there, Penny! And the champagne fountain, all ready to go. I've never seen one in real life before.'

The champagne fountain had been Matt's idea and although it had taken ages, not to mention a steady hand to assemble it, Patsy had to admit that it looked amazing and was a fabulous centrepiece for the bar.

More guests began to arrive and once everyone started chatting, Patsy slipped away to check on the food and to make sure the champagne was out of the fridge and ready to go down to the backstage bar for the fountain. There was no-one she could ask to carry it down there, everyone in the kitchen was busy and although she had bar and waiting staff they were all out serving drinks and prepping for the food service. Never mind, it'd only be a couple of trips for her to take it herself.

Patsy put a couple of bottles under her arm and took one more in each hand and headed through the kitchen to the backstage bar. She gave the barman, Simon, a grateful smile and seeing that he was snowed under with making drinks, offered to serve the couple of guests that were waiting.

As she waited for a pint of draught lager to pour, she glanced around at the guests, wondering who might be coming that she knew from the town. She spotted Rosemary with Linda and Steph from the library, who gave her a quick wave and Jess was there but Patsy couldn't spot the man she'd planned to invite..

She began pouring another pint and looked up in time to see a man approach Jess and wrap his arms around her from behind, making her laugh. Patsy smiled, thinking how nice it was to see Jess with someone and looking so happy. The man twirled her around and leaned in for a kiss. When he pulled away, Patsy's face fell, along with the glass in her hand.

It was Dan.

Muttering some incoherent excuse to Simon, not even noticing that she was leaving a smashed glass and a puddle of lager in her wake, Patsy stumbled out from behind the bar and back into the corridor that led to the kitchen and foyer.

She leant against the wall, her breath heaving and her heart hammering in her chest. What was he doing here? Was he really with Jess? It couldn't be that simple. Not where Dan was involved.

She managed to get her breathing back to normal and tried to think about what she was going to do. The plain fact of the matter was that she was running the party and couldn't slope off to avoid him. And what had she said about being strong enough to cope if he turned up again? Well, she was going to have to pull herself together, somehow try and make sure that when she walked back into that room that she was prepared to see him, not let him see that she was rattled, and she would treat him like any other guest at the party.

But first she needed to check that she looked the part after the shock she'd had. She walked through the kitchen to the foyer and retrieved her bag from the cloakroom, heading into the ladies but bumping into Ed who was coming out of the gents.

'Are you alright?'

'Yes, I'm fine. I thought I'd better touch up my lippy.' She couldn't let on that Dan was here. If Oliver or Matt found out, they'd want to throw him out and at the very least, a scene like that could ruin the party. No, better to keep it to herself. But she wished more than anything that Matt was here. He was at a planning meeting at the council so was going to be late. All she wanted to do was be in his arms where none of this stuff mattered.

'Come on,' she said looking at her reflection in the mirror. 'He can't do anything to you.' She just wished she could make herself believe that. She practised a bright smile but could see in the mirror that she was struggling to look calm. At least people would think she was stressed out about the party. But if she went in looking like this, Dan would know he'd rattled her. She forced herself to drop her shoulders and took a few calming, deep breaths into her belly instead of anxiously into the top of her chest.

Patsy handed her bag back to the cloakroom assistant and took a deep breath before she headed back into the stalls.

'Hey, Pats.' Oliver was walking towards her and she felt a wave of relief that she didn't have to face Dan alone.

'I think it's time to do the champagne, Ollie.' She grabbed his hand before he could disappear anywhere else and they walked down to the backstage together. Patsy stationed herself next to the champagne fountain and Oliver stood next to her which meant she could concentrate on him rather than allow her eyes to wander to see where Dan was.

'Alright, Pats?' He rubbed his hands together with anticipation. 'God, our first proper event. Crazy isn't it?'

She nodded. 'You do your speech now and then can you help me pour the champagne?'

Patsy kept her eyes on Oliver as he spoke. She didn't hear his speech because all she could think about was Dan. But she tried to keep a smile on her face as she watched Oliver's joy, wishing she was sharing it.

Then everyone cheered as Patsy and Oliver carefully began pouring champagne into the glass at the top of the pyramid and it flowed just as Patsy had hoped it would, into all the glasses below. Everyone was clapping and watching. It should have been a relief that things were going to plan, but all Patsy could feel were Dan's eyes boring into the back of her, even though she had no idea where he was actually standing.

Once all the glasses were full, Oliver and Patsy began handing them out to the guests and people started to help themselves once the first couple of layers had been dished out. Then Patsy took the opportunity to leave the room to catch her breath again.

Matt would be here soon and in the meantime she could seek sanctuary for a few minutes in the projection box. At least Oliver was around now to help manage things and there was still half an hour until the food came out.

'Cleo.'

She turned around to find that Dan had followed her out into the stalls. There was no-one else around.

'I can't stop,' she said, sounding as matter-of-fact as she could manage. 'I don't know what you're doing here but I'm working. You should leave.' She carried on moving towards the door to the foyer but he kept coming towards her. Could she make a run for it? Run up to the projection box and lock herself in with Ed?

'It was a genuine invitation, pure coincidence,' he said with a smug smile. He continued moving towards her as he spoke.

'Right. Well you'd better get back to the party then.' She felt for a split second that she was finally gaining control of her emotions. Maybe she could hold a conversation with him without having a panic attack.

'It's quite something you've got going on here. I've been hearing all about it from your friends in the knitting club. Landed on your feet, haven't you? Perfect time for a divorce. Get rid of me before you have to start sharing.'

'You've got a nerve! After all you took from me…' She was suddenly so angry, that tears were threatening and she didn't want to give him the satisfaction. She took a deep breath and said, 'I don't owe you anything and I don't want anything from you other than a divorce.'

'Hey, Patsy.'

She turned to see Matt heading towards her and had never felt so relieved to see anyone in her life.

'Sorry, I didn't mean to interrupt.' He smiled at Patsy and she realised in horror that he was going to walk straight past her to the backstage bar. So much for telling him she didn't need rescuing.

'No worries, mate. I was just catching up with my wife.'

Patsy stared in horror at Dan. But it had stopped Matt in his tracks and he came back and stood in front of her, allowing her to move away from Dan.

'I didn't recognise you, 'Matt said coldly. 'And I'm certain you weren't invited.'

'He's with Jess,' Patsy said in a low voice behind him.

'Patsy, perhaps you could let Jess know that her escort has left without her.' Matt began to walk towards Dan, forcing him to back up to the top of the stalls.

He was holding his hands up, 'Look, I'm not here to see her.' He almost spat with vitriol in Patsy's direction but now that Matt was in charge, she could see the smugness evaporating from Dan.

'I don't know what other reason there would be.' Matt said.

Dan braced himself on the door frame and ended up chest to chest with Matt who was physically leaning into the doorway to stop Dan from flying back in.

'You owe me, Cleo! I want that fucking laptop back!'

Matt finally shoved him out into the foyer, causing Dan to stumble backwards and fall.

'Matt! Be careful!' She ran to the foyer, terrified that Dan would turn on Matt and they'd end up fighting. But Dan was walking out of the door, with his hands aloft.

'I'm going, okay?' She heard him say to Matt.

Matt turned to her. 'Don't worry,' he said, with a reassuring nod. 'I'll make sure he goes.'

Patsy nodded back, then stunned, she went to find Jess. What did he mean about the laptop? It was an old laptop that she'd known he never used. She'd been so sure that he wouldn't even have noticed it was gone, otherwise she wouldn't have taken it. But now she wondered why he was interested enough in it to mention it. If that was the reason he'd tracked her down, there was more to it than a crappy old laptop.

Jess was sipping a glass of champagne with the Knit and Natter group but Patsy could see that she kept looking around, wondering where her boyfriend was.

'Jess…'

'Patsy! This is brilliant, a real step-up, even from last week's practice. Congratulations.' Then she frowned. 'Are you okay?'

'I need to talk to you.'

She led Jess into the stalls where thankfully there was no sign of Matt and Dan but people were beginning to take their seats ready for the film. It wasn't the place for such a conversation.

Patsy took Jess through the corridor that  bypassed the stalls and the foyer and they headed upstairs to the circle which was out of bounds for the night to everyone else.

Patsy sat down with her back leaning against the wall and Jess sat next to her.

'What is it? Has something happened?'

'It's about Dan.'

Jess looked puzzled and smiled in confusion. 'Sorry, who's

Dan?'

'Your boyfriend.' Of course he hadn't used his real name. If Jess had had the presence of mind to google him, which she might well have done, Dan James would probably have resulted in the truth coming out.

'Joe. He told me his name was Joe.' She sighed in a way that said she wasn't all that surprised. 'You know him?'

Patsy nodded. 'He's my husband.'

'Oh my god. Your husband?'

Patsy told Jess everything and in return Jess told her what she knew. Between them they worked out that Dan had appeared on Tinder right after he'd shown up in Croftwood the first time.

'He'd have known that if I lived near a knitting shop I'd be in there,' Patsy said.

'And I had knitting on my profile. It's not the most attractive trait but I always thought if it didn't put someone off, it was a sign they were one of the good ones.'

'I'm so sorry, Jess.'

'It's not your fault. I'm sorry I was part of bringing him back into your life.'

Patsy shook her head. 'He'd already done that anyway. I don't understand why he involved you.'

Jess shrugged. 'Even so, he's still not up there with the worst Tinder date I've ever had. What does he want?'

'I honestly don't know but I'm going to find out.'

The lights dimmed and the film began. Patsy stood up.

'I need to go back down and help. Let's see if Oliver will walk you home.'

'No need. I'm going to go down and watch the film with the girls.'

They hugged each other and then headed downstairs.

Oliver appeared when they were halfway down. 'Hey, Pats, I've been looking everywhere for you. Can you give us a hand with clearing backstage while the film's on?'

'Sure. Have you seen Matt?'

'No. Why? Everything alright?' Oliver asked as they went downstairs.

'Yes, of course,' she said, with what she hoped was a reassuring smile. Now wasn't the time to tell Oliver. They needed to concentrate on the rest of the evening. There would be plenty of time to talk later.

# 32

After the film, when all the guests had left, Oliver and Patsy were tidying up the stalls while Ed was packing the film up to send back.

'What happened to Matt?' Oliver asked. 'I thought he was coming after his meeting.'

Patsy was worried about him. He hadn't come back after he threw Dan out and she had been telling herself all evening that Matt was a grown man, more than a match for Dan and quite capable of looking after himself. But still, he should have been back by now.'Something happened tonight, Ollie. Dan turned up with Jess. Matt threw him out and I haven't seen him since then.'

Oliver shook his head. 'What? Dan came here and you didn't tell me?'

'I didn't want it to overtake the launch night. I thought Matt was making sure he'd gone and then he'd be back.'

'But he isn't. Christ, Pats. You should have told me instead of letting Matt deal with it on his own.'

That's exactly what she should have done, it was obvious now. There was nothing more important than making sure

248

Matt was safe and she'd let him go off with Dan alone and said nothing.

She sank down onto the floor and started sobbing. 'I'm sorry,' was all she could manage to say.

Oliver sat down next to her and put his arms round her shoulders, pulling her close. 'I'm sorry. It's not your fault. I'm just worried about Matt. Let me try calling him.'

They sat there as the phone rang and rang but Matt didn't answer.

'Let's finish up here and go back to mine,' Oliver said.

'Ollie, Dan wants my laptop. There's something on there that he wants and I need to find out what it is. That's why he's come back.'

'Right, we'll go to yours first and you can get the laptop and pack some stuff. You're staying with me until we know what's happened.'

Patsy nodded. It was a huge relief that Oliver was taking charge of the situation. Whatever she'd thought about being strong in the face of Dan, all that had fizzled away now that Matt was missing. She was sure that the only reason he hadn't come back was because Dan had done something to stop him.

Ed came down to find them. He'd packed the film away and was on a bit of a high given that it had gone so well.

'Wow, that was amazing! I think we pulled it off!' He was grinning from ear to ear in a way Patsy had never seen him do before, yet another testament to the fact that he was more interested in the cinema than he was in her but she didn't care anymore.

'Thanks for everything you've done, Ed,' said Oliver, giving him a brief man-hug. 'You've gone above and beyond for us. I could do with having a chat sometime about whether you and Hayley would be up for training some projectionists for us?'

'Sure, be happy to.'

Oliver ushered him out, with Ed explaining about how he'd arranged for a courier to collect the film they'd shown that night, before he said goodbye.

'Okay, the door's locked. Let's finish up and get out of here.'

Later on, Patsy was sat on the sofa at Oliver's, poring over the laptop to see if she could work out what Dan was after. Oliver had called the police and explained what had happened. They were going to look into the terms of Dan's release from prison but it was too soon for Matt to be considered a missing person, even in the circumstances, so that was as much as they could do for now.

'If we haven't heard back from the police tomorrow, perhaps you could call the probation service or something. They'll have to tell you what the situation is, won't they?'

'I think so.' It was something she should have done weeks ago when Dan had first appeared. Perhaps then none of this would have happened. She might have been able to stop him.

Oliver handed her a glass. 'It's brandy.'

'Thanks. Should we go to Matt's house? See if he's there?'

'I think he'd have come back to the cinema, Pats. Don't you? He definitely wouldn't have told Dan where he lived, or gone home without coming back to let you know everything was okay.'

Oliver was right. After what had happened between them, she knew that Matt would have come to her. If he could.

Some hours later, Patsy was still searching the computer for anything that might give her a clue as to what Dan was up to, interspersing it with some bug hunting to break the monotony. The bug hunting wasn't going as well as she'd hoped. She had managed to find a vulnerability in one website but it turned out someone else had beaten her to it and had got the reward instead, not that it would have been enough to have made any difference. Amy's deadline was fast approaching and they were no closer to being able to pay across the money. After tonight, Patsy was starting to feel hopeless.

Oliver had fallen asleep on the sofa beside her. She'd pulled a blanket on top of him, grateful that he'd wanted to keep her company. At about four in the morning, his phone which he'd left on the coffee table began buzzing.

'Ollie,' she shook him to wake him. 'Ollie, someone's ringing you.'He shot upright, grabbing his phone with one hand and rubbing his eyes into focus with the other.

'Oh, thank god,' he said, after he'd listened for a few seconds. 'Okay.' A few more okays and thank yous later, he hung up.

'That was Matt's ex-wife. He's been found.'

Patsy threw her arms around Oliver, feeling elated before she realised that his ex-wife was calling because he couldn't.

'Is he okay?' She didn't want to hear the answer but at the same time, she did.

'He's in hospital. The police found him on the Worcester Road and his ex-wife is still the emergency contact in his phone apparently. He's awake though, and asked her to call me to let us know he's okay.'

'Can we go?'

Oliver shook his head. 'He's resting and we've had a drink. We'll go tomorrow, Pats. I'll ask Jack to work and we'll both go.'

'Did Dan do this?'

'I don't know anything, except that he was unconscious and it does look like he was beaten up. I don't think he's said anything about what happened, from what she said.'

Patsy started crying. 'It's all my fault. I did this. If I'd faced up to the situation and sorted things out with Dan straight away, this wouldn't have happened.'

'Come on, you can't know that. If he's willing to dupe one of your friends into going out with him just so that he can get close to you, god knows what he's capable of. Did he ever do anything like that before? You know, get violent?'

'Not with me but I always thought he was capable of it. He threatened it enough times… I was sure he was going to one day. That's why I had to leave because that's what happens, isn't it? People want to believe it'll never happen to them but I knew he was taking everything from me. I wasn't myself anymore and as soon as he started being investigated for fraud, he was like a caged lion. Angry all the time, and it was only a matter of time before he got to the point where all of the threats would turn into something else.'

Oliver hugged her. 'It's so hard to imagine anyone being able to make you, of all people, feel like that. It tells me just how evil he was.' He took the laptop from her and closed the lid. 'Come on, now you know he's okay, try and get some sleep.' He insisted she take the bed and she slipped into a deep sleep as soon as she pulled the duvet over herself.

Patsy was awoken the following morning by Oliver tapping on the door and delivering coffee and a pain au chocolat to her bedside.

'Jack's already here. I called the hospital and we can visit this morning.'

Patsy leapt out of bed into the shower, leaving the coffee and pastry until she came out. She wound her damp hair into a bun and was ready to go in less than ten minutes but then ended up waiting impatiently for Oliver to finish in the bathroom.

The drive to Worcester was torture. Patsy was desperate to see Matt but terrified that he would blame her for what happened. Oliver had been reassuring her that Matt wouldn't hold her responsible but somehow, her mind had flipped back to when she and Matt had been at odds with each other over almost everything and in her mind, that was the Matt that was lying in hospital. Not Matt who she'd shared the most impossibly wonderful night with. Not Matt who had lovingly whispered about her constantly surprising him. She was so sure that the Matt who liked her would have disappeared into a black hole created by Dan, that by the time they got to the hospital, she was ready to persuade Oliver to go in alone while she waited in the car.

'He'll want to see you, not me,' Oliver said kindly. 'I have an inkling that he likes you.' He smiled and rolled his eyes.

'He might not now my husband has beaten him up.'

'I'm not sure that'll make any difference, Pats. Come on.' He held his hand out and she took it. It was the right thing to do, face up to what had happened; what she'd caused. At the very least she owed Matt an apology.

Matt had his eyes closed and aside from his hair, he was barely recognisable. His face was bruised and his left eye was hugely swollen. He had a dressing on his forehead and his right hand was bandaged.

Not caring that Oliver was watching, Patsy reached out and gently pushed his hair back from his forehead, repeating the motion again and again, finding it soothed her as much as she hoped it was soothing to Matt. He began to stir, moving then wincing before he woke up, his one eye too swollen to open.

'Hey,' Patsy said gently.

He turned his head carefully and gave her a smile when he recognised her.

'Patsy.' He reached for her hand, then his expression darkened. 'Are you okay? Did he hurt you?'

'No, no. I'm fine. How are you feeling?'

'Bit sore.'

'Hey, mate. Is all of this an excuse to get out of tidying up last night?'

Matt smiled. 'I'm sorry I missed it.'

'No worries. You're on the rota for next time.' Oliver squeezed his arm. 'Thank you.' He looked at Patsy. 'I'll wait outside.'

She nodded, unable to pull her gaze away from Matt. The longer she looked at him, the less she noticed his injuries.

'What happened?' She was desperate to know but then maybe he didn't want to talk about it.

'I just wanted to make sure he'd gone.'

She rubbed her thumb back and forth across the back of his hand as he carried on.

'I wanted him to get on the bus to Worcester. He said that's where he lives. I wanted to make sure he was leaving.'

He was looking at Patsy, willing her to understand.

'And then he attacked you?' she said gently.

He nodded but a tear slipped out of his good eye, betraying how he was really feeling. 'I'm okay.' He managed another smile but then closed his eyes for a minute while he squeezed her hand. 'Nothing like that has ever happened to me before. It was terrifying.'

She nodded. 'I know. I'm so sorry. I had no idea he was capable of anything like that.' To anyone other than her.

'You couldn't have known.'

Patsy put her hand to his forehead again and began stroking it with her thumb, hoping that it would convey how she was feeling when her heart was too full to turn it into words.

'I love you, Patsy,' he murmured before dozing off.

He had said it. That was what she had wanted to say to him but even after everything that had happened, had worried that it was too soon.

'I love you too.' He was asleep which might be for the best.

He wouldn't remember that either of them had said it.

It was too soon.

But it was what she had needed to say to break the ball of emotion that had sat at the top of her chest ever since she'd realised he was missing last night.

'Okay?' the nurse asked Patsy quietly while she checked his temperature and pulse, noting down the numbers on his chart.

Patsy nodded. 'Can I stay?'

'Only until the end of visiting time.'

Patsy wondered whether Nicole would be visiting him. They didn't have the most amicable relationship from what Patsy had gathered and she wondered who would look after him? If Nicole was still his emergency contact, it suggested that he hadn't had anyone else to take on that role. And it made sense because of the children. It was right that he and Nicole were still there for each other. But Patsy wanted to do that for him now.

'Can I leave my number? In case he needs anything.'

'You're not his next of kin?' It was a statement more than a question.

'No, but I'm not sure he has anyone.' Patsy whispered, and handed over her number, hastily written on the back of a receipt she'd found in her pocket. 'Check with him when he wakes up, I think it'll be okay.'

The nurse smiled and put the receipt in her pocket, then wrote some things down on the chart.

Patsy kissed his forehead and went off to find Oliver.

# 33

Matt was allowed home after a couple of days. His ex-wife, Nicole, was adamant that the twins shouldn't see him until his face had healed and he'd reluctantly gone along with her plan to tell them that he was away for work. It meant he was going home to an empty house and the doctor had said that he shouldn't be by himself for a couple of days as a precaution since he'd been knocked out.

He'd wanted to get a taxi home but the hospital had insisted he needed someone to collect him so Oliver and Patsy had gone. They watched as Matt assured the nurse that he would be staying with a friend while Oliver and Patsy looked at each other, their facial expressions questioning each other as to whether he'd asked one of them if he could stay and soon realising that he was telling everyone what they wanted to hear.

Oliver helped him into the front seat of his Mini — not the easiest car to get into with bruised ribs — and Patsy leaned across and pulled the seatbelt around him since his one hand was too sore.

'So Pats and I have decided that she's going to come and

stay with you for a couple of days.'

'There's no need—' Matt began.

'The options that I've already ruled out for you by the way are, you stay at Patsy's which has three flights of stairs and a bathroom in the eaves so you'll have to duck your head in the shower. No offence Pats,' he added, grinning into the rear-view mirror at her. 'The other option is staying at mine which I think we both know neither of us would enjoy.'

Matt raised an eyebrow, then winced. 'Fine.'

'It's not like you don't have the room and I'm sure you'd rather sleep in your own bed.'

'I said fine,' he snapped.

'I'll drop your stuff over later, Pats.' Oliver had worked all of this out without a word to Patsy about whether she was happy with his plan but in fact she could think of nothing better than holing up at Matt's for a couple of days. She could look after him while she carried on trawling through the crap on that laptop for whatever Dan was after.

'Did you speak to the police, Matt?' She couldn't believe it had taken her until now to wonder about that.

'Yep. There wasn't much I could tell them. I don't know where he lives or his full name. They asked me to let them know. Could you do that?'

'Of course I can.' It was the least she could do. 'Will they charge him?'

'I don't know.' Matt leaned his head back and closed his eyes, signalling an end to the conversation.

Matt's house was incredible. It was at the end of the cul-de-sac, set back from the large turning circle at the end of the road. It was, as all the houses were, clad in wood to give the impression of them being log-cabins but the size of them was impressive and Patsy was quite excited to see what it was like inside.

Oliver pulled onto the driveway which was gravelled and

had a path made of railway sleepers set into it that led to the front door. Matt took his keys out and opened the door while Oliver grabbed his bag from the boot.

The hallway was enormous with a double-height ceiling and stairs which led up to a balustraded landing.

'Wow, this is amazing,' Patsy said. It looked like something from Grand Designs, which was perhaps the point since Matt was an architect.

'Thanks,' he said, before heading into the kitchen and sitting down at the table. It was covered in blueprints, drawings and files.

'I can see you are about as tidy as me,' Oliver said. 'Anything else I can do before I go?'

'No, thanks Oliver, for everything.'

Oliver shook his head. 'It's nothing, mate. I'll drop your stuff over when I've closed, Pats.'

They stood in silence for a minute while Patsy gazed around and then took her coat off.

'So how long have you lived here?' She put the kettle on and started checking through the cupboards for mugs and teabags.

'Far left. Do you often go through people's kitchen cupboards?'

'I'm a guest so I think it's allowed, and I am looking after you.'

He smiled. 'I've lived here about four years. Nicole and I moved in together but it wasn't long after that when things came to a head and she moved out. It's always felt more like my house than ours and I don't think the twins know anything other than that their parents have always lived apart.'

'I bet they love coming over here,' Patsy said, looking out the window to the garden which had a trampoline buried in the ground so that it was level with the lawn and a rope swing in a huge tree down in the bottom corner where the garden met the woodland beyond.

'They love it. Sammy's desperate for a treehouse. I should have got started on that before the summer. It feels a bit late now.'

Patsy could hear the guilt in his voice. 'Come on,' she said, spooning the teabags out of the mugs. 'Have you got somewhere more comfy we can sit?'

He led the way into the lounge which had a huge fireplace made out of enormous pebble-like stones reminiscent of a ski lodge, and even in the middle of summer made Patsy want to start a roaring blaze in there.

'That fireplace is amazing.'

'Isn't it? Brings out the caveman in me. When I moved in, I lit a fire every night and I pick up kindling on my walks in the woods.'

'So is this the kind of house you'd design for yourself?'

'I did design it. I was the architect for this development.'

'Oh my god, I remember Ollie telling me that. That's got to feel good, living in a house you designed, everything exactly as you want it.'

'Apart from the fact that it's a family home…'

'You're missing the children.' He was down in the dumps. Obviously, he was black and blue, probably sore all over and he wasn't allowed to see the twins for as long as he looked like he'd been in a fight, which Patsy guessed could be a couple of weeks.

'Why don't you give them a ring?' she suggested.

'We always FaceTime. They'll think it's weird if they can't see me.'

'Don't be defeatist. You could legitimately be somewhere where the WiFi's terrible and it's not possible to video call.'

'I don't know what Nicole's told them. Where they think I am.'

He might be understandably feeling sorry for himself but nevertheless, it was exasperating.

'Ring, or text Nicole and ask her. Tell her you want to speak to the children. It's not rocket science.'

'Christ, is there no peace?' he said, but she saw the hint of a smile which he quickly suppressed. He reached for his phone and sent a text as she'd suggested. A minute or so later his phone rang and his face lit up as he chatted in turn to Sammy and Flo. From what Patsy heard of Matt's side of the conversation, they weren't that interested in where he was or what he was doing, instead telling him all about what they'd been doing at school and that they'd been to a party at the outdoor swimming pool in Droitwich.

'In two weeks, that's about ten more sleeps,' he said in response to a question from one of them. 'I know, but we'll do something exciting. You and Sammy have a think about what you'd like to do. The seaside? We'll have to wait and see if it's going to be a sunny day.'

Once he hung up, he looked a lot brighter.

'Thanks. I don't know why I thought that not being able to see them meant I couldn't contact them at all.'

Patsy shrugged. 'You had a bash to the head. Of course you're not thinking straight.'

'I think I might go up and have a sleep. I don't suppose you'd be able to ring the police would you?' He stood up pulled a card out of his back pocket.

Patsy stood up too and took the card. 'I'm so sorry, Matt. You shouldn't have been involved in any of this.'

He took her hand and lifted her fingers to his lips. 'It's not your fault. I riled him up by insisting on making sure he went on that bus. I should have left it.'

'He's angry with me though and you got the brunt of it.'

'If he didn't beat me up…it might have been you.' He bent and gently kissed her cheek. 'That would have been much worse.'

Although she'd feared Dan for years, it hadn't reached the point where she thought he would have laid a finger on her. She had always been frightened of that possibility but there were other things he did to her which were worse. He'd very effectively driven a wedge between her and anyone she cared about. Her parents hadn't understood why she'd kept putting them off when they wanted to visit and why she never visited them and eventually they had stopped suggesting anything like that. Their relationship was reduced to cards at birthdays and Christmas. In her heart, Patsy knew she could repair that relationship when she was ready but her friendships weren't so easily mended. All of that seemed far worse than taking a beating that would heal in a couple of weeks so yes, it would have been better if it were her instead of Matt.

'Sleep well. I'll call them now.'

He headed upstairs while she took his spot on the sofa which was still warm and called the number he'd given her. Aside from confirming Dan's name and current address, it was a conversation she wished she'd had when he first showed up in Croftwood. All of this might have been avoided. They said that any threatening behaviour or criminal activity could mean he may have to go back to prison for fourteen days because he was out on licence and this offence, if Matt wanted to press charges, could mean that at least was likely. After hearing her story, they also recommended that Patsy look into taking out a non-molestation order against him.

Oliver arrived with her things while Matt was still asleep and once he'd gone, she'd opened up the laptop and started searching again. An hour or so later, Matt came downstairs in search of food.

'Takeaway?' he asked, pulling a handful of menus out of the coffee table drawer and chucking them on the middle seat of the sofa.

'I could eat a pizza,' Patsy said. She was ravenous and that was a hole that only pizza could fill.

'Pizza it is.' Matt picked up his iPad and ordered on the app. 'What are you so involved in?'

Patsy could feel her eyes had that quality of having looked at the screen for too long without a break. 'I think there's something on this laptop that Dan wants. I've looked and looked and so far, there's nothing obvious.'

'What do you think it could be? I have no idea about stuff like that. Do you?'

'I used to be a software engineer.' She'd been used to people looking surprised when she told them but it had been a while since she'd told anyone, so she'd forgotten. Besides, Matt's expression also told her that he was impressed.

'A constant surprise,' he murmured, reminding her briefly of the night they'd spent together. 'So if there's something, you'll be able to find it.'

'I hope so. Knowing him, it has to be money.'

'Like a bank account or something?'

'Mmm. I don't know. I was thinking a crypto currency wallet or something like that but there's nothing.'

'You mean Bitcoins?'

She nodded. 'That's what I was expecting. It has to be something that is stored on here, rather than something that could be accessed remotely from any computer.'

Matt gingerly settled back into the opposite corner of the sofa. 'Could it be as simple as a password that's stored on there?'

'It could be but I've checked all the obvious things. I need to think outside the box. He's always been good at hiding his tracks.'

'Until he wasn't and ended up in prison.'

Patsy giggled. 'Good point. Perhaps I shouldn't give him

too much credit. I think I need a break from it though, maybe then it'll come to me.'

'Do you fancy watching a film?'

'Can I light the fire?'

'It's August.'

'It's gone a bit chilly now the sun's going down,' she argued, desperate for it to be as cosy as she imagined it would be with the fire.

'Go on then, but you'll have to fetch some logs in. The log store's by the back door.'

With the fire lit, the pizza on their laps and The Day After Tomorrow on the television, Patsy was in her element. But sharing all of it with Matt was the best part.

# 34

'You don't have to go,' Matt said on the morning of Patsy's second day at his house. His eye was beginning to open and some of the bruising had started to turn to a lighter shade of purple.

'I think you're okay now, though. It's been two days.'

It had been a challenge to take a step back from where they'd been heading on the night of the dry run at the cinema. But that's what they'd been forced to do, because Dan had come between them physically and emotionally. Neither of them had spoken about how they felt since that night but Patsy longed to be held in Matt's arms again. When they sat next to one another on the sofa, watching movies and old box sets of 24 and Breaking Bad, she could almost feel something fizzing in the space between their hands. It would be so easy to reach across the seat between them and see if that was still something tangible, not lost to all that had happened since that one incredible night. To see whether if she touched him, the feeling that had been building inside her again since the I love you in the hospital would be released like it had been then.

Matt, she knew, was battered and bruised, not only where she could see it on his face, but all over. He was still careful when he moved, wincing less now but still sore. And she wanted all of him, not just the bits that Dan didn't hurt, so she was willing to wait.

'I think I might die of boredom if I've got no-one to watch telly with.'

'As much as I'd love to stay and watch telly with you for the next goodness knows how many days, I do have a life and a cinema to run.'

'What day is it?' he said, a look of confusion on his face.

'It's Saturday. And—'

'And it's your first proper day of the cinema running. I'm so sorry, Patsy. God, you must have had so much to do and I've been keeping you here.'

'No, not at all. Ed's got the film ready, the pizza is all prepped and ready to bake, so all I have to do is open up and supervise.'

'What film is it?'

'Toy Story.'

'Classic! The twins love that.' His face fell. Patsy knew he'd love to have been there with them.

'Bring them next week,' she said, gently. 'It's going to be Madagascar. I bet they'll love that too.'

He nodded. 'But you will come back and stay tonight?'

Patsy was surprised to see that he almost looked like he was pleading with her. Then it dawned on her that he hadn't been alone since it had happened.

'Of course. I'll bring something back for dinner.'

'As long as it isn't pizza,' he said, managing a smile.

'Don't look a gift horse in the mouth.'

'If I'm going to eat pizza twice in one week, it'd better be pepperoni, that's all I can say.'

'I'll see what I can do.' She kissed his cheek and went

upstairs to get ready.

It couldn't have gone better. Patsy's new front of house person, Alice, was brilliant. She seemed to be everywhere she needed to be before Patsy had to ask. Between Alice, Ed and the two kitchen staff who had to keep churning the pizzas through the ovens, everything was covered, which left Patsy feeing very much in control and able to enjoy the first proper showing. She spent the time chatting to customers before the film started, delivered pizzas and drinks to their tables, then discretely helped to tidy up once the film started. It wasn't a quiet affair, but it wasn't supposed to be and when everyone left, they were full of praise for how relaxing it had been to come as a family to enjoy a film in a slightly different way.

They saw the last of the customers out and then it was all hands to the deck to tidy up. A cleaning company was due to come in a couple of times a week so all there was to do was tidy up and straighten the furniture, make sure the kitchen was clean and all the washing up had been done. By the time Ed came down after rewinding the film, they were just about finished.

'Do you want to take some pizza?' Patsy asked him. 'There's loads left.'

'Thanks, that'll save me deciding on what take-away to go for tonight.'

He followed her into the kitchen and helped pop some takeout boxes into shape then leant on the worktop next to her while she filled them with as many slices of pizza as they could take.

'Thanks for projecting today, Ed. We've started advertising for projectionists so hopefully we won't take up your Saturdays for too much longer.'

He shrugged. 'I don't mind and I'm happy to train whoever you find.'

'Thanks. And I meant to say, you could mention it to Hayley in case she'd like some shifts?'

'Will do. Right, I'd better go before I miss the next bus. Are you okay?'

She knew he was asking if she'd be okay alone. 'Thanks, Ed. I'll be fine.' It was the middle of the afternoon so she would be. The park would be busy as well but even so, she was starting to feel like Dan was losing his grip on her and she wanted to lean into that feeling.

She packed her boxed-up pizza into her bag, made sure all the lights were off and stepped out into the sunshine. Not only was it glorious but it was even more so for the fact that she was heading back to Matt. Hopefully she could persuade him to sit in the garden for a while or maybe even venture into the woods for a stroll before they got stuck into whatever they decided to watch tonight.

Patsy locked the door, double-checked it and headed off through the park in the direction of Matt's house. It was a longer walk than to her's, but still a lovely one, taking in the outskirts of town where the pavements were bordered by hedgerows full of rosebay willowherb and cow parsley. By the time she'd reached Matt's road, she was hot, and ready for a cold glass of beer or wine.

She heard a noise behind her and turned, thinking that something might have fallen out of her bag. She caught sight of someone diving behind a tree. Her breath caught in her throat. She was fairly sure it was Dan because who else would be following her in broad daylight? She stayed where she was, ready to see when he moved again. There was no way that she was going to lead him to Matt's front door.

Thank god she hadn't got that far.

After a couple of minutes, she almost felt like laughing. The thought of him hiding behind the tree seemed to take away the menace and was quite funny.

'Dan!' She began to walk back up the road towards the tree. 'I know you're there. You might as well come out and say whatever it is you're here to say.'

She'd almost reached him, her heart beating hard now at the thought of actually confronting him. She sounded a lot more confident than she felt. He stood up from where he'd been crouched and stepped out onto the path.

'What are you doing?' she said, her voice full of derision.

'Look, all I want is the laptop.'

She could see that he was struggling to keep his temper under control and that scared her but she'd been in this situation before, many times.

'I don't have it.' Well, it wasn't with her.

He exhaled impatiently and took a step towards her, his fists clenched.

'Haven't the police been in touch? I would have thought beating someone up was against the terms of your licence?' It took everything she had to stay where she was, sounding like she was in control.

He looked shifty for a second, then said, 'There's no proof.'

Patsy laughed. 'I'm not sure your word against his is going to go in your favour to be honest, especially when I tell the police that you've been intimidating me as well.' It was a bold move. It could have gone either way, and as soon as she said it, Patsy felt like an idiot for even thinking about provoking him but it went in her favour and surprisingly, and much to her relief, he began walking away, backwards.

'I know you've got it. I'll be back for it, Cleo, sooner or later.' Then he turned and Patsy watched him until he was out of sight, certain that he wasn't going to see where she was going. It took all of those few minutes for her to gather herself but the overwhelming feeling she had was triumph. Finally she'd stood up to him and he'd backed off. Sadly, she also wondered whether if she'd had the guts to do that years ago, things could have been very different.

By the time she got back to Matt's, the enormity of what had just happened started to hit her. Now that the adrenaline had worn off, she realised how lucky she'd been to manage to see him off.

'You should have called the police,' Matt said. He was cross. 'He never should have been out, I thought they'd have recalled him to prison by now.'

'It was fine,' she said, trying to reassure him when all he could think was that she could so easily have ended up like him. Beaten black and blue. 'All he wants is that laptop. I need more time to find out why.'

Matt ran his fingers through his hair, tugging it in frustration. 'Give him the bloody thing, if that's what he wants. Whatever it is, it isn't worth putting yourself in harm's way.'

Patsy went to him and gently cupped his face in her hands. 'Matt, I can't let him win again. This is the only thing that he's wanted that I've ever been able to hang onto. He took everything from me. Everything. I have to do this.'

Matt took her hands in his and gently pushed them away. 'I can't be part of this, Patsy.' He had tears in his eyes. 'I can't expose the twins to this, to the fact that he might be following you. If I was okay, they could have been with us today. They could have ended up being another bargaining chip in his bid to get that bloody laptop.'

Stunned that she hadn't realised before, she said, 'I'll give him the laptop.' Nothing was more important than making sure the twins were safe. Matt was right, they could have so easily got caught up in this mess. Dan could have found out where Matt lived and they couldn't risk that happening again.

With tears beginning to run down her cheeks, she nodded and stepped away from him. 'No, you're right. I totally understand.' She rubbed her eyes with the back of her hand. 'I'll get my stuff and go to Ollie's. It's safer that way, just in case.' Before Matt could say anything, she turned and went upstairs, managing to hold in the sob that was ready to engulf her until she had closed the door to the spare room she'd been sleeping in and was safely locked in the ensuite bathroom.

She sobbed for what could have been. For what she might have had with Matt if only she'd been able to face up to her past and deal with Dan sooner. For wasting three years doing nothing except hiding. Of course he was going to catch up with her one day. If not now, next year, the year after and whenever it was, it was always going to be like this. An unwelcome intrusion, something she should've faced three, four, five years ago.

When she'd stopped crying, she splashed some cold water on her face, not that it helped. Her eyes were bloodshot and swollen. Matt wasn't an idiot. He knew it was going to be hard for both of them to walk away from something that had felt so full of promise. But he was doing it for his children, and Patsy loved him even more because of that.

'Okay, well ring us if you need anything,' she said as brightly as she could manage before she shoved her sunglasses on and picked up her bag.

Matt got up from the sofa. His eyes were still so bruised, it was hard to tell if he'd been crying or not. He took her in his arms, his hand on the back of her head. It felt like more than a goodbye and Patsy choked back another sob.

'I'm sorry,' he murmured.

She pulled away without looking at him again and headed for the front door as quickly as she could without running. She didn't look back, but heard Matt lock it behind her.

# 35

Although she'd told Matt she'd go to Oliver's, all she wanted was the space to wallow by herself. Being at home alone didn't seem quite so frightening now that she knew that the threat of the police was enough to keep Dan at bay. And besides, nothing he could do was as awful as knowing that she had been within reach of everything she'd ever wanted and had lost it because of her inability to face up to the past.

She had drunk a whole bottle of wine by herself as she sat on the roof terrace watching the sun set over Croftwood in a blaze of pink and orange glory. When she began to get chilly, she went inside and curled up on her bed, still in her summer dress, feeling the warm breeze lick at her skin until she fell into a deep sleep.

She awoke to a persistent noise which it took her a moment to realise, wasn't her phone alarm but her doorbell. Stumbling down the stairs, cursing her landlord for not having a doorbell that you buzz people in with, she ended up stood in the hall nervously wondering who would be on the other side of the door.

'Hello?' she called, feeling like a total idiot but also

unwilling to risk having to deal with someone barging in at… whatever time it was, on a Sunday morning.

'It's Oliver, Pats.'

She opened the door and could see by the pity in Oliver's face that he'd spoken to Matt. She turned before he could see the tears emerge again and headed back upstairs to the flat, Oliver following her.

'Let me get changed,' she said, heading to the bedroom and looking at herself in the mirror before she pulled her dress off, swapping it for cropped leggings and an old, comfy oversized t-shirt with a faded logo of Joseph and his Amazing Technicolour Dreamcoat on the front. She half-heartedly brushed her hair and pulled it into a loose bun. Yesterday's mascara was sitting underneath her eyes so she dampened a cotton pad with some cleanser and sat for a moment, enjoying the soothing feeling of it on the skin around her eyes, raw from too many salty tears.

When she went back into the lounge, Oliver had made coffee for both of them and had laid out an embarrassment of pastries on a plate.

'Breakfast on the terrace?' he asked.

She nodded, glad of the legitimate excuse to wear her sunglasses and dragged a couple of blankets out of the window while Oliver managed the breakfast.

'So you spoke to Matt?' she asked, as she pulled pieces of pastry off a pain au chocolate to get to the middle.

'He called last night to make sure you got to mine safely. Don't worry, I told him you had.'

She gave him a grateful look, her mouth full of chocolate.

'And then I came round to make sure you were here but you didn't answer the door. Your neighbour said she'd seen you though so I knew you were okay.'

'Sorry, I should have told you. I needed to be by myself.'

'Matt said you'd seen Dan again yesterday.'

Patsy had almost forgotten that had been the catalyst for her life imploding. All she'd been thinking about was how she'd almost led Dan to Matt's house. If she hadn't realised he was following her…

She nodded.

'Matt called the police. They're going to pick Dan up on the assumption he was going to find Matt.'

Patsy shook her head. 'He didn't know I was going to Matt's. He was following me to get the laptop. I wish I'd given it to him. Like Matt said, nothing on there is as important as us being safe.' Her voice broke and Oliver shuffled towards her so that he could put his arm around her.

'Come on, Pats. It'll be okay.'

'I don't think so, Ollie,' she sniffed. 'Everything started to seem possible. The cinema is amazing, things were going well with Matt and now, because I kept putting off what I needed to do to get Dan out of my life, it's all ruined.'

'You're being too hard on yourself. Look what happened when he first appeared, you were a mess. And look at you now. You stood up to him and he backed off. That's huge, Pats. It wouldn't have happened a couple of months ago. From where I'm standing, you've taken on this huge project with me, totally pulled it off and at the same time gained the confidence to face the most difficult thing in your life. That is all you. And walking away from Matt to protect him and his kids, that shows how much you love him.'

Oliver knew. Of course he did, he'd probably seen it coming before she or Matt had. 'I do love him, Ollie. I have no idea why because sometimes he's the most frustrating person in the world but… he's the first person I've felt like that about, ever.'

She had no idea how to start dealing with the fact that they couldn't be together because who knew how long it would take to settle things with Dan. She couldn't expect Matt to put his life on hold, waiting for her. Her own life had been on hold for the past three years and now that she could look back and understand that, it wasn't something she wanted for him, or for herself.

At least she could throw herself into the cinema. There was so much to do, so much potential to tap into and  being able to focus on that was what would save her.

'You're right, Ollie. It will be okay. Maybe not today, though.' She smiled and took a gulp of coffee. 'Thanks for breakfast.'

Patsy spent the rest of the day bug hunting. It was something she could lose herself in and before she knew it, it was late afternoon. She stood up and stretched, pondering the next thing she could try for the website she was working on. She made a cup of tea and took it out onto the roof to get some fresh air. As much as she wanted to spend all day out there, the laptop needed charging and she didn't have a long enough extension lead, so she'd had to make do with periodically sitting indoors beside the open window. As the sun warmed her face, she had an idea about what she was going to try next. She stepped back inside and went to the file explorer on the laptop. She wanted to set up a virtual machine inside the laptop but it was so ancient, she needed to check whether there was enough space on the disk. She clicked onto the C drive which was supposed to be 240GB but was showing as 200GB. Patsy frowned. Why would the size of the disk be showing differently? She wasn't puzzled for long, realising almost straight away that something was amiss, and whatever it was that was taking up this mysterious 40GB was probably what Dan was after.

Around an hour later, Patsy had discovered a hidden partition on the laptop, where she found a single file with 'wallet' in the name, but it was password protected. Years before, she'd been on an ethical hacking workshop that had explained how to attempt brute forcing of passwords and even though she was rusty on the details, there was one thing in her favour. The fact that she'd had the laptop for three years and it had been sat on a shelf gathering dust for at least another three meant that the password had been chosen before anyone cared about two-factor authentication or special characters, which made attempting to crack it a lot easier.

The next several hours went in the blink of an eye for Patsy. She had never been more focused or more determined to get to the bottom of anything in her life. A plan was formulating at the back of her mind that she wouldn't allow herself to pay any attention to until she knew that she could get access to this wallet. She downloaded a password cracking tool to help her get there faster, frustrated knowing that if she had a better computer, it really would be faster. The size of the memory on the ancient laptop meant that everything was slow. As soon as she added the word list — basically a dictionary of possible passwords — into the tool and defined some rules to use, the pace slowed to glacial. But finally, at a bleary-eyed three o'clock in the morning, she did it. The password was R1chDan1988.

Patsy could hardly believe she'd managed to get into it. Thank god she'd been practising her skills for weeks with all the bug bounty hunting she'd been doing. Otherwise, coming at it cold, it could have taken longer than she had. Realistically, it was only a matter of time before she'd have had to face Dan demanding the laptop again and it would have been gutting to have handed it over without knowing why he wanted it so badly.

She held her breath as she looked at what was held in the wallet. It was no wonder he had wanted the laptop back. He had close to twenty Bitcoin. A quick google search told Patsy that when he'd bought them in 2016, he'd paid around £2,000 for them and now they were worth over £300,000. At their peak in November 2021, he would have been within spitting distance of being a millionaire. That thought filled her with glee, imagining him in prison, unable to sell and seeing the value drop like a stone before he was released.

She knew exactly what she was going to do.

# 36

As soon as it was an acceptable time to call round to Oliver's, Patsy let herself into the coffee house, raced up the stairs and rapped on the bedroom door.

'Ollie, are you awake?'

'Christ, Pats! What's happened?' He came bursting out of the bedroom, half-asleep, trying to pull some jeans on over his boxer shorts. He didn't look amused when Patsy started laughing.

'I've got a present for you.'

He did up the fly on his jeans, collapsed on the sofa and sat with his head in his hands. 'It couldn't wait until a more civilised hour?'

'Check your bank account.'

'Seriously, Pats. It's way too early to be this demanding. Can I have a coffee first?'

'Ollie! Look at it and then you can have a coffee.' She needed one herself, having been up all night, but she was fuelled by adrenaline and the need for closure.

He picked his iPad up from the coffee table and found the app for his bank account. He rubbed his eyes and blinked as he saw the balance.

'Is that enough to pay Amy?'

'Where did this come from?'

'Is it, Ollie?'

'It's more than enough, Pats but I don't understand. Where did it come from?'

'It came from me.'

'But…'

'This is what Dan had on the laptop. That's why he wanted it. He had a crypto currency wallet hidden on there with Bitcoin in it.'

'Is it legal? How do you know it isn't the proceeds from his fraud thing?' Oliver asked.

'Because this happened at least a year before that, and although it's worth a lot of money now, it was worth £2,000 when he bought it.'

Oliver still looked dubious.

'That £2,000 was mine. To start with, all of my money went into a joint account which he syphoned off the minute it went in there. Then when I tried to change my account details so that my wages would go into my own account, because he worked in the accounts office, he used to change the bank details on the file that got sent to the bank from mine to his. It took me ages to realise that's what was happening because every time I confirmed my details with the payroll system, they were correct. And even if I'd known, I wouldn't have been able to do anything about it. Not then.'

'Okay.' Oliver still wasn't looking as thrilled as she'd hoped.

'It's fair.'

Oliver stood up and put his arms around her. 'I know it is, Pats. You deserve this, that's why you can't give it to me.'

'I already have. I don't need all of that money, Ollie. I don't want anything from him except for him to leave me alone.'

'If you give it to him, he will.'

'No. He doesn't deserve it. You do. This way, we all benefit. The cinema gets off to a much sounder financial start because you won't need to take any money out of it after all. And you get a clean break with Amy.'

'While you're stuck in that tiny flat with nothing to show for any of this.'

'I love my flat, thanks very much,' she said, smiling despite his dig at her little sanctuary. 'I can get paid properly for running the cinema and,' she took Oliver's hands in hers and stared him right in the eye so that he would know how important it was to her, 'I'll have closure.'

'We'll be business partners in the cinema. That's the only way I can accept this. Equal partners.'

She flung her arms around his neck. 'Yes! That's perfect, Ollie!'

Finally, she allowed Oliver to make coffee for them both while she sat on the sofa, finally able to relax after her hours of hard work and before the kettle had boiled, she had fallen asleep.

She woke a couple of hours later to find Oliver had laid a blanket over her. She could hear the noise of the coffee machine downstairs which meant the coffee house was open. Once she'd freshened up as best she could and made one important phone call, she went in search of more coffee and something to eat, feeling as if a weight had lifted off her.

Oliver was busy serving but she spotted Toby sat at his usual table so she made coffee for herself and Toby, grabbed a cinnamon swirl and headed over to talk to him.

'Morning, ready for a refill?'

'Thanks, you're a mind reader,' he said with a grateful smile. 'Look, I've been meaning to say, I haven't had the papers back from your husband yet. I don't suppose you've heard from him?'

'I have. I'm going to try and see him so I'll get him to sign them and I'll bring them back with me.'

'Right...' Toby sounded doubtful.

'I've got something he wants back so I'm hoping that'll give me some bargaining power to get everything sorted out once and for all.'

'You sound confident. Are you sure it's a good idea after what you've told me about him? You're not worried about how he might react?'

'I think it'll be okay once he sees what I have.'

'Okay, I'll leave it with you then. But just for my own piece of mind, will you make sure someone knows where you're meeting him. Maybe even think about taking someone with you.'

'He's been recalled to prison. They picked him up yesterday so I've put in a request to visit him. Hopefully it'll be tomorrow.' She'd phoned his probation officer before she'd come downstairs.

'Wow. Well, that makes things easier for you. Best of luck.'

Patsy finished her breakfast and headed home after promising Oliver she'd be back to help with the lunch rush. The plan that had been in the back of her mind the night before was fully formed. All she needed now was the okay to visit Dan and it'd all be over.


'Patsy Clements,' called the prison guard, checking her identification before he let her through to a large room where Dan was already sat at a table by himself. All the other tables were empty. She'd been allowed a special visit arranged by Dan's probation officer and the police sergeant who'd been dealing with Matt's assault case.

He was wearing a grey sweatshirt and jogging bottoms and looked thoroughly pissed off at her being there.

'Happy now?'

'Not yet but it's a good start.' She saw the look of surprise in his eyes as she stood up to him. It helped being in the prison, knowing she was protected if he did take exception to anything she said. But that comment was as far as she'd go anyway in terms of winding him up. That wasn't why she was there. 'I've just picked these up from your parents' house.' She pulled the divorce papers out of her bag and laid them on the table between them.

'I'm not signing those.' Dan leaned back in his chair and folded his arms.

'I found the Bitcoin.'

His eyes briefly widened in shock but he didn't say anything.

'I'm sure we can come to an arrangement.' She pushed the papers further towards him.

'I'm not telling you the password.'

'I have the password.' Seeing yet another shock register made Patsy certain that she had the upper hand now. The hold that he'd had over her was well and truly over and even if she hadn't had the trump card she was yet to play, she was fairly sure he wouldn't be coming looking for her again.

'What do you want?'

'I want you to sign these.' She looked over at the guard who came over with a pen and stood over Dan while he signed the pages that Toby had helpfully indicated with sticky tabs. The guard took the pen and went back to stand near the door. 'Thank you.'

'So I can have the money?'

'Not all of it. I hope you'd agree that the way you treated me, I probably deserve to keep all of it but I'm willing to make a deal.'

For the first time in the whole time that Patsy had known Dan, he looked slightly ashamed. He wasn't going to break down and beg her for forgiveness but it was enough to see on his face that he acknowledged that what she'd said was true.

'I'm listening.'

Patsy took a piece of paper out of her bag and passed it to him. It had already been checked on her way in and was okayed by the prison. Not that it was probably much use to him until he was out again, anyway.

'This is a crypto wallet that I've set up for you. I've emptied the old one and I'll transfer the value of half a Bitcoin into your wallet every year for the next ten years. But in return, you have to agree not to contact me, not to contact anyone I know and to have no interest in me or my life for the rest of yours.'

'So you can go off into the sunset with the lion's share of my money and your new man?'

'Yes, exactly.' She paused, wondering how he could have gone from looking ashamed to being remorseless so quickly. 'You might think I'm taking your money but you took most of my money for years along with my self-confidence, self-respect and most of my friends and family. Then you came back, terrorised me and my friends purely because you wanted literally the only thing that I'd taken from you. And I really did think it was a crappy old laptop that you wouldn't miss. This is karma, Dan.' She stood up and waved her arms expansively at the room before leaning towards him and saying, 'And this is karma.'

She walked out into the sunshine feeling like she finally had closure. She had signed divorce papers in her bag and she knew that there was no way that Dan would jeopardise the deal they'd made because he was too desperate for the money. By the time ten years came around and the deal was over, hopefully he'd have moved on and forgotten all about her.

Instead of catching the bus back to Croftwood, she jumped

on a train to Ledbury and spent the rest of the afternoon mooching in some of the independent shops. She treated herself to a few things to brighten up the flat from a wonderful Scandinavian homewares shop which she normally wouldn't even set foot in because it would be too expensive. But today, she was treating herself with her little windfall from Dan. Now that she'd given some of it to Oliver to repay him for the kindness and support he'd given her over the past three years she felt that it had done some good. It would enable him to move on as well and it meant that both of them could move forward with the cinema on an equal footing. Patsy finally felt as if she'd contributed to its regeneration instead of feeling as if Oliver was involving her out of pity.

She wandered back down the high street towards the train station and caught sight of a sewing machine in the window of a charity shop. It was like a sign. She could do one of Jess's sewing courses if she had her own machine. A new hobby would be just the thing to start this new chapter of her life and would fill the hours that were hers again now that she wasn't bug hunting, projector cleaning or project managing.

Luckily the machine was relatively modern and light so she managed to carry it home on the train, although by the time she plonked it on the floor in her flat she felt as if her right arm had stretched by a few inches. She unpacked the rest of her goodies which included a new tea towel with bright Scandi flowers on it, a little tray and matching coasters for the coffee table and a vase, then she flung open the window and took a blanket out onto the roof terrace so that she could lie in the sunshine.

What a day. It was the end of everything she'd been running away from and the start of something wonderful. When she thought of wonderful, she automatically thought of Matt and was overwhelmed with sadness that things hadn't worked out between them. It would be so easy to go to him, tell him what she'd done to get Dan out of her life and walk into the sunset together. But that wasn't fair. She had no assurance that Dan would stick to the deal. She was pretty sure the temptation of the money would be enough to keep him away and she was very happy with the level of certainty that gave her, but Matt had other considerations. How could he trust that it was over for good? Trust her enough to know that his children would be safe? That Dan wouldn't get greedy and turn up to threaten him again?

Accepting that she had to leave Matt was the hardest thing she'd ever done and it was going to take some time to forget, if she ever could, how she'd felt for the brief time they'd spent together. How for the smallest of moments, she'd begun to believe that someone loved her again and that she wasn't broken, hadn't been ruined forever by that man who had taken everything. Because she knew now that he had never taken her heart. That was Matt's at the moment. Although she wished with every part of it that she wouldn't, one day, have to contemplate moving on and giving it to someone else. But after everything she had been through, she knew she wasn't going to hide anymore. She was going to pick herself up, allow herself time to come to terms with the fact that she was alone again, and then get on with her life. She'd waited long enough.

# 37

Patsy was in the projection box alone, lacing up the projector with the first film she would be responsible for showing for paying customers. Luckily her debut projectionist gig was for Purl at the Pictures, a matinee showing with the lights not fully down, so that people could bring their knitting or other craft and do it while they watched the film. Hopefully the audience would be kind if there were any problems.

The available and relatively cheap film was One Fine Day with George Clooney and Michelle Pfeiffer which seemed appropriate for what Patsy fully expected to be a roomful of women.

Once the film was weaving in and out of the projector and back to the tower, she got her checklist, which was looking pretty dog-eared by now, and went through it to see if she'd missed anything. So far so good. A glance at her watch told her she had ten minutes to sort it out before they opened the doors. Was ten minutes long enough to play the start, to make sure she'd put the five separate reels of film together in the right order? It would mean lacing up again afterwards but maybe that was okay. It was important to have peace of mind.

Once she'd put the lamp on and started the film, she forced herself to acknowledge that it would still be okay if she wasn't standing watching it run through the projector and ran downstairs to the circle balcony to check the sound was working and that it looked okay, which it did. She clapped her hands together in gleeful relief and headed back to start all over again.

By the time she got down to the foyer, Alice, was waiting on the doorstep.

'Sorry I was late letting you in,' Patsy said apologetically. 'I was just checking the film for the last time.'

'No problem.' Alice skipped past her. 'Where do you want me?'

They were severely short-staffed. 'This is going to be a bit of an experiment but I thought if I sold the tickets and you did the drinks to start with, I'll go up and start the film and then come back down to help once it's on. Will you manage with the tickets and drinks once I've disappeared?'

'Yes, I'm sure I will. I expect most people will be here by the time you go to start the film.'

'Hopefully, yes. It's hard to know how many we could expect for the first time.'

Patsy went and sat in the ticket booth while Alice manned the bar which was well stocked with cakes, since a drink and a cake were included in the ticket price. She looked at her watch. Half an hour until the advertised start time of the film. It took another ten minutes before she heard footsteps on the steps outside, by which time she was wringing her hands with worry that no-one was going to turn up.

'Hello!' It was Linda from the library.

'Hi Linda, welcome to Purl at the Pictures!'

'Oh, I have been so looking forward to this, Patsy. How many have you got so far?'

'You're the first,' she said, trying to sound as if that was okay but secretly terrified that Linda may end up having a private viewing.

'I'll be able to get the best seat then,' she said, making Patsy want to lean out of her booth and hug her for being so optimistic.

While Linda was collecting a coffee and cake from Alice, Sue and Mary arrived followed by a young woman and a young man, students Patsy guessed. When she'd come up with the idea she'd envisaged most of the customers being of retirement age but she had been into knitting and crochet when she was a student, although not as publicly as this, so perhaps she shouldn't have been surprised.

'We weren't sure you were actually open. This is a brilliant idea,' said the girl. 'I always think I'd love to take my knitting to the cinema but it's too dark. Imagine the stress if you dropped a stitch?'

'Exactly,' said Patsy, smiling.

'Any chance we could swap the coffee for a pint?' her friend asked.

'Yes, of course you can,' she said, catching Alice's eye and giving her the nod that it would be fine. That would have been her perfect outing; a good film, knitting and a pint, even if it was only eleven o'clock in the morning. In fact, it appealed despite that.

By the time there was a lull in customers, it was almost time to start. Patsy left Alice in charge of the foyer and headed upstairs, the adrenaline beginning to surge as the time approached to start the film. She wished Oliver had been able to come with her for the first time but Jack couldn't cover the coffee house today so she was on her own. She'd brought her knitting but she was starting to think that was wishful thinking and that even once it was underway, she'd be on the alert for an emergency.

The lamp was on, the tower was on. She was ready. This

was it. Her heart was beating out of her chest as she switched the projector on, hoping that there was nothing catastrophic that she'd forgotten. It whirred up to speed, the film making a satisfying flicking sound that Patsy had learned sounded right. She opened the shutter, peered through the window and saw the film showing on the screen exactly as she had hoped, with only a tiny adjustment to the focus being necessary. She turned the house lights down to what she hoped would be the perfect level, having now realised she forgot to check what that should be, then cast an inexpert eye over everything to make sure it all seemed okay still before she ran downstairs to see how Alice was doing.

'We had a couple more but I think that's probably it now. I think there are twenty-four altogether,' she said proudly.

'That's great. Are you okay to stay out here in case anyone wants another drink? I'm just going to pop in and see how it's going.'

Patsy opened the door to the auditorium and slipped inside. She sat in the nearest chair and took a look around. Most people had opted to sit about halfway down the room and were grouped around tables with nobody sitting alone, even if they'd arrived by themselves. The light level seemed perfect and she could hear the gentle click of needles when the film was quiet but it wasn't irritating, particularly not to a knitter. Yes, everything was as it should be.

She took a photo of the back of everyone to post later on Instagram and sat back to enjoy the film for a few minutes before she went out to the foyer and told Alice she could sit inside until a few minutes before the end of the film. Patsy sat in the little ticket booth and spent the time doing some social media and working on the website she was in the process of building. When Alice came out near the end of the film, Patsy ran upstairs to get ready to put the lights up and to finish off.

'I've tidied up and cleaned the bar.' Alice said, putting her head around the door of the projection box about ten minutes later. 'Is there anything else you want me to do before I go?'

'No, thanks Alice. I think that went really well. See you on Friday night?'

'Sure. Bye, Patsy.'

Patsy began to rewind the film, gently cleaning the inside of the projector with a cloth while she waited. Something caught her eye through the little window that looked out over the auditorium. She peered more closely but there was nothing. She laughed at herself for getting the heebie-jeebies in the middle of the day but she couldn't help worrying that Alice may not have dropped the latch on the front door.

Once everything was switched off, she headed downstairs, stopping to pick up a random Post-It note that someone had dropped on the stairs.

She loves me, was printed on it. That was weird. They still didn't have the circle open so it must have been Alice that dropped it.

A few steps further down, there was another Post-It note. She loves me not.

Intrigued, Patsy continued, picking up another two Post-Its. She loves me, she loves me not. On the ground floor, she paused to check the front door. The latch was down but it didn't put Patsy's mind at ease. There were three more Post-It notes making a trail that led into the stalls. She had stopped picking them up but carried on following them all the way down to the door at the side of the screen that led into the backstage bar. As soon as she opened it, the back door slid across and it was filled with sunshine and her favourite people in the world.

Oliver was stood there, grinning, having just pulled the back door aside. Matt, Flo and Sammy were standing outside, under the dappled shade of the trees, holding a big daisy made out of cardboard and covered with lovingly scribbled colourful petals.

The children could barely contain their excitement but must have been under strict instructions not to say anything.

'Hey,' said Matt, smiling and beginning to walk towards her, his hand out ready to take hers. His face looked back to normal and she realised how much she'd missed him.

'What's going on?' She could hardly get the words out. The anticipation and hope that he was here for her was almost too much.

'Oliver told me what you did. You weren't going to tell me?' He looked at her questioningly but with the same look in his eyes that told Patsy he was curious, not cross.

'I wasn't sure it would be enough.'

'It's more than enough. Sending you away… it nearly killed me, Patsy. I don't think I knew until then how I felt.'

'Daddy! Ask her!' Flo said, pulling on Matt's arm. 'Patsy, we made this for you.' Flo whipped the daisy out of Sammy's hand and shoved it at Patsy.

'Thank you, I think it's the most beautiful flower I've ever seen.' Her heart swelled as the children looked at each other with huge pride.

'Look at the back!' Flo said, excitedly.

'Okay…' she said, grinning at Matt, before turning it over and finding the last Post-It.

She loves me.

'I hope she loves me.' he whispered quietly enough so that only she could hear, his eyes firmly on hers, filled with emotions that mirrored her own exactly.

She nodded, 'More than I know how to say.'

'I feel the same,' he said. 'Hence the Post-Its.'

'Daddy!'

Matt turned and smiled at his daughter. 'What did I say?'

'Wait nicely,' said Sammy solemnly.

'Well done, Sammy. You've been very patient. Patsy, the

children and I have something to ask you. We wondered if you'd like to come on holiday with us.'

'We're going to the seaside!' The children began jumping around, unable to hold it in any more.

'Wow, that sounds exciting,' Patsy said, her eyes searching Matt's. It was a big step, introducing someone into their lives. A holiday felt like a step too far and Patsy was suddenly worried that he was offering her something he wasn't ready for.

'Hey Sammy, Flo, shall we go and see if the swings are free?' Oliver held out his hands and the twins obediently took one each and went with him.

'Before you say anything,' Matt began, 'it's all sorted. Even Nicole's on board. Said she'd never seen me so miserable and is quite happy for you to join us on holiday. I know it's not the most romantic thing in the world, asking you along to a kids' beach holiday in Tenby but we have got a lovely little cottage on the harbour and I'll insist the twins are in bed by six so we'll have the evenings alone.'

'Your kids are great. In fact, they're the biggest selling point of the holiday,' she teased.

'You won't be saying that when they jump on the bed at six in the morning. Oh. Is that a yes?'

'It is.'

Matt took her face gently in his hands and drew her towards him. The kiss was even better than she remembered the last one being, although a lot had happened since then. And it felt as if all of the longing, the days and days of hopeless loss and bleak thoughts of a life without him, all came together in that moment and Patsy knew that this holiday was the start of everything being good in her life again.

'Shall we go and find them?' she said, once they'd finished kissing. For now.

Matt pulled the door across, put his arm around Patsy's shoulders and she leant into him, tucking her hand into his back pocket as they headed out into the late August sunshine towards the playground. She turned to look back at the cinema. That was where all of this had begun, the good, the bad and everything yet to come.

The End

**Notes from the Author**

Thank you for visiting Croftwood! It's a fictional town, loosely based on my home town, Great Malvern in Worcestershire. Malvern is famous for its hills whereas Croftwood is flat, something that is very desirable when you have a tricky garden on the side of a hill, but many of the other things about Croftwood, like the park, the church and the high street are very similar to Malvern. Working in Malvern Cinema was my first job when I left university and I absolutely loved it. Writing this book brought back memories of the feelings of high anxiety and adrenaline which I imagine were the same for most projectionists in the days before digital cinema and to my shame, I was once that person who went to say that the film was out of focus in another cinema. It definitely was.

I hugely appreciate you choosing to read my books and am astounded at how many of you have taken the time to leave ratings and reviews on Amazon and Goodreads. It means the world to me and I'm immensely grateful for every single one.

The biggest thank you this time goes to my husband, James, who not only read this book before anyone else and in record time, he also wrote a few bits of the technical computery stuff for me when he thought my descriptions were unrealistic. I rolled my eyes, accepted the help but did have to heavily edit his writing to avoid Patsy 'mounting' something. That's a technical term that I thought best to avoid.

Wonderful Berni Stevens came up with the perfect cover design, yet again giving me what I didn't know I wanted. Thank you to Catrin for proofreading and editing for me, I couldn't do it without you. Thank you to Rachel at Rachel's

Random Resources for organising my blog tours and to all the amazing bloggers and reviewers who do a fantastic job of flying the flag for all the romance books out there. Last but not least, huge love and hugs to all my family who are my biggest cheerleaders. You're all ace.

For the latest news about new releases and all sorts of other things, follow me on Facebook at Victoria Walker - Author, follow my Amazon page and check out my website www.victoriaauthor.co.uk

## Sneak Peek of the next Croftwood book - coming Autumn 2023

Croftwood Library was housed in a grand Victorian building with an overgrown, slightly neglected garden at the front. The windows were so high up that there was no way to sneak a look inside so Lois Morgan propped her bike against the wall, locked it up, and took a deep breath as she stood in front of the heavy oak doors.

When she'd gone to work that morning at the Hive, a city library in Worcester and one of the biggest in the Midlands, it had been a normal day. Now here she was in a little town that was only five miles from Worcester but which in terms of the library might as well be the other side of the world, it was so different from the huge library she was used to.

As she took a step closer to the doors, they opened automatically and the scent of an old library which was ingrained in Lois's memory enveloped her and briefly transported her back to the Saturday mornings of her childhood. It was a combination of things that were indescribable and had been lost from the library where she worked now because it was too new. It was stillness, silence, time and so much more, as well as the books themselves all wrapped up in that smell that hits you when you walk into a library of a certain age.

She inhaled deeply and took a second to enjoy the nostalgia that washed over her as a million tiny memories flashed through her mind too quickly to dwell on but leaving her with a sense of contentment at being somewhere that felt so familiar.

The information desk was centred in the entrance so that customers were channelled down one side to enter and deposit their returned books and the other side to exit. It was like entering a time warp. It was a long time since she'd been in a library like this one. She could see why it was listed for closure because it was so behind the times. It had been forgotten and overlooked in the wave of modernising and computerising libraries and Lois knew it would be impossible to get any funding to get it done now. It would always be cheaper to close it.

'Are you a member?' a woman barked from behind the desk.

'Yes,' said Lois, extracting her Worcestershire Libraries card from her purse.

The older woman peered at the card through her half-moon reading glasses. 'No,' she said.

'Sorry, no?' The card allowed membership to all the county's libraries.

'We don't accept those new-fangled cards here. You will need to join this library.'

Lois wasn't about to start an argument which she wasn't sure she would win, even though she knew she was right. 'Okay, thank you. I just wanted to browse today.'

The woman tutted and went back to what she was doing. Lois took that as a sign she was permitted to enter and hurried past the desk.

She spotted another lady re-shelving some books in the fiction section.

'Hi, can you recommend a good crime novel?' Lois asked, smiling.

The woman looked like a rabbit in the headlights. 'Can I recommend a crime book?'

Lois suddenly felt like she was in an alternate universe where libraries weren't what she thought they were at all. If not that, it was certainly like stepping back forty or fifty years in time.

'Or whatever you've read recently that you enjoyed?' Maybe it was the crime request that had thrown her.

'Gosh, I can't remember the last time anyone asked me to recommend a book to them. How lovely,' she said in hushed tones. 'I don't read much crime but I very much enjoyed 'The Flatshare' by Beth O'Leary.'

'Oh, I've read that, it's brilliant,' said Lois. 'Clever concept.' Lois would never have expected that to be on this woman's reading list which just went to show that you should never judge a book by its cover.

'I have to admit,' she said, glancing over her shoulder before she continued, 'I love contemporary women's fiction.'

'Do you have a section for that here?'

'Goodness no. Barbara Taylor Bradford is about as contemporary as we get in these parts.' She smiled, then realising she had relaxed for a nano-second too long, immediately became flustered and said, 'Anyway, I must get on.'

'It was nice talking to you,' said Lois, slightly stunned to hear that less than five miles from Worcester, contemporary fiction was considered racy.

The only nod to modern times was a large table with a cluster of four elderly computer terminals and a printer on it, all of which were switched off. Not that there was anyone in the library to use them. Despite the nostalgia that Lois had felt when she walked in, now she felt like it was quite a sad and lifeless place. Could she bear to spend the next six months here?

'I've had a request from County Libraries,' her boss, Robert had said when he'd called her up to his office earlier that morning. 'It seems they are suddenly lacking a librarian in Croftwood. I have been tasked with lending them a capable member of staff until such time that it's resolved.' He'd looked expectantly at Lois.

'Oh right. So, you want me to fill in for a couple of weeks?'

'Actually, it's a little longer than that. To be completely frank, Lois, Croftwood Library is on the list for closure. Their librarian is retiring and they need someone to step in for a few months. Just until the decision is made one way or the other.'

It was always sad when a library faced closure and Lois's heart had gone out to the little town that could lose its hub, but now that she had seen it for herself, she could understand why the decision had been made. It could be a particularly depressing secondment with nothing to do apart from wait until the end came.

'Can you do without me here?' Lois had asked, uncomfortably. She hated to over-estimate the value of herself to the Hive but could they really lose a deputy manager without noticing?

Robert had exhaled loudly and kneaded his forehead with his finger and thumb.

'The thing is, I'm between a rock and a hard place. There is always the pressure to cut costs here and you're right, we can't do without you but moving the cost of a deputy manager off my payroll for a few months would make all the difference. Obviously, it will be very difficult to work around your absence but the library in Croftwood needs a solid librarian, old school as it were. I could send Andrew but you know how awful he is at cataloguing and he hates re-shelving. I would hate to inflict that on any other library. I appreciate it's a big ask, Lois but you're the only person who fits the bill.'

Lois hadn't been sure whether she was flattered or offended but as she snuck out of the exit of Croftwood Library a few minutes later, breathing a sigh of relief at managing to avoid the scary librarian, she couldn't help but think that Robert had picked her as the person who would make the least fuss.

'Take tonight to think it over, and why not take the afternoon off and pop over there,' he'd suggested.

The bike ride in the autumn sunshine had turned out to be the best thing about the visit and she wasn't sure what she was going to say to Robert.


Oliver Jones began every week at his eponymous coffee house expecting Monday to be quiet whereas, in fact, Monday could sometimes be busier than Saturday, not in takings but in footfall. People were lingering, meeting friends, easing themselves into the week which meant the exact opposite for him.

'One-shot espresso, please,' his next customer said. An unusual request after midday but one that Oliver sympathised with.

'Drink in?' It definitely would be. No-one had take-outs on a Monday.

'Yes please.'

Oliver put two espresso cups under the porta-filter and once he'd handed one to his customer he took the other himself, leant against the counter and gazed out of the window, taking advantage of the nearest thing he was going to get to a break for another few hours.

There was a steady stream of people walking up and down the high street. Croftwood wasn't a big town but it was a loyal town and the high street was thriving compared to other places. It heartened Oliver to know that, having sunk every last penny of his savings into the coffee house and the local cinema, the town was behind him.

He was drawn out of his trance by the sight of a woman riding an old-fashioned bike past the window. She was wearing a floral dress and Doc Marten boots both of which were at odds with the safety helmet she also wore. The basket on the front of the bike was only just containing a sweater; the sleeve was hanging down, threatening to become caught in the spokes. Something about her lifted his mood and he smiled to himself.

A couple of customers later, he checked his phone. He tried not to look at it too much during the day because he liked to emit a laid-back vibe for his customers. If he stood there checking his phone it was hardly attentive and he prided himself on his customer service. It was the only thing that set him apart from the chains.

Amongst the numerous emails from companies he had been interested in for a fleeting second and whose emails he kept meaning to unsubscribe to, there was an email from Amy. It was the first time he'd heard from her in a while. The subject was 'Catch Up?'.

'Skinny latte please and a chocolate muffin.'

'Sorry.' Oliver dragged his face into a smile and pushed his phone into his apron pocket. 'Drink in?'

'Yes please.'

'Take a seat, I'll bring it over.'

He turned to the coffee machine and went through the familiar motions while his phone burned against his hip, willing him to look at the email but it would have to wait.

Printed in Great Britain
by Amazon